Speechless

Stephen Puleston

ABOUT THE AUTHOR

Stephen Puleston was born and educated in Anglesey, North Wales. He graduated in theology before training as a lawyer. Speechless is his first novel in the Inspector Marco series

www.stephenpuleston.co.uk
Facebook:stephenpulestoncrimewriter

OTHER NOVELS

Inspector Marco Novels

Prequel Novella– Ebook only
Dead Smart
Novels
Speechless
Another Good Killing
Somebody Told Me

Inspector Drake Mysteries

Prequel Novella– Ebook only
Devil's Kitchen
Novels
Brass in Pocket
Worse than Dead
Against the Tide

ISBN-13: 978-1532734205
ISBN-10: 1532734204:

In memory of my mother
Gwenno Puleston

Chapter 1

Grey clouds drifted over the early-morning sky as the city stirred. Looking out over the Bay I warmed to the prospect of my first day off in a week: lunch with my parents, which meant my mother's *ravioli con funghi,* enquiries about my health and complaints that I didn't visit enough.

Yesterday's unread supplements sat on the worktop behind me, and two tickets for Cardiff's Premiership game against Chelsea that afternoon were propped against the Gaggia coffee machine, which made a comforting hissing sound. After the match I'd have dinner with Trish, tell her about lunch and roll my eyes, describing my mother's comments and then we'd return to the flat and freshly laundered sheets.

It promised to be a typical Sunday until Boyd rang.

'Boss, there's a floater in the Taff.'

'Who's the duty inspector?'

'Detective Inspector Hobbs and he's investigating a rape in Grangetown. He told me to ask for you.'

'Is there nobody else?'

'Sorry, boss.'

I fumbled for a pen in the drawer under the worktop before tugging at a piece of paper from a notepad and writing down the details.

'The ambulance and the fire brigade are on their way,' Boyd said.

'When will they arrive?'

'Half an hour.'

I looked at my watch and knew that after the body had been fished from the Taff and the formalities concluded in the morgue I'd be at my parents' home in good time for lunch.

I was chewing on a piece of toast and watching the espresso dribbling into a cup when my mobile rang. Trish's number appeared on the screen.

'Missed you last night, John.'

'And me you,' I said. 'But I was so tired I couldn't walk straight. Your mum okay?'

'Yeh, she's fine. Are you still all right for later?'

'I'm looking forward to it. But I've just had a call about a body in the Taff.'

'I thought you were off duty?'

'So did I but I should be finished mid-morning. How about coming with me for lunch?'

'I wouldn't want to come between an Italian boy and his mother now, would I?'

I rang off and swallowed the last of the cold espresso. I tidied the kitchen and checked around the flat. I chose a pair of well-pressed denims, a red cotton shirt and, from the bottom of the wardrobe, a pair of brogues with a deep-brown shine. Before I left I picked up the remote for the television and fiddled with the controls until I'd pressed the right button to record *Top Gear*. By the mirror near the apartment door, I drew a hand through my hair and pulled on a light fleece before walking down to the car park.

I found an Elvis CD in the glove compartment of my Mondeo and pushed it into the player. I turned the volume up and 'Heartbreak Hotel' filled the car as I fired the engine into life. The traffic was quiet as I passed the tinplate works, thin plumes of white smoke drifting from its chimneys. A patrol car – lights flashing, siren blaring – shot past me, followed by a couple of taxis heading for the hotels in the Bay.

I stopped at the traffic lights by the prison, a dark Victorian relic, and watched as a couple of joggers ran in front of the car. I turned towards the centre of the city and overtook a council refuse lorry crawling along the street collecting the Saturday night rubbish. Eventually I spotted the fire engine as it drove down into Wood Street and I followed it towards the Taff and the Millennium Stadium. The tender flashed its lights before stopping behind an ambulance and I pulled up on the pavement a little way behind it. I walked over towards two paramedics standing by the railings, peering down into the river.

Boyd walked towards me, sipping from a takeaway plastic cup. Empty burger boxes and chip papers blew around the concrete; a chilling wind whipped around the stadium and cut through my fleece..

The fire tender's reversing alarm sounded and the paramedics stopped their chatter and turned to watch. I stepped up to the railings and looked down into the Taff.

The body was floating face down, caught by a piece of wood wedged against an outfall that was dribbling a dirty-coloured liquid into the river. A heavy, fishy smell hung in the air. The tender finished its manoeuvre and parked by the railing. The fire crew and paramedics were joking and talking as though fishing a dead body out of the river was an everyday occurrence.

'There it is, boss.'

Boyd leant over the railings and pointed towards the Bay. The sound of the outboard was clear and we watched as an inflatable bobbed up and down. A diver dropped into the water from the small boat and, once he'd secured the corpse, waved a hand to the crew above him.

The tender hummed and the cradle lifted clear of the river, a stream of water cascading onto the surface. The fire crew lowered it onto the concourse, and I stepped towards the body. I looked down and then up at the troubled faces of the paramedics.

***

'I have never seen anything like it.'

Dr Paddy MacVeigh, the Home Office pathologist, sounded as though he had something else to say so I stood and waited. The paunch that strained at Paddy's white coat suggested that late-night curries and too much lager had gone into developing the spiders of burst blood vessels on his face. He looked down at the corpse in front of him: the clothes were sodden and small pools of brown water had gathered on the mortuary slab. He leant forward and looked up at me.

'Have you seen his mouth?'

I shook my head and looked down at the bloated features of the face.

'The tongue's been cut out.'

'Are you sure?'

He gave me an exasperated stare.

'Of course I'm sure. We found the tongue in his pocket.'

'What?'

'It was cut out somehow. I'll show you.' He turned to a trolley by his side.

I held up a hand. 'Thanks, Paddy, but you keep it.'

I felt a tacky sensation in my mouth. I drew my tongue over my lips and realised that without my tongue, I couldn't eat, or speak, or wet my lips, or …

'Can you tell if it was cut out before he was killed?'

'Should be able to, once we've finished the tests,' he said, without any emotion. Then he reached over, picked up the dish with the tongue, and looked at it as though it were a rare orchid on the verge of extinction.

'The tongue is really fascinating,' he said, tilting his

head to one side. He opened his mouth to continue.

'I need a smoke,' I said, making my way towards the door.

'But we haven't really started.'

I pulled the door open and as it closed behind me I heard him say that I had to stay, as the senior investigating officer, and that I should know better. I found the small office at the end of the corridor, opened a window, and let the fresh air fill the room. From my rear pocket I took out a crumpled packet of cigarettes and placed the first of my five-a-day between my lips. I sparked my Zippo, just as Paddy came through the door.

'You know it's illegal to smoke in here.'

'So call the police.'

'Very funny,' he said, sitting in the chair by the desk. 'I've never seen that sort of injury. Must be some sort of ritual.'

The mortuary assistant came in, clutching a tray of belongings that he dropped onto the table before turning his back and walking out.

'Michal Dąbek,' Paddy said, switching on his computer.

'Is that his name?'

'Polish identity card and driving licence in the pocket with the tongue.'

I felt relieved that someone else had found the identification. The Poles had moved to Cardiff by the thousand once the regulations allowed. The hotels and bars were full of them and the factories paying minimum wage couldn't survive without them. I looked down at the tray and wondered what else there was to his life.

I started picking at the contents of the tray. There was a leather wallet, a Polish identity card and driving licence and some loose change. The mobile was an old

Nokia, its sides scratched. A red handkerchief was a sodden mess.

'Any chance of forensics from the body?' I asked, still pushing at the contents of the tray with a biro.

Paddy shrugged. 'Difficult to tell. Depends how long he's been in the water.'

'Cause of death?'

'You're joking,' he said. 'Strangulation would be a wild guess.'

'OK, OK … You know how it is.'

I drew on the last of the cigarette and tossed the butt-end out of the window. I pulled on a pair of latex gloves, opened the leather wallet, and emptied the contents. A wedding band and a cross on a chain fell out. Tucked under a flap in a small pouch was a brass key. There was a membership card for the Rumney library, a season ticket to the sports centre, also in Rumney, an old cinema ticket and then a family photograph taken by a bench in a forest. I could make out two men and a woman all in their thirties, drinking from tall bottles of beer, broad smiles on their faces. A young boy sat at the end of the table with a girl younger than him, both smiling self-consciously.

'Is this him?' I asked.

Paddy mumbled a reply.

I turned the image round in my hand. I tried to guess who the people might be, but the rear didn't help – no date, or name. The clothes looked modern and I guessed the younger man was Dąbek.

From the inside compartment of the wallet I pulled out a slip of paper but as I unfolded it the damp material tore. I cursed under my breath and laid out the remainder on the office table. The words were faded and all I could make out were figures in various columns.

Paddy finished on the computer and stood up.

'You coming to watch?'

'Give me a minute – I've got an urgent call.'

He buttoned up his jacket and headed back to the mortuary. I found my mobile in my back pocket, tucked against the tickets for the game. The telephone rang a couple of times before my mother answered.

'John?'

'Really sorry,' I said. 'I won't be able to see you for lunch. Something urgent came up. A body in the Taff.'

'But you said—'

'There was nobody else.'

She paused and I could hear my father in the background asking her what was wrong. She shouted at him not to interrupt her.

'Look after yourself, John, and make sure you get enough to eat. You're working too hard.'

My mother always thought I worked too hard.

As I walked over to the mortuary I could hear classical music and when I pushed open the double doors, the sound of an orchestra thundered through loudspeakers.

'Wagner,' Paddy shouted. 'I can't work without it.'

'I prefer Elvis myself.'

Paddy gave me a brief smile and got straight back to work. Once he was finished he heaved a sigh and looked up at me with a satisfied look in his eyes, those of a man contented with his lot in life.

He promised to send me the report and warned me I'd have to wait for the results of the forensic tests. I trundled outside, pleased to escape the suffocating atmosphere of the mortuary. The sun was warmer, the wind had died down and the day was beginning to take shape. I had Michal's possessions in a plastic pocket in my left hand, and the car keys in my right when my mobile rang. I reached the car, put the plastic pocket on the roof and picked up the call.

       'Marco.'

       'Boss, where are you?'

       'By the car.'

       'What are you doing now?'

       'Get to the point, Boyd.'

       'Is the floater called Michal Dąbek?'

       'How the fu—'

       'I've got his boyfriend in the office now.'

Chapter 2

Queen Street police station was long past its demolition-by date but it had a homely feel, like an old jacket you couldn't face giving to the charity shop. I punched in the security code and let myself in. On the third floor, I pushed open the door to the CID office and met Boyd who was fidgeting with the water dispenser.

'Dąbek's boyfriend came in first thing,' Boyd said. 'He got suspicious when Michal didn't return this morning.'

'Why didn't he report it last night?'

Boyd shrugged.

'What's his name?'

'Kamil Holter.'

'How did he take it when you told him we'd found the body?'

'He went to pieces. He started sobbing and crying.'

I walked over to my office, put the bag of exhibits on the table and slumped down on the chair by the desk. Stale air hung in the room so I got up and opened the window, hoping the smell of chip fat and curry spices from the restaurants in Queen Street hadn't lingered all night. Working night shift in the summer was worse, when the stink could drill its way right up to the highest reaches of my nostrils.

Boyd had followed me, notebook in one hand, and water beaker in the other. I knew that Boyd's every instinct was to wear a suit and tie, so it must have been difficult getting accustomed to my shabby-chic-casual look. That morning he had a pair of navy denims and a white button-down shirt, the sort Marks & Spencer sell by the million, and a tie. A dark-blue version with red spots.

Normally the first thing we had to do was to secure the crime scene and preserve the evidence, but not knowing where Michal Dąbek died made that difficult. All we could do was wait for the forensics results. In the meantime we had a bag of exhibits here and a tongue in the lab.

'Is that all of the exhibits?' Boyd asked, pointing at the plastic wallet.

'And his tongue. It was cut out.'

He grimaced.

'So what's the story from the boyfriend?' I asked.

At six feet Boyd was a couple of inches taller than me, and several inches wider around the waist and chest. Boyd's straight hair was combed neatly back off his face and it reminded me of how I'd always wanted a fancy haircut to attract the girls, instead of the unruly wavy mass brushing my collar.

'He tried Michal's mobile last night but it didn't answer. Then he called at Michal's bed-sit first thing this morning. They don't live together. At least that's what he said, boss.'

Now we had the basics about his life – where he lived, who his lover was – but the photograph in the exhibits wallet and the key to some cupboard or cabinet might tell us more. I glanced at my watch; I still had plenty of time before the game.

'Where is he?' I asked.

'He's in interview room three.'

'Has he eaten anything?'

'The uniformed lads got him some chips earlier, but he left most of them. He said he wasn't hungry.'

I drew a hand over my mouth and thought about the ravioli my mother would be making now. The smell of the mushrooms and herbs would linger in the house and I could imagine her shaping the pasta with a lightness that years of practice had perfected.

13

I guessed lunch for me now would be another bag of chips or a pasty from the chippy down the road. But there was always the burger van by the gate to the City of Cardiff Stadium before the game and I was having dinner with Trish, so maybe I should skip the chips.

It was a short walk down the corridor to the interview room. I heaved open the door and looked down at the frightened face of Kamil Holter sitting on a plastic chair, chewing his lip.

He wore a thin, white, v-neck sleeveless top that opened halfway down his chest. From the bottom of the V small specks of grey hairs protruded. His hair was trimmed neatly, his face so pale and his cheeks so hollow it looked like something had sucked all the goodness from his body.

After a flaccid, lifeless handshake he carried on chewing his lip.

'Detective Inspector Marco,' I began.

He blinked hard and nodded an acknowledgment.

'I understand you knew Michal Dąbek.'

Another nod.

'What was your relationship?'

He flashed me a frightened look, ran his tongue over his lips, and sipped on a beaker of water.

'We were friends … good friends. He was my …'

'Boyfriend?' I said.

After half an hour Kamil stopped and drew breath, apparently relieved to be telling someone what had happened. He had been with Michal for three months but their relationship had been a secret, even from their closest friends. They both worked in an electrical components factory on one of the industrial estates on the outskirts of the city. It paid minimum wage but they still managed to send money home to their families in Poland.

'Do you know where Michal went last night?'

He brushed away a tear. 'He work hard. It is not fair.'

'Where did he go last night?'

'I not know for sure. He not tell me.'

'Where did you think he was going?'

He tossed his head to one side and looked away. 'Michal not tell me everything.'

'You must have some idea.'

He avoided my stare. 'I come for better life.'

I decided to try another approach. I opened the exhibits bag and picked out the photograph, pushing it over the table.

'Is this Michal's family?'

He squinted, then gave out a small whimper.

'His mother and father.'

'Do you know where it was taken?'

He shrugged and pulled out a pouch of roll-your-own tobacco.

'No smoking,' Boyd said.

'It looks like a forest somewhere. Where is it?' I asked.

'I not know.'

I asked about Michal's parents and although Kamil had never met them it sounded like he knew them well from the intimacies Michal had shared with him. I pushed over the small key. He raised his eyebrows and a flicker of recognition passed over his eyes. He moved his hand towards the key and then drew it away.

'Do you know what this is for?' I asked, half-believing he knew the answer.

'It is key.'

'Don't be clever.'

Kamil gave me a hurt look. 'Like I say, Michal not tell me everything. I not know what it is.'

'Well, has he got a cabinet in his flat?'

He shook his head.

'Does he have a cupboard where he works?'

Another shake of the head, this time slower. I looked at my watch, trying to justify not visiting Michal's flat and thinking that Boyd could do it on his own or that we could leave it until the morning. And thinking that I really didn't want to miss the game and that today was supposed to be my day off. But there was something about Kamil, something that wasn't right that made me realise I had to be present.

He threw his hands in the air. 'It could be anything.'

'So where did Michal go last night?'

'He was working.'

'What, at the factory?'

Kamil looked away again. 'Sometimes he work part-time, in club in town.'

I moved my chair closer to the desk.

'Which club is that?'

'Four Seasons.'

Boyd whistled under his breath.

The Four Seasons belonged to Frankie Prince.

And that meant trouble.

Chapter 3

'How's it going?'

Dave Hobbs could make the most innocuous question sound mysterious. He sat on a chair in the main office, his feet propped on the desk, and as he stared at me his eyes bulged. I'd walked in with Boyd and was making for my room, hoping I could ignore Hobbs.

'I hear it's a murder inquiry,' he said.

He rolled his 'r's, softened every vowel and I longed to imitate his North-Walian accent back to his face, but I'd probably find myself at the wrong end of a bullying complaint.

'Early days, Dave.'

'It should be my case. I was the duty DI.'

'The post mortem's been done and we've just finished interviewing the next of kin.'

Calling Kamil the next of kin stretched it, but I wasn't going to let Hobbs think there was any scope for interference.

'It's all under control, Dave. How was the Grangetown rapist?'

His lips twitched – the best attempt he could make at a smile. 'Waste of time. The WPC is with the girl now. Saturday night date that went wrong.'

'We'll have the floater cracked in no time.'

I glanced at Boyd, who was draping his jacket over the back of a chair and he nodded confirmation. Hobbs narrowed his eyes and I knew he didn't believe me, but there was nothing he could do. I could see his mind working, cursing himself for having passed up a murder investigation for a rape that was going nowhere. It would be back to burglaries and thefts for him next week. But he was thinking of every angle to get the case reassigned. I'd seen the look before and decided that I had to talk to the Superintendent. Hobbs adjusted his tie, moving it back and forth before returning it to its original position and then he pushed out his chin.

'Going to the game, Dave?' I said.

'Reports to write,' he said, lifting his feet off the desk before standing up and turning on his heels.

I walked into my room and sat down on the chair. I could hear the activity from the takeaway restaurants, that were preparing for another day, drifting up from across the street. I glanced at my watch and realised I had to get moving with the search of Michal's bed-sit. But first I had to see Superintendent Cornock.

It was a short walk through the corridors to his office and once I'd knocked I heard a muffled shout. Cornock was leaning over a tank of goldfish when I entered, not the sort you buy in a bag at a funfair but large multi-coloured ones that looked well fed.

Spencer Cornock had a short back-and-sides in the old-fashioned style, his shirt was white and the tie a solid-blue. In fact his shirt was always white, he always wore a dark-blue suit and it was difficult to tell whether it was the same one each day.

'Good morning, John.'

'Morning, sir.'

'Fish are very soothing you know.'

I nodded.

'That's why they have them in doctors' waiting rooms.'

He obviously went to a different surgery from the one I used. All I could bring to mind was a waiting room with stacks of out-of-date magazines, the sound of babies crying and the coughs and splutters from chronically sick people. Cornock lived in Cyncoed, where houses were detached and trees lined the roads, where the doctors had more time for their patients, and presumably their waiting rooms had tanks with fish, probably tropical.

'I took a call this morning about a body in the Taff. Down by the Millennium Stadium.'

Cornock stepped back towards his desk and sat down before giving me a quizzical look. 'I thought you were off duty.'

'Dave Hobbs was the duty DI but he didn't want to take the call. He went to Grangetown for a domestic.'

He pinched his lips and his eyebrows almost met above the top of his nose. I continued, rather pleased with the reaction. 'I've done the post mortem and collected the exhibits. And we've interviewed the next of kin, well sort of.'

'Sort of?'

'The dead man's boyfriend. He was really cut up.'

'Can he do the identification?'

'He should do. But there was a Polish identity card on the body.'

'Ah,' he said. 'The realities of modern Europe, John. Keep me informed.'

I got up to leave and as I did so I told him about Frankie Prince.

He gave me a wintry gaze. 'Be careful, John.'

I mumbled a reply as I left Cornock, who picked up an expensive-looking pen and peered down at the mass of paperwork on his desk. It was the best I could have achieved in the circumstances, as procedure made it clear that once a senior officer had been allocated to a case, it wasn't normally reassigned. I smiled, considering what Cornock might make of Hobbs turning down a murder investigation in favour of a domestic.

Passing an open window, I saw rain-threatening

clouds drifting over the sky and hoped that any showers would keep away until after the game. Boyd was fiddling with a set of car keys in his hand when I walked up to his desk.

He looked bored. 'Ready, boss?'

We collected Kamil on the way to the car park and after Boyd unlocked the unmarked police car we climbed in. Kamil looked relieved to be leaving the station. We threaded our way through the city centre towards Newport Road and then took a right towards Splott. Kamil sat in the back, dead quiet.

Along the streets delivery vans were disgorging boxes of clothes and trinkets for the pound shops. Children on small bikes toured the pavements surrounding the terraced houses. I knew that most of the Eastern Europeans in Cardiff had found their way to the cheap bed-sits owned by landlords who crammed two into a bedroom.

After twenty minutes Boyd pulled over and parked.

'Is this the place?' I turned to Kamil who was leaning forward.

'Yes.'

I held the palm of my hand towards him. 'Let's have the key then.'

He put two Yale latchkeys into my hand.

'The one with green tape is for front door,' he said.

I pushed a small rusty gate to one side and, choosing the green key, opened the front door. Two old bicycles were propped up against the bottom of the staircase: the air smelt stale and vinegary.

'What's that stench?' Boyd asked, wafting a hand in front of his face.

'Red cabbage and sausage,' Kamil said. 'Polish food.'

The smell lingered and my mouth took on a strange, salty sensation.

'Where's Michal's room?' I said.

Kamil pointed upstairs. 'Second floor.'

A threadbare carpet covered the stairs and the handrail rattled against the spindles.

'It's through here,' Kamil said, as we reached the second floor.

A plastic number seven hung at an angle in the middle of the door. I fumbled for the other key.

I took two steps into the room, Kamil immediately behind me. Covering the bed were the contents of several flimsy wooden drawers, which had been thrown in a pile by the window. At the far end of the room the doors of the makeshift kitchen units hung limply from their carcasses, bottles and sprays spewing out over the floor.

When Kamil saw the destruction he put his hand to his mouth and said something in Polish – it sounded hard; I didn't need a translation to understand what he meant. Boyd pushed his way past Kamil and let out a low whistle.

'Better call the CSIs,' I said to Boyd.

Kamil walked around the bed, piled high with ripped clothes and the remains of cushions and pillows.

'Don't touch anything,' I told him as he leant down and fingered a piece of clothing. He looked me in the eye and straightened up. 'This is a crime scene,' I said, raising my voice.

Boyd stepped back into the room. 'On their way, boss.'

I walked over to the wardrobe, a decrepit wooden one, good enough only for firewood, and pulled open the doors. Some old T-shirts were draped on hangers, all cut to shreds.

Kamil bent down and picked up a box, of a fancy purple-speckled colour. He fiddled with the green ribbon tied in a bow on the lid. It looked like a container for carrying expensive Belgian chocolates.

I looked over at him and said, 'I thought I told you ...'

He held it tightly in the palm of his hand and tugged at the ribbon. It fell away; he lifted the cover.

And then he screamed.

The box shook in his hand as he gulped for air. I stepped over the discarded piles of clothes and took the box from his hand. I looked down and for the second time that day I saw a dismembered tongue.

Chapter 4

I groaned when I heard the voice on the stairs.

Alvine Dix was the fussiest crime scene manager attached to Southern Division of the Wales Police Service and usually made no attempt to hide her irritation at police officers' contamination of a crime scene. Her voice, a couple of decibels too loud, echoed around the empty stairwell.

'I don't want anyone leaving the building until we've established the outer perimeter.'

I guessed she was talking to the crime scene investigators who would be following in her slipstream. She stopped shouting instructions when she reached the landing and gave me a curt smile.

I nodded at Michal's room. 'In there.'

She pushed open the door and stood for a moment, surveying the carnage. 'What a mess.'

'There's a tongue in that box.' I pointed to the floor, where the box now lay.

After removing its lid she held the container in the palm of her hand and looked down at the contents as though she couldn't quite believe what she was seeing. Turning to one of the investigators standing at the door, she dictated a long list of instructions, so when she paused for breath I made my excuses and left. On the landing I met Boyd who'd returned from taking Kamil home.

'We need to talk to all the tenants,' I said.

'Sure thing.'

'Somebody should have heard or seen something.'

Boyd would work down from the top floor and I headed downstairs to start from the ground floor. I tried the first room and the door edged open. I flashed my warrant card and saw an unshaven face and thick glasses through the narrow gap.

'Police. I need to talk to you.'

The door eased open and a thin man with buckteeth looked at me. 'What you want?'

The accent was Polish or Hungarian or Latvian – I could never tell them apart.

'Did you know Michal Dąbek?'

'Sure.'

'Michal is dead.'

'Too bad,' he replied, without a flicker of emotion crossing his face.

'What's your name?'

He spelt his name slowly as I wrote it down in my pocketbook. I glanced at the name and attempted a pronunciation but he corrected me. He started to close the door but I shoved my foot over the threshold.

'I know nothing.' He even managed to sneer.

'Did you hear anything last night?'

'Like I say, nothing.'

'There was someone in Michal's bed-sit, turned the place over.'

'Turned over?'

'I'll need to see inside.'

'What for?' He raised his voice a fraction. 'You have warrant?'

I could hear the television blaring in the background and guessed that he watched too much TV police dramas.

'We'll need to interview you properly.' I tried to sound menacing.

He shrugged and pushed the door closed.

As I moved down the corridor towards the rear of the house a sensor picked up my body heat and a dim light came on. A small, narrow window that badly needed cleaning filtered a smudge of sunshine onto the walls.

Leon, the occupant of the second room, was more

cooperative and he slumped on his bed, yawned violently, rubbed his eyes, and then scratched the makings of a beard that seemed to dribble over his chin.

'You wake me,' Leon said, explaining that he'd been working nights.

His eyes widened in shock when I told him about Michal, and his face lost what colour it had.

'When was this?'

'Found in the river this morning.'

He had no more information than the occupant of the first room – seen nothing, heard nothing. I got Leon's date of birth, checked his identity and left, warning him he could expect to see us again.

The final door opened against a chain and the face of a young girl peered under it. There was a grain of apprehension in her eyes. I held out my warrant card for several seconds, trying to reassure her. She eased the door closed and I heard the chain falling away.

I could still see the uneasiness in her face after I entered her bed-sit. It was neat, tidy – just as you'd expect from a girl living on her own. There was a small bunch of fresh flowers in a tall plastic mug and the place smelt clean. She even had some picture frames on a table in one corner. I tried to pronounce her surname from the passport she pushed into my hands.

'Sob …?' I began.

'Dagmara Sobczak.'

'Is this your hometown?' I nodded towards the photographs.

'Sure. I am from Warsaw. Lots of Polish people come to England from Warsaw.'

I felt like telling her that this was Wales, but let it pass.

'Do you know Michal, from room seven?'

'Yes. Of course. he comes from Warsaw too.'

'I've got some bad news for you. Michal has been killed.'

She blinked hard several times before fidgeting with her hands, wrapping them over each other and then her eyes filled with tears.

'This is awful.'

'How well did you know him?'

'What happened to him?' She looked me straight in the eye; her English was good and her accent clear.

'We pulled his body out of the river this morning. He was murdered.'

Her eyes opened wide. 'This is awful.'

'Michal's room was trashed last night. Did you hear anything? Did you see anyone?'

'There are lots of different people living in this house,' she said, sadness in her voice. 'Lots of people come and go. It is difficult to know who lives here.'

After I scribbled down the details of what she could tell me I left and heard the chain being replaced once the door closed behind me. Boyd was waiting for me by the front door.

'Let me guess – nobody heard anything or saw anything or wants to get involved,' I said.

'That's right, boss.'

I needed to catch up with my five-a-day habit so I stepped outside onto the square of concrete that passed for the front garden. A couple of limp weeds were clinging to life around the edges and the tape marking the outer perimeter of the crime scene waved silently. The road was quiet, too quiet. I saw the vertical blinds on a nearby window flicker as a hand drew them to one side.

'So. Nobody saw nothing,' I said out loud.

'Poland must be a shit place to live,' Boyd said,

kicking some loose pebbles with his shoes.

'Living in a dump like this can't be fun.'

'All the hotels are full of Poles and Hungarians. There must be thousands in Cardiff.'

'Nothing we can do about it, Boyd. We're all in the EU together.'

'I know, but only last week a cousin of mine in Llanelli went for a job interview and all the rest were Poles. Some of them could hardly speak a word of English. And then my cousin was asked in the interview if she could talk Welsh. Something isn't right ...'

I put the second cigarette of the day to my lips and held it between my teeth as I searched for the lighter in my pocket. I glanced at my watch, remembered about the tickets for the game, and knew that Robbie would kill me if he missed the match. There was no way I could leave the scene while Alvine Dix was around. She'd have complained to the Chief Constable that I'd left for a football match – more than my career was worth.

'Boyd, give one of the uniformed lads a shout.'

He went back into the house, returning a moment later followed by a young constable who looked like he hadn't yet started to shave. The constable seemed relieved when I explained that I needed him to deliver an important package to Queen Street, and I passed him the football tickets in an envelope.

I finished the cigarette, tossing the butt into the street. Then I fumbled for my mobile and texted Robbie, telling him to collect the tickets at the police station.

After two hours making preliminary house-to-house enquiries I leant against a garden wall, realising it would be a marathon task getting the evidence we'd need. I tried to imagine what Michal must have thought of this place and why he had chosen a life here and not in Poland. I suspected that Kamil was probably the answer. Boyd was walking towards me down the opposite side of the street and I knew from the look on his face that the result of his house-to-house was just as fruitless as mine.

The investigators were finishing photographing and bagging up the exhibits from the scene when I returned to the second floor.

'There are prints all over the place,' Alvine began.

I saw the dust covering the surfaces. There were piles of clothes, all stacked into a corner and the furniture had been tidied. 'Find anything?'

'What exactly are we looking for?'

I shrugged.

'Well if you don't know – how can you expect us to mind-read?'

I left Alvine and found Boyd talking to one of the other occupants. I heard the words *civil liberties* and *human rights*. Boyd was looking frustrated – arms crossed, head pitched to one side – but he kept his cool.

'We'll be here as long as it takes,' he said.

'But I need shit.' The voice was thick and accented. For some reason there were CSIs working in the bathrooms.

When I saw the time I realised that the second half had just begun, so I sent Robbie a text. Moments later my mobile beeped and, reading his reply, I smiled. It was a goal each and the Chelsea fans were chanting for the manager to be sacked – nothing changes.

In the car journey back to the station I could feel the tiredness aching at the bottom of my back. I wondered if Cardiff had scored again and then I realised that dinner with Trish would have to wait. I tapped out a text to her, explaining about Michal and the reply came seconds later – *Indian later?* I sent a reply as Boyd pulled into the car park.

We spent another hour notifying the hospitals

about the dismembered tongue. It was difficult to imagine someone turning up at Accident and Emergency with their tongue missing. I knew we had a body to find but we still had procedures to follow.

It was after nine when I finally left Queen Street. In the car I retraced my steps from early that morning. Back home I slumped into the sofa and picked up the television control. *Top Gear* filled the screen and I began to relax as I watched the introduction, trying to imagine what I would do if I could afford a Porsche.

I heard the scratch of the key in the door and then Trish's voice as she walked in, carrying a takeaway. I told her about my day as she heaped dollops of chicken curry onto a plate, then rice and some chapattis and poured chutney into a bowl. We sat watching television after finishing the meal until Trish gave me a light kiss on the lips.

'Fancy a shower?' she asked.

I paused the player. Clarkson could wait until later.

Chapter 5

When I needed breakfast therapy I went to Ramone's. It was the best greasy-spoon in Cardiff and probably the best in Wales. I raised a hand to Greg, standing behind the counter, and he nodded back. I always had the same order so I didn't need to remind him. At a table by the window I cleared the condiments to one side and turned to the sports pages of the *Western Mail*. In the end Cardiff had lost by one goal and the report suggested it might have been more. It was a poor start to their first season in the Premiership and I hoped they weren't going to be relegated at the end of it.

A waitress in a white apron smiled at me as she put the plate down on the table.

'All right, John?'

I smiled back.

'You OK for sauces?' She sounded tired, even though it was the start of the day. I nodded.

The bacon was perfect, the hash browns crisp and the beans sweet and tomatoey. The waitress came back a second time and left a mug of tea by my plate. I was sweeping a piece of bread around the plate, gathering the last of the tomato sauce and egg when I saw Terry walking towards the café. He had a lopsided gait and kept darting his head from side to side, as though he expected a car to mount the pavement and collide with him. He pushed open the door, gave me a hesitant smile, and made his way over to my table. He eased himself into the bench seat opposite me.

'Do you always have to sit in the window?'

'It's the best place. I can see the world go by.'

'And the whole fucking world can see us.'

The waitress reappeared and Terry ordered a full

breakfast.

'So, what's the story?' Terry asked.

'A floater in the Taff last night.'

Terry shrugged. 'So. Thirty pints of lager and he can't walk straight.'

I gave him an executive summary – just enough for him to know more than he'd learn from the television news, but nothing prejudicial to the inquiry. The waitress returned with Terry's meal and a mug of tea. He turned three spoonfuls of sugar into the steaming liquid and began shovelling the food into his mouth.

'So why call me?' he said, mumbling through a mouthful of bacon and egg.

'Frankie Prince.'

Terry stopped eating and gave a furtive look out of the window. He took a tissue from the dispenser on the table and dabbed the corner of his mouth, removing a drop of ketchup.

'Frankie Prince,' he repeated slowly, as though the name itself was contaminated. 'What's he got to do with a body in the Taff?'

I raised my eyebrows. He knew I couldn't tell him any more.

'I want to know what the latest is about him.'

'The latest?' Terry spluttered. 'He's into everything. Drugs, property, massage parlours, nightclubs.'

'Nothing new?'

'You want me to start asking around about Frankie Prince?' His eyes widened, incredulity in his voice.

'That's it. You owe me, remember.'

'That was a long time ago.'

'I've got a good memory. And I bear a grudge.'

Terry stopped eating for a second. 'For fuck's sake. I'd better check my life insurance. In fact I haven't got any fucking life insurance. And I quite enjoy not being dead.'

Terry finished the last of his beans and took a large slurp of the sweet tea.

'It's important, Terry.'

'Yeh. Of course, of course,' he replied. He sidled out of the seat and threw the paper napkin onto his plate before leaving. Through the window I watched him put a mobile to his ear as he picked up the pace of his stride. After paying, I raised a hand to Greg, thanked him for breakfast and promised to be back soon. Outside, a cool autumn breeze blew along the road and a group of students in thin T-shirts and jeans snaked down towards the university.

When I arrived at the station I nudged my Mondeo into a narrow space between a patrol car and a Scientific Support Vehicle. I took the staircase to the third floor at a leisurely pace, the sound of muffled conversations and one-sided telephone calls filling the stairwell. I ignored a glance from Hobbs that said *late again* and made my way to my office.

Boyd had been working with me for the last three months. At first I hadn't been sure what to make of him. He always wore a suit, shirt with a tie and shoes that kept themselves clean. His personnel file said he'd studied law at Swansea University and that he was *committed to a career with the Wales Police Service.* Because I became a policeman by accident when I was twenty I didn't understand how he could have wanted his whole life carved out in careful steps. He'd married young and Mandy now wanted children. But he was conscientious and I could rely on him.

He knocked on my door and I waved him in.

'Have you heard from the factory where Michal

works?' I asked as he sat down.

'Not yet.'

'Then call them again. We need to find out everything about his friends and work colleagues.'

Boyd nodded. 'What do you make of Kamil?'

'If they were lovers, then he's our best chance of finding someone with a motive for Michal's death. And we need to talk to the Polish community in Cardiff. Is there a community centre?'

'There's a Polish pub down the docks.'

I'd seen some of the intelligence reports on the place. No drugs, just industrial-scale boozing; and they sorted out any trouble themselves.

'I thought there were Polish shops in Cardiff.'

Boyd nodded. 'And there's one in Newport. They sell massive jars of gherkins, funny-shaped biscuits and dark rye bread.'

'How do you know so much about Polish cuisine?'

'I had a Polish girlfriend in college.'

'Really.' I wondered whether Mandy knew. 'And is there a Polish priest?' Even I knew that Poland was a Catholic country. 'We need to get into the Polish community. Somebody must know something.'

'This could take a long time.'

Before I could agree, the telephone rang.

'Is that Inspector Marco?' It was a whiny tentative voice. 'This is Matt Lloyd. I'm Michal Dąbek's supervisor. You left a message yesterday. It was Sunday.'

'You've heard about Michal?'

'Yes, of course. Terrible. I can see you this morning if it helps. But I'm going on holiday this afternoon. My wife and I have booked two weeks in the Canaries. We always go this time of the year. And the weather—'

'We'll be there as soon as.'

I heard him say something about the traffic jams as I put the telephone down. I grabbed the car keys and shouted to Boyd.

After twenty minutes we turned into the industrial estate off the link motorway and eventually we found the car park of the electronics factory. I ignored the small notice saying *Reserved Braggins* screwed to a pole in the ground and we walked over to the office.

A girl with straw-coloured hair and a very short skirt sat behind a reception desk with a glass top..

'I'm here to see Matt Lloyd,' I said.

'Have you appointment?' she drawled. The accent was different from the Eastern Europeans I'd heard yesterday but it still sounded foreign.

I explained about Michal and her lower lip fell slightly.

'Sit, please,' she said, before speaking into a telephone.

The reception had magazines about holidays in the sun and the latest gadgets and toys. After a few minutes a door opened at the far end of the reception area and a tall man with a high forehead came out towards us. He smiled, shook our hands and told us his name was Matt Lloyd.

'Morning, Inspector. Awful about Michal.'

We followed him through various corridors to a small room looking out over the production line. The smell of grease hung in the air and the faint hum of machinery filled the room.

'What can you tell me about Michal?' I asked, once we'd sat down.

He shuffled some papers on the desk. 'He was well liked and conscientious. They all are—'

'They …?'

'Poles. Eastern Europeans in general.'

'What exactly do you do here?'

'We build components for the electronics industry – plugs, switches, consumer units. All low-tech stuff. We pay minimum wage and the Poles don't complain. That's the only way we keep the business here. Otherwise it would have gone to the Far East a long time ago.'

He scribbled on a notepad when I asked for a list of Michal's work colleagues. From an inside pocket I took out a small plastic pocket with the key we'd found on Michal's body and showed it to Lloyd.

'Do you have any idea what this key might be for?'

He shrugged. 'No idea.'

'Do you have lockers for the staff?'

'Yes. But I don't think this key fits.'

'Can we see the locker room?'

He found two hard hats from a box behind his desk. 'Health and Safety.'

As we got up the door burst open and a short man with shiny hair and arms that looked like he'd been hung from a height for a long time walked in. He shouted something I didn't understand and then threw his wiry arms in the air.

'Mr Lloyd. The locker room,' he said eventually, between lungfuls of breath. 'Come quick.'

Lloyd left the room and we followed him through the shop floor. We threaded our way, passed the machines punching out metal boxes with deafening regularity, until we reached a door that said *Staff Room*, which he pushed open.

Two girls sat by a table in one corner, comforting each other. One of them wiped away the remains of a tear; the other looked at Lloyd and nodded over at the two open lockers.

Lloyd grabbed a locker door and it squeaked open.

I stepped over towards him and saw the disgust on his face.

I looked into the locker at another dismembered tongue.

By the time Alvine Dix had finished, she'd found two more.

'Animals, of course,' she said.

'Can you tell what animal?'

'What difference will it make?' she asked, an exasperated look on her face.

'Well ...' I struggled.

Alvine carefully tried every locker but Michal's key fitted none of them. She piled the contents into an exhibits bag, which she handed to one of the CSIs in her team.

'We've got work to do,' she said.

After a couple of hours gathering the details of everyone on the shop floor, Boyd and I stood to one side of the yellow perimeter tape by the door to the locker room, looking at Alvine.

'Are you two finished?'

I nodded.

'Then bugger off. I've had my fill of people gawking at me. All the staff took turns to look at me as though I was a performing seal.'

Back at the station we sat in silence in my office, Boyd passed me his list of the staff and I noticed Leon's name from Howick Street. I'd seen him from a distance but he'd looked away, as though he didn't want anyone to notice he'd recognised me. Now we had five tongues, a dead body and a lot of work to get through.

The usual post-lunch torpor hung in the atmosphere at

Queen Street like a thin sea mist in a horror movie. Yawns were stifled, shoulders rubbed, and arms stretched. I dropped a ham and cheese sandwich onto my desk with a bottle of flavoured water. I ran through the notes on my desk. So much for the paperless office. I gnawed at the sandwich and flushed a large piece of cheddar down with a mouthful of the coloured liquid that was supposed to taste of oranges.

There'd been a voicemail and a text from Cornock telling me he wanted to see me. I couldn't ignore the requests for too long. I threw the remains of the sandwich into the bin and headed for his office.

When I knocked there was the sound of papers scuffling from inside the office and a loud shout that I took to be an invitation. Cornock was on his knees gathering files that had fallen on the floor. When he stood up, clutching the papers in one hand, he smoothed down an imaginary loose hair with a gentle sweep of his free hand. I'd known Cornock for years but now he was beginning to look old and worn out. His skin was pale and the wrinkles around his eyes creased deeply. The ageing process had hit him hard, and earlier than most, once his daughter became a drug addict and he'd abruptly stopped talking about her nursing career.

'Sit down,' he said, nodding at the chair in front of his desk. He cleared his throat. 'You'd better bring me up to date.'

'We visited Dąbek's place of work and there was another tongue in a locker. In fact we found three today – Alvine reckons they're all from animals.'

Cornock nodded as though he knew it all. He raised his eyes and shuffled the papers some more.

'How are you, John?' He managed to give every word more emphasis than he needed to.

I could see where this was going.

'If you need help with the investigation I want you to tell me.' He gave me an intense, challenging stare.

He rested back in his chair and played with a pen in his right hand. We both knew what he really wanted to say, but he was finding it hard to confront the difficult question. I'd been dry for over a year now and the longer I stayed that way the better it felt. Not that I didn't find it hard, sitting in a pub looking at a pint of Brains, but the pain of remembering how I could be always came back to haunt me.

'I could assign Dave Hobbs to assist ...'

I could see Hobbs worming his way into the investigation by suggesting I wasn't up to it.

'Not necessary.' I held up my hand to stop his train of thought. 'I haven't touched a drop for over a year. My mother would kill me if I did.'

He made a narrow smile, relieved that I had mentioned the drinking and I knew he'd go no further. Cornock had faced the pain of dealing with a family crisis. He never mentioned his wife, but talk was that she was a recluse who wouldn't go out of the house after what happened to their daughter.

I spent the rest of the day working my way through the results of an internet search for *amputating tongues*. Saddam Hussein had, my search told me, been a keen exponent of this form of torture and there were graphic accounts of how his gangs would nail people's tongues to tables and then torture them before amputating other bits of their bodies. It made me feel sick that amputating tongues was an accepted part of the arsenal employed by Russian Mafia gangs – inspired by torture methods from the

Middle Ages – who especially liked to keep their victims alive; they used old-fashioned razors. In the States there was a story about a young boy who'd fallen and bitten clean through his tongue, but after it having been stitched back, he made a full recovery.

I could hear Boyd in the CID office talking to Accident and Emergency departments. It was obvious from his replies that nobody was taking him seriously.

Then I read about the cases of cancer where tongues had to be amputated to prevent the disease spreading and then reconstructed with skin from the hands and wrist. It was long process and one patient had been on the operating table for fourteen hours. I looked at my hand – it was difficult to imagine what it would feel like to have skin from my hand in my mouth. Queen Street emptied as the evening drew in and I closed the window against the falling temperatures. I worked through the unopened emails in my Inbox. The forensic report confirmed that the tongue in Leon's bed-sit was human and that the three in the factory were animal.

Boyd had loosened his tie when he appeared at my door, his hands full of folders. 'I've got more paperwork on the Claudia Avenue burglaries.'

I sat back in my chair. The investigation had been ongoing for months, but the residents were still annoyed and I had to placate them somehow. I pointed towards the pile of papers on the corner of my desk and Boyd dropped the files on top.

He yawned and then stretched his back before adding, 'The local Polish priest is going to call me tomorrow. And I've done all the hospitals in Cardiff and Newport. There's been no reports of anybody turning up without a tongue.'

'I didn't expect so,' I said. 'It must be a ritual. The

killer's sending a message. Telling someone not to talk.'

Chapter 6

I sat outside the Four Seasons and watched the sun reflecting off the bonnet of the silver-blue Aston Martin Vantage. I looked around the inside of my car, realising that being a professional criminal promised the chance of a better motor than a policeman's salary could ever afford. The Aston had personalised plates of course – no self-respecting successful businessman would be without them. It had eight cylinders, a 4.7-litre engine and could do 0–60 miles an hour in 4.9 seconds. The upholstery would be leather with pieces of walnut veneer along the dashboard. I could almost smell it. But all I could really smell was the tired and dirty fabric of my Mondeo with its collection of stones and shingle in the footwell that would be more at home on the beach in Barry Island.

Frankie Prince was as well connected as the national grid – and when he flicked a switch things happened. If Michal had been working for Frankie then I had to know what he'd been doing. I left the car, pointed the remote and squeezed hard until the lights flashed.

The gossip in Southern Division had been that it had been Frankie's wife who had christened the club – she thought the name would add class. The trials of everyday life had left Lucy Prince behind when she got married and she'd slipped into a life of indulgence and luxury, one that included her own health club and art gallery.

An illuminated sign sparkled above the main door, which opened easily, despite its size, and I stepped inside. It was a barn of a place with high ceilings, tall windows and various walkways suspended from the ceiling with strong chains. A short woman came towards me with a swagger that suggested she wanted to be taller. She had a dull, resigned look on her face, as though she was expecting me to be a photocopier salesman who she could get rid of in seconds. I flashed my warrant card.

'Is Mr Prince available?'

'He's very busy.'

I cocked my head as if to say that she'd have to try harder than that.

'It's important.' I gazed around the club. 'I'll wait. Can I get a cappuccino?'

She turned her back on me and walked to the rear of the club. I walked around, running my hands along the leather-trimmed sofas and chairs. The table tops were chipped and the surfaces cracked, but I guessed that when the lights were dimmed and the music thumped no one would notice. It wasn't long until a door at the far end opened and the same woman called me over.

'Mr Prince will see you now.' She made it sound like an audience with the Pope.

I followed her into a well-lit corridor and I noticed the image of Gareth Edwards running in his famous try for the Barbarians, alongside photographs of every Wales rugby team since the golden era of the nineteen seventies. For a short woman she walked quickly and as I dawdled she disappeared from view. There were pictures of the Arms Park and the old Stradey Park in Llanelli. I stopped when I saw the picture of Delme Thomas carried shoulder-high by his teammates after their win over the All Blacks in 1972. My father had been at the game and once a year he would produce the programme from a plastic pocket where it was kept like a sacred relic.

The girl reappeared by my side and cleared her throat. 'This way, please.'

There was the faintest sound of classical music from the room ahead of us. She gave the door the gentlest of knocks before walking in.

Frankie Prince was standing with a remote control in his hand, pointing at a stereo system and the music softened to a background hum. The collar of his shirt closed perfectly around his neck and the sleeves fell to just above the wrist. A little shorter than me, he held out his hand and I felt his damp palm against mine. I sat down on a leather chesterfield that could have seated the whole of the Cardiff City team and caught him wiping his hand against his trousers, which were held in place by a thick and immaculate brown leather belt.

'What can I do for you, Inspector Marco?' Frankie said, sitting down behind an enormous mahogany desk.

'I'm investigating the murder of Michal Dąbek. He worked for you.'

'I employ a lot of people,' he said, without averting his eyes and as an afterthought added, 'Sorry to hear that. How did it happen?'

'The body was found in the Taff, Sunday morning. Strangled.'

Frankie raised his eyebrows. 'Terrible. Does he have a family?'

'What did he do for you?'

The short girl was standing by the desk that dominated one corner of the room. She was fiddling with a smartphone that was making a beeping noise.

'Your next appointment is here, Mr Prince,' she said, right on cue.

I stayed where I was – Frankie wasn't going to succeed with that old trick.

'We have reason to believe he was employed here at the Four Seasons. What did he do?'

'I really don't know. You can check with the manager.'

'Can you get him here? Now.'

Frankie shot me an impatient look and then nodded at the nameless girl. I made myself comfortable and wondered what he'd think if I lit the second of my five-a-day. I scanned the table top for an ashtray but the room smelt clean and tobacco-free. I tried small talk. 'Do you employ many Eastern Europeans?'

'They're good workers. Loyal and hard working. They understand what hard work means, Inspector.'

Frankie was enjoying his own rhetoric. 'We've lost that work ethic.'

I flinched – Frankie talking about ethics was akin to Genghis Khan talking about forgiveness and loving his enemies.

'How many Poles do you have working for you?'

'Quite a few. The exact numbers …' He drew his hand in the air as if remembering was beneath him. He probably knew exactly how many and all their names and history and how many of them owed him. It was the sort of information that Frankie's business thrived on.

The door opened and slid over the deep pile of the carpet. A man in a crumpled shirt, his sleeves rolled up, entered, looking flustered.

Frankie got up and stepped from behind his desk. 'This is Jim White, the manager of the club. I'm sure he'll help.'

I was being dismissed, passed to a minion and Frankie was hoping that I'd be out of his club soon enough. I got out my notebook and found a biro in my jacket pocket. I sensed Frankie's frustration and the sly glances around the room.

I struck a friendly tone. 'Jim, what can you tell me about Michal Dąbek?'

He glanced at Frankie. 'He worked here as a doorman.'

'When did he start?'

'I'd need to check the records.'

'How often did he work?'

'A couple of nights a week. Sometimes more; it depended.'

'On what?'

'On how much he wanted to work and how busy we were.'

'Was he working on Saturday night?'

'Yes. He left the club at two. Said he wasn't feeling well.'

I asked about the names of the other doormen who'd worked that Saturday, knowing that all the answers had been too sudden, too easy. I felt set up, as though they had expected me. I wrote down all the names in the notebook and doodled a bit on a page, killing time, waiting for Frankie to say something about his important meeting. I was disappointed when he waited for me to finish. Then the girl, still tapping into her smartphone, was instructed to take me through to the main entrance.

I walked past the Aston and over towards my Mondeo. My alloys needed cleaning and I noticed two new scratches on the paintwork by the passenger door.

I sat in the car and looked up at the club. Getting a story right can take time and trouble and thinking ahead. Once White hadn't asked why I wanted to know about Michal, I knew that something was wrong. Frankie was probably in his office right now shouting at him.

Chapter 7

'Who lives in number ten?'

I asked the question without thinking. I'd spent a couple of hours reading statements and surveillance reports that had been sitting on my desk for days. Occasionally the thought that they needed my attention had caused spasms of guilt. Michal's death had pushed them further down the list of priorities.

'The prime minister,' Boyd said.

When I raised my eyes and looked at him I could see that the self-congratulatory smirk on his face was developing into a smile. I had decided long ago that comedy was definitely not Boyd's strong point and that the attempt at humour by junior officers should be a disciplinary matter.

'Very funny,' I said, not twitching my mouth a millimetre.

'You did ask.'

'Claudia Avenue,' I said, reminding him of the task in hand.

In the leafy suburbs of the Heath, the residents of Claudia Avenue, with yachts parked in Marbella and children with Audis, had been plagued by a spate of burglaries. A man with a string of stars tattooed around his neck and a strong Scottish accent had been caught in various gardens, protesting that he was '*looking for Geoff*' and could the occupant help. The call to Area Control room came as soon as he left.

But the mysterious sneak thief had proven elusive and the pressure was on. Cornock wanted results, presumably as a consequence of telephone calls from concerned residents and local politicians. It was near where he lived and at our last review he'd made the position clear. 'Can't have this sort of thing going on.'

The only house that had been spared was number ten. I wondered about the prime minister and all the security he had and whether the residents of 10 Claudia Avenue could afford the same level of protection.

'You won't believe it,' Boyd said, as though he was the sole guardian of some important secret.

'Spit it out.'

'Granville Tront.'

He let the name hang in the air.

Tront and Tront was one of the leading firms of defence solicitors in Cardiff and Granville was its senior partner. The speed at which Granville worked earned him the nickname GTi and I first got to know him fifteen years earlier as a young constable interviewing a suspect on a drugs charge. The sergeant had tried to warn me, but then the colour behind my ears was a deep green and when the case got before the stipendiary magistrate GTi tore it apart.

'How much are the houses worth?' I asked absently.

'A million, easy.'

'Doesn't Frankie Prince live in that area?'

'Moved to the Vale last year. What's the Four Seasons like?'

'Haven't you been?'

'Mandy'd kill me.'

'Frankie knows something. I could tell.' I lay back in my chair, curling my arms around the back of my head. 'Everything was ... staged.'

'Do you think he was involved with killing Michal?'

'Frankie Prince is capable of anything. Aren't we all, if the circumstances push us to extremes?'

Boyd nodded.

'What have we got on the Scotsman?'

'We haven't got much. Twenty houses all done over in the small hours when the owners were out. It must have been a surveillance job.'

'Did anyone see any vehicle parked on the road?'

Boyd shook his head.

'And there's no forensics and the chances of recovering the stolen televisions and stereos are non-existent. The Scotsman can't be that stupid if he can disable the security alarms.'

'They probably weren't turned on, boss. You know how people can be.'

I was always amazed how many people didn't use their alarms, as though they expected them to go off by magic.

'Have we traced anything?'

'You're joking.'

'Off chance.'

I hated paperwork and the more I fingered the various coloured pieces of paper, the more despondent I became. I could feel my stomach turning. I had to eat.

'So what do we do, boss?' asked Boyd, as he followed me out of the station.

'Have lunch and think about it.'

It was a short walk to Mario's through the midday shoppers.

'Should we increase the surveillance?' Boyd asked, as we weaved past pedestrians.

My mind was already thinking about food. 'Sorry?'

'Surveillance in Claudia Avenue.'

'Yes, of course. And do a memo to Cornock telling him.'

I pushed open the door, quickly ordering a bacon sandwich. Boyd chose the tuna baguette – no mayo – and a side salad, instead of his usual portion of chips. We found a couple of seats in the back room, which we shared with a crowd of girls. I could hear the giggles and roars of laughter when they mentioned various boys' names.

'Half rations?' I said.

'Got to watch my diet. Mandy complains like hell. Tells me I have to cut out all the crap I eat.'

'Really?'

'She's convinced that my diet will affect my sperm count.'

'How does that work?'

'I don't know. She's read all these articles.'

A waitress appeared with two plates. Boyd picked up the tuna baguette and stared at it, before prodding the lettuce and tomatoes on the side of the plate.

'Salad's good for you.'

Boyd chewed a mouthful of tuna.

'I thought you were looking into IVF?'

Boyd shook his head before swallowing.

'Might do. For now she's into keeping charts of her temperature and her cycle. Best time for it. I know days in advance.' He sounded unenthusiastic. Most men would have gladly swapped with him. 'She's got everything planned. The birth, the nursery. Everything. Did you have time off?'

'Sorry?'

'Paternity.'

'No. Maybe a couple of hours to go to the hospital.'

I chewed on the sandwich and thought about Dean, realising I couldn't remember a thing about his birth. He'd been an accident and after five years, when things hadn't been working out, Jackie left. Eventually she got married to an accountant and moved to Basingstoke. After Jackie there'd been Pauline and now Trish. I wondered if they all laughed about me like the girls at the table opposite.

I was never good at expressing condolences. The words always seemed to come out in a jumble. And I was useless at writing Christmas or Get Well or In Sympathy cards.

Trying to do it with a family from Poland stretched the limited resources that my training and experience had given me. The interpreter that Operational Support had arranged only heightened my embarrassment, as I offered my *profound sorrow* and *sincere regrets*.

Veronika, the interpreter, was sitting at the far end of the table in one of the conference rooms. By her side was Michal's mother, dressed in black, deep shadows under her eyes, hair the colour of sea foam and the consistency of dried straw. She seemed tired of the world. Her husband had massive hands that were cupped together and placed firmly on the desk.

At the other end of the table, next to the family liaison officer was Magda, Michal's wife. She had a bewildered look on her face and she kept blinking and then looking down at her feet. In front of me, on the desk, was the plastic wallet with the remains of Michal's life. His father opened his hands and waved them in the air as he said something in Polish. His hands looked even bigger now and the voice sounded angry.

Veronika turned to me. She had high cheekbones and eyes wide apart. In fact, they all had. 'Mr Dąbek wants to know if you have caught anyone yet?'

'Too early.'

She translated, but she spoke so much that she must have added to my reply.

'What can they tell me about Michal?'

The older woman's face clouded over as she replied, until Veronika had to stop her so that she could interpret. I started making notes, fearing that this was going to take all afternoon.

Michal had done well at school. The translator tried to explain the Polish schooling system, about *gymnasiums* for the fourteen to eighteen-year-olds and how all students got a good grasp of English before they left school. It explained how all the bar staff and cleaners in the big hotels of the city could speak passable English. Most people in the UK managed English well enough, but adding the ability to speak another language was too much of a struggle. I remembered how I had hated my Welsh lessons at school and how I had loathed all that singing and poetry in the school eisteddfod. My mother had tried to get me to learn Italian but all I could manage were a few words of greeting.

I focused my attention when Veronika said that once Michal left school, he'd gone on to study computing before enrolling in the army.

'What did he do in the army?' I asked.

More Polish.

'He was an engineer. Working on special computers.'

Michal's father interrupted her mid-flow and sounded animated, making a turning motion with his hands.

'He says Michal was in Special Forces. He was very proud of his son. He was very well trained and could kill with his bare hands.' Veronika made the same circular motion.

Magda was still looking at her feet. I pushed towards her the image of the family photograph in the forest. I could just make out the similarity between the face, smiling broadly into the camera, and the grieving woman sitting in front of me.

'When was this taken?' I asked.

Veronika translated and then nodded as the woman replied. 'Two years ago, before Michal came to England. It was taken in a forest park near to Warsaw.'

It must have been important for Michal, but was it just a family photograph? I couldn't help feeling that it had more significance. 'Who's the man sitting down?'

Magda moved in her chair and surprised Veronika when she replied to me directly.

'It is Jo. He is friend of Michal from army. He is good friend.'

'And the children?'

'Pawl and Carrie.'

The names sounded English, too soft to be Polish.

'Children miss him,' she added under her breath.

I had been skirting around the problem of how to tell them about Kamil. Boyd had suggested we didn't need to tell them. But it would come out soon enough, and there was only one way – simple and to the point.

'Did they know that Michal was gay?' I spoke directly to the interpreter.

She stared at me and blinked a couple of times before turning to Michal's parents and Magda. She spoke slowly this time and there was sensitivity through the guttural tones. I watched as the look on their faces turned from incredulity to anger. Michal's father stood up and abruptly fisted both hands, which he smashed onto the table, and then he leant towards me, bellowing something in Polish. He kicked the chair from behind him and it fell to the floor. He said something to his wife and they stormed out.

Magda spoke rapidly until she slumped back. I watched as Veronika ordered her thoughts.

'It is a lie,' she said simply.

'Is that all?'

She swept her hand in the air and blew out her cheeks. 'Lot of other stuff about Michal being in the army and always being a real man. Michal's father said a lot of things about gays that you would not like to hear.'

Magda fumbled through a bag on her lap and picked out an envelope that she thrust towards Veronika, spluttering a long mouthful of Polish at the same time. Veronika extracted a single sheaf of paper from the envelope, raised her eyebrows and dropped her chin as she read its contents.

'This came for Michal last week,' she said, pushing it over the desk.

It was a bank statement: the words made no sense although even I could interpret the figures.

'Magda knows nothing about this,' Veronika said. 'There are 100,000 zloties in the account.'

I nodded. 'What's the exchange rate?'

I could see her making a mental calculation.

'It's about £40,000.'

When I arrived back in the CID office two civilians were sweating heavily as they moved a large notice board into one corner. Then I remembered the memo circulated by Cornock to everyone in the team – basically Boyd and me – telling us that the office had been designated as the Incident Room. Once they'd finished I went over, pinned a photograph of Michal onto the board, and stepped back. It always made me pause, that moment when the face appears on the board, a reminder, not that we needed one, that a body was lying dead in the mortuary and that we had a killer to find.

Boyd looked at his watch.

'We're late, boss,' he said. 'The priest will be waiting.'

The traffic was light as we wound our way through the one-way system towards Cathedral Road and then down towards Grangetown. I was thinking about Magda and Michal's parents as Boyd explained about the priest. I'd seen grieving families before, but losing a child in some foreign country must be hard – and then added to that not being able to understand what was happening.

'He's been in Cardiff for three years,' Boyd said, raising his voice.

'Who?'

'He came from Poland. Apparently the Catholic church is training thousands of priests in Poland. I can't see it myself. All that celibacy stuff and living like a hermit.'

I'd never been much interested in religion but I knew that my mother drew comfort from the rituals. 'My mother says it's the mystery that's important.'

Boyd didn't reply; he was negotiating past a pizza delivery van parked on a pedestrian crossing. A shower of rain drenched the car as we turned into the car park of the church. I pulled the collar of my jacket up against my neck as we ran for the front door.

Father Aurek Podolak was waiting for us and he took us through into a large office. I was surprised how young he was – mid-thirties, strong jaw and a firm handshake. He could have been a solicitor or an estate agent.

'I was very disturbed to hear about the death of Michal Dąbek,' he said, his English confident.

'Did you know him?' I asked.

'No. But I do know a lot of the Polish community and some of his friends come to mass regularly. I have spoken to them.'

'The Polish community keep themselves to themselves.'

'There is a large community from Poland here in Cardiff. They are mostly young and looking for short-term work. Long hours at minimum wage, but they save and then go back to Poland.'

'And have your parishioners heard anything?'

He sat back in his seat and looked out of the window before replying.

'In the last two years, maybe, I think things have changed. There is much going on that I do not like. The Polish people are not so happy.'

'What's wrong with them?'

He raised his hands in the air. 'It is nothing maybe, but I have heard of bad people coming into the city.'

'What do you mean, *bad people*?'

'There are criminals from Poland who want to take advantage of the young people. You have to remember, Inspector, that most have come here for better life. A lot of the Polish people here in Cardiff are from Warsaw. There is not much work there and the wages are poor.'

'We need something specific we can go after,' I said. 'We can't go on innuendo and rumour. We need something positive.'

Father Podolak shook his head slowly and gave me a hard look.

'It is difficult.'

'A man has been killed.'

'There are always circumstances that make it difficult for a priest.'

I could sense Boyd tensing by my side, moving to the edge of the hard wooden chair.

'If you know of any crime then you have an obligation to report it to us,' I said.

Father Podolak cast his gaze over the room towards a cabinet full of leather-bound volumes.

'My obligation is to the vow I gave to God and to my parishioners ...'

Before I could debate the finer points of Roman Catholic doctrine, I felt my mobile buzzing in my jacket. I read the message about a fracas in the Polish club and, when the name of the suspect appeared, my heart sank.

'We'll have to leave this for another day.'

The lights on the unmarked car were broken so we had to suffice with the siren and Boyd's regular blast of the horn to clear the traffic. The Polish club was an old public house in the docks that had been closed for three years before a community group took it over.

After half an hour we drew up beside the building, which was surrounded by derelict houses and boarded-up shops. A marked police car was parked at the pavement. When I left our car, I noticed a smell of decaying food and rubbish hanging in the air. A large shrub was growing out of the gutter and water had darkened the wall underneath it. Through the open door I could hear the sound of music thumping and then the sound of voices raised.

Inside there were two uniformed officers standing by various upturned tables. There was a dark stain on the wooden floor and shards of glass by the edge of the bar.

The shorter of the officers had her hair pulled back into a pony tail that swung briskly when she moved her head. She had her pocketbook open in one hand.

'PC Gladwyn. Glad you've arrived, sir,' she said, the relief evident in her tone. 'This is PC Marshall.'

The second officer was tall and thin with enough pimples to pass for a teenager. I noticed his pronounced Adam's apple. 'Sir,' he said under his breath.

There were two men behind the bar and another three sitting down by one of the round tables in the middle of the room. One of them had a bruise over one eye that was beginning to turn a crimson colour.

'This is Stefan Majewski, the manager,' Gladwyn said, nodding to the fatter of the two men behind the bar.

'He was fat pig of man,' Majewski said.

'Who?' I said.

'He come inside and wanted to speak to Kamil. Say he kill him. And he show hands and say that he killed many men with bare hands.'

I stepped nearer the bar.

'We have no trouble here until now.'

The man next to him nodded his head; the others sitting by the table mumbled agreement.

'He Michal's father. You know, man found dead in water.'

'What happened?'

'Fat man come into bar. It quiet – we have good time; some men watch football on TV.' He gesticulated towards the large screen in the corner. 'He was much angry and banged on table saying he wanted to speak to Kamil and to other friends of Michal.'

I turned to Boyd. 'Find out where he's staying.' Boyd nodded and, fishing his mobile from his pocket, stepped outside. Majewski was whispering to the other man behind the bar when I looked over at him.

'We'll need statements from you and your friends.'

'We no want trouble.'

Gladwyn moved towards me and showed me the notes she'd made in her notebook. 'There are two men who've gone to A&E, sir.'

I glanced up at Majewski. 'Do you and your friends want to make a complaint or not?'

'We want quiet place.'

We left Gladwyn and Marshall taking statements and contact details and headed for the hotel where the

Dąbek family were staying. The hotel was on a business park near an office block and a builder's merchant. The car park was empty so we pulled up by the front door. The building looked like one of those timber-framed constructions bolted together in a few days. A man sat behind a small counter watching television as we entered, and he jumped to his feet, obviously pleased at the prospect of custom.

'What can I do for you guys?'

I carded him.

His eyes opened wide. 'Wow. Do you guys really want someone here?'

'Dąbek family.'

He scrambled through some paper records on the desk. 'I shan't keep you guys waiting any longer than a couple of seconds.'

A woman pushing a trolley laden with various cleaning materials passed us.

'Got it. Room 316. Third floor and you guys can find the lift just behind the door to your right.'

'Thanks.'

We took the stairs two at a time. The room was in the middle of the corridor and we thumped on the door, knowing there was someone inside from the music we could hear.

A woman's face appeared at the door.

'Is your husband here?'

She gave a mournful sort of wheeze and let go of the door that had begun to close in my face. I stepped into the room, Boyd following, and we tried to make ourselves understood to her. It wasn't successful and eventually we gave up and left.

Outside I cracked open a new packet of cigarettes, found the lighter and then let the smoke sweep through my lungs.

'Where to now, boss?'

I took another long drag. 'We drive around.'

'Drive around?'

'Yes. Until we find him.'

'Where exactly?'

'Well, we're not going to Roath or the Vale, are we?' I was beginning to feel frustrated with the prospect of chasing an angry Pole around the city. 'Have we got Kamil's mobile number?'

'Back in Queen Street.'

I gave Boyd a concerted look that said we needed it. Within a couple of minutes he was speaking to Kamil, warning him about Michal's father. I was contemplating another cigarette before he'd finished.

'He'd heard. BlackBerry messaging service has been full of it.'

I nodded. 'Let's see if we can find Dąbek.'

My office was crammed and hot and sweaty. Gladwyn sat on one of the chairs by the desk; Marshall stood behind her. Boyd stood by the door and Veronika leant against the wall. I sat bolt upright in my chair.

'So we don't have a complaint of any sort?' I said.

'That's right, sir. None of the injured parties wanted to make a complaint. They'd both sustained injuries but they didn't want to cause trouble.'

'So we don't have grounds to detain Antoniusz Dąbek.'

'No sir,' Gladwyn said, even though it hadn't been a question.

Dąbek had been apprehended in a takeaway kebab restaurant, hungry and tired. His wife and daughter-in-law were in a witness room downstairs drinking weak tea and stale sandwiches from the canteen.

'When's the next flight to Poland?'

Boyd had done the research. 'Three hours from Bristol.'

'Is it to where they live?'

'No, sir. The next one to ...'

I raised a hand and said to Gladwyn. 'You and Marshall take them to the airport and make sure they catch the plane.'

The regular monthly meeting was a comforting routine. I needed that extra assurance. Confirmation that others were like me. Other people who didn't want to go back to the old ways. Others who wanted to recapture the love of their families, the loyalty of friends and the respect of work colleagues.

Pity and sympathy were all well and good. People who'd said that I should pull myself together didn't understand. It was such an infuriating thing to say. It never worked. And it never made me stop drinking.

I would usually start with a couple of lagers after work with the lads and then by the time I'd got home it had become five pints and I was public enemy number one. Jackie would fly into a rage so I'd drink more and blame her for being selfish and unsupportive. Once I started on the wine I had to finish the bottle and then look for another, before finding the vodka.

Most drunks just fritter away their lives until the Grim Reaper comes knocking. Families exchange knowing looks at the funeral, making comments like *suicide by drinking* or *sad waste* and then get on with their lives.

When I woke up in a Garda station in the port of

Rosslare I knew something had to change. First of all I thought that one of the lads had played a practical joke and locked me in a cell overnight. When I'd heard the unfamiliar accents outside the cell door a dull knot had formed in my stomach. I'd fiddled with my clothing, trying to find my ID but the pockets were empty.

I'd pissed in my pants and I reeked. The shirt I was wearing had a large stain down the front – I couldn't remember how it got there. I'd felt the stubble on my chin and realised that I must look awful. I'd noticed a pool of vomit by the toilet in the corner.

There was loud jolt as the key found its place in the door of the cell. A guard stepped in and gave me a sideways look.

'Jesus. You were fucking shit-faced last night. Heavy night was it?' he'd asked.

Truth was, I couldn't remember. Nothing. Not a fucking thing. I'd gone out for one drink after work. And I'd woken up in a police cell in the Republic of Ireland.

'What ...?' I'd stammered. My tongue had felt like sandpaper.

'We picked you up on the ferry. Truly fucking pissed and fighting like a tinker.'

I'd felt for my watch. 'What's the time?'

'Two. Do you want something to eat?'

I shook my head. I'd wanted a hot shower and to clean my teeth. My lips were clung together with saliva.

'Water,' I'd said and even that took effort. 'Has anybody ...?'

'Don't worry. We rang your boss. He didn't sound too pleased. Said he'd call your missus.'

I could explain it, of course. I always could, to myself at least.

On the journey home I knew things had to change.

I poured the vodka away and went to the first Alcoholics Anonymous meeting of my life. The three words had stuck in my throat like an enormous piece of stale bread and I had fled the meeting, deciding they were poor, pathetic idiots who didn't have enough willpower.

But I had gone back a month later and every month afterwards. Tonight was no different.

Once I'd parked the car walked up to the hotel. I found the room at the back and sat down, nodding and smiling to the others. By the time it was my turn to speak I was ready.

'I'm John. I'm an alcoholic.'

Chapter 8

'Inspector Marco?'

I didn't recognise the voice.

'Yes.'

'Sergeant Parkes. BTP.'

Normally I never dealt with the British Transport Police, whose task it was to police the railways and trains.

'Yes.' I sounded disinterested.

'We've had a break-in at the left luggage lockers in Cardiff Central.'

'I'm sorry. How …?'

'I was told you might have an interest in this incident …'

'Maybe,' I said, remembering our alert about unusual burglaries. 'But how do you know if the locker …?'

'All of them, Inspector.'

'Sorry.'

'All of the bloody lockers were crow-barred last night. They even had guards posted at the entrance explaining that it was a routine security check and that nobody could access the area.'

I slammed the phone down after telling the sergeant I'd be there as soon as I could. At first I walked but then I broke into a mild jog with Boyd panting behind me. Buses weaved their way down St Mary Street towards the castle and we turned into Wood Street, slowing as we saw Central Station.

A couple of BTP officers stood by the entrance – arms folded, intense stares – in front of the flickering crime scene tape. I flashed my warrant card and asked for Sergeant Parkes. One of them spoke into his radio and soon Parkes appeared from inside the station.

'Our scene of crime officers haven't finished,'

Parkes said, motioning for us to follow him. The Transport Police were still in the twentieth century; even the Wales Police Service had CSIs.

A voice boomed through the station tannoy, announcing a train for Birmingham and then another for Plymouth. The left luggage lockers had been added to a corridor lined with gaudy green tiles and SOCOs were working through the contents strewn all over the floor. Before leaving Queen Street I'd picked up the plastic pocket with Michal's key, so I took it out and turned to Parkes.

'Any idea if this might fit?'

He shouted at one of the SOCOs. 'Dave, over here ...'

A man with a dark ponytail unfurled his legs from his seating position and walked over towards us. I showed him the key.

'Can I see if this fits any of the locks?'

'You can try the lockers from the far end,' he said, but then he looked down at the key and shook his head. 'Doesn't match any of the keys I've seen.'

He was right and after we'd tried every lock I stood and thought about Michal. Why had he kept the key in his wallet? If the key was that important, why hadn't the killer taken his wallet? Perhaps we were one step ahead of the game. But we couldn't work out which lock the key fitted. Somebody else was wondering the same.

Boyd used all of the twenty minutes it took us to walk back to Queen Street to explain about the doormen working in the Four Seasons who we were going to interview later that morning. There were Poles, a Latvian, but mostly lads from the Valleys who had clean records.

The civilian on the desk gave me a puzzled look when I walked in. 'I've been trying to get hold of you. Tried your mobile a couple of times.'

I cursed when I realised I'd left the mobile in my office.

He continued. 'Only we had a call. DI Hobbs took it. Left in a hell of bloody hurry.'

I drove too quickly, failing to block out the red mist clouding my mind. Dave Hobbs was out of line and I'd see to it that this was the last time he'd make that mistake. The blue lights and the siren helped to clear the traffic but it was still a few minutes before I reached 14 Howick Street. This time it was a crime scene and the Scientific Support Vehicle was parked outside; a uniformed officer stood outside, scanning the street.

I ducked under the perimeter tape and entered the house. When I heard the North-Walian twang to Dave Hobbs's voice, it immediately set my nerves on edge.

'That's not the way to do it,' he said.

And then I heard the voice of Alvine Dix – it sounded melodious and almost attractive alongside Hobbs's voice.

'The correct procedure is quite different,' Hobbs continued.

Alvine was going to swear any minute.

I took the narrow stairs two at a time and found Dix and Hobbs arguing outside one of the bedrooms on the first floor landing. I clenched my jaw and realised I was ready for a fight. Two officers emerged from one of the rooms down the corridor and I could hear the crime scene investigators inside the bed-sit.

'Alvine, you'll excuse DI Hobbs and myself. Protocols to discuss,' I said, grabbing Hobbs by the arm and pulling him towards the stairs.

On the second floor I pushed him down the corridor, checking that no other officers were present – wouldn't do for junior officers to see two DIs arguing.

Hobbs was shorter than me, but he'd puffed himself up like some exotic bird on heat. I clenched my fist and then thought the better of it. It could wait for a dark night when he was pissed. I unclenched my fist and prodded him with my middle finger.

'You're way out of line, Dave. You know this is my case.'

'I took the call. Trying to help, seeing that you were unavailable.'

He brushed my hand away from his jacket. He buttoned his coat and straightened his tie in one smooth movement, as though he was preparing for an interview.

I carried on prodding. 'You can just fuck off back to the station before I make a formal complaint about you breaking *protocols*. How would that look on your file?'

He cleared his throat and moved his face closer to mine. I could smell the cheap aftershave and see the hairs growing from his nose. 'Think you're up to it, Marco? Think you can handle the pressure? Not going to have another *incident* are we?'

I clenched both fists this time, but the sound of movement downstairs spared Hobbs a kicking and me from facing an assault charge and an early exit from the Wales Police Service with no pension.

He smirked at me and then swaggered down the corridor; even the back of his head smirked at me.

'There's an eyewitness,' he said, over his shoulder.

I wanted to change my mind and beat the crap out of Hobbs, but I walked calmly along the corridor and down the stairs.

'Where's DI Hobbs?' Alvine asked.

'Urgent call from Area Control. Cat stuck in a tree ... You know how it is.'

A flicker of emotion crossed her eyes and her lips quivered.

The bed-sit had been trashed like Michal's but the difference was the body lying across the bed. Leon's neck had been snapped like a twig in a storm and lay at an odd angle against the pillow, a trail of blood along the bedding.

'Has his ...?' I asked.

'No, his tongue has not been amputated,' she said.

Now I had two deaths from the same house, but there was still another body without a tongue. Nothing was making sense except the certainty that somebody had lost something very valuable indeed.

'Where's the eyewitness?' I asked.

'Girl in room five.'

I left Alvine and the other CSIs to their work and walked down to the ground floor. The door to room five was ajar.

'DI Marco,' I said as I knocked on the door.

The room was little changed from the last time I'd seen it. Dagmara was sitting on an old Lloyd Loom chair, her legs tucked underneath the seat. The flowers in the vase had died a little and there was a stale, air-less feel in the room. I noticed the double locks of the window, firmly secured.

I held out my hand and Dagmara gave it a limp, lifeless shake. 'I understand you saw something.'

She nodded and I sat down on the bed. It was soft and sagged under my weight.

'What can you tell me?'

'It was very early.'

'What time?'

'Four. Maybe a little later.'

'What were you doing at that time of the morning?'

'I was with a friend until late.'

She avoided eye contact. Her eyes were set high in her face and slightly at an angle that made her face look like an animation. Her skin was clear and her mouth was wide.

'I came back towards the house and heard the voices when they came out ...'

'Did you hear what they said?'

'No.'

'What language were they talking?'

'English.' But she sounded tentative.

'Did you see them?'

I heard my name being called and knew that I'd have to speak to Dagmara again so I arranged a time to see her in the station. I heard the scraping of the chain on her door as I walked away down the corridor.

Dr Paddy MacVeigh was kneeling by the side of the bed when I entered Leon's room. A sharp smell, like dirty clothes on someone in need of a shower, hung in the air. I couldn't tell if it was Paddy or Leon or both.

He glanced over and nodded. 'Good morning, John.'

I nodded back.

'Lost the power of speech?' he said.

'Not funny,' I said. 'Not even sick-funny.'

'Looks like a single blow with a sharp knife or blade. He's been dead a few hours. No obvious sign of a struggle.'

Paddy didn't stay long. He didn't need to. Leon was dead and the CSIs had work to do. The post mortem would tell us more. After he left, Alvine turned towards me.

'Something you should see.'

One of the CSIs passed over an exhibits box. Inside was another mass of pink and bloodied flesh.

Chapter 9

The preliminary forensic report was on my desk and I'd managed the first couple of pages before Alvine arrived. She looked different somehow. Perhaps it was the absence of the all-white one-piece suit but then I noticed her hair had been drawn back behind her head, making her chin more pronounced. She had a touch of blusher on her checks and that got me thinking she must have a date later.

When I met Alvine years ago she was single and made a point of telling me that she hated her name – both of them, in fact. 'It's like the name of that big old car,' she'd said. 'And Dix sounds like it came out of a James Bond film.'

Perhaps that's why she went into forensics. A brief marriage to a librarian she met online had ended after a couple of years, and I'd heard some strange rumours about his nocturnal habits. Alvine wasn't the same for a while. Now, she was married to her work.

'The tongues aren't human. Apart from the one in Michal's pocket and the one in his flat.'

'What are they?'

'Dogs. At a guess Alsatian or Labrador.'

'So why cut out the tongues from dogs?'

'Beats me. You're the detective,' she said, glancing at her watch. 'Do you want to go through the rest of the forensics or are we going to talk about dogs?'

'Are you due elsewhere?'

'None of your business.'

Must be a date. Poor unsuspecting bastard.

She cleared her throat and gave me a summary of the forensics in Michal's bed-sit. Fingerprints on the door casing and cupboards. She guessed they'd be Michal's or Kamil's or possibly the others from the house. In executive summary-speak, it was a mess. All the clothes had been taken to the lab but the results would take a week, maybe two.

The locker in the factory was no better. 'Shit place to work,' she said.

'Boyd thought so too,' I replied.

'There are prints on the door, on the lock and all over the inside of the locker, but nothing else. I hope you've got more to go on,' she said. 'All I have are a pile of cheap clothes and most of them will be Polish.'

'What difference will that make?'

'Tracing the clothes,' she said, with incredulity in her voice. 'I heard about the lockers at the railway station. Think they could be connected?'

'Somebody's lost something. And they want it back badly enough to warn people off with tongues from dead dogs.'

'Think they know you've got the key?'

I drew breath and paused. Eventually I shrugged. Alvine got up and left me to finish reading the reports.

If they knew that Michal had a key in his wallet it must have been careless leaving it with his body or else the killer didn't know he had to find something until after he'd killed Michal. If only I knew where to look.

'Why didn't they cut Leon's tongue out?'

Boyd had a strained look on his face.

I was reading the paperwork on my desk and preparing for the interviews with the doormen working at the Four Seasons.

'Maybe the killer was disturbed,' he continued.

I looked up at Boyd. 'Or maybe it's a different killer. Different MO and Leon's killer doesn't have the stomach for amputating tongues.'

Boyd didn't seem to have thought about that possibility, but then he nodded slowly.

There were ten names on the list. Three of them were names with multiples of 'x's and 'z's, making them unpronounceable and the others looked straightforward UK surnames. There was even a Benedetti and a Jones. Against each name Boyd had written a date of birth and confirmed whether the individual was '*known*'. He'd printed off the Police National Computer checks for each man.

The first doorman had a neck like a tree trunk and a clean-shaven head. He wore a polo shirt a size too small that had Four Seasons printed over his left nipple. He called Frankie 'Mr Prince', but he didn't know Leon or Michal, who worked different shifts from him and generally he didn't like the Eastern Europeans. The second doorman was from Merthyr, like the first, and he had tattoos over his arms but his neck was a normal size.

'Were you in the forces?' I asked.

'Welsh Cavalry, and proud of it. I did two tours in Afghanistan.'

'Did you know Michal Dąbek?'

'No. Never met him.'

'And Leon Ostrowski?'

'No, sir.'

The next three were the same and it was clear that Frankie had been coaching them well: none of them knew Michal. It wasn't until the first doorman from Poland sat opposite me that things changed.

'Michal good person.'

'How long did you know him?'

He shrugged. 'Months only. It is bad and Mr Prince is upset too.'

Janek Symanski was tall and slim and built like an athlete. But his eyes darted around, looking at me, then

Boyd. I took a mouthful of the coffee Boyd had organised after the previous bouncer.

'Did you know Leon too?'

'Yes.'

'Did you work with them in the Four Seasons?'

'Yes. I work with them all the time and they are good men.'

'Do you know of anyone who would want to kill them?'

He glanced around again and raised his hand briefly in the air.

'It is very sad. Michal and Leon they ...' But he hesitated and didn't finish.

I took my time to finish the coffee as I tried to cajole more information out of Janek, without success. He knew more than he was telling so we'd have to see him again.

We got back to the Incident Room just as a CD of the CCTV camera from Cardiff Central station arrived. Boyd loaded the CD into a computer and fiddled until the flickering images filled the screen. There was a time display in one corner and then a series of bustling images as the station concourse filled the screen. A crowd of teenagers in T-shirts and jeans ran in. One of them stopped to look at the monitor and I saw him mouthing something to the others before they ran up the stairs. After this a couple of drunks staggered through, lurching all over the floor. Then three men marched over towards the lockers and I moved closer to the screen.

One of them must have been six foot three and not much less around the chest. He had a massive head, and shoulders like gravestones, and he walked purposefully. He knew exactly where he was going as he headed for the lockers. The other two followed him and then he stood upright at the entrance to the locker area.

I watched the man blocking the entrance for a moment until someone came up to him. He turned, without showing his face, and the passenger moved away. It was like this for a couple of minutes but it felt longer.

'Why the bloody hell doesn't someone complain?' I said, exasperated.

Then the shed-like man twisted around and for an instant the camera captured an image of the other two.

'Stop it now,' I shouted and Boyd froze the image of Janek's face on the screen.

Chapter 10

'What's so special about Uncle Gino?' Trish asked.

I was scraping low-fat butter substitute on a piece of wholemeal toast, instead of my usual breakfast of white sliced bread an inch thick, with butter and strawberry jam. Trish said I would feel better for eating it but I had my doubts as I prodded the hardened bread with my knife. Trish was wearing an 'Old Guys Rule' T-shirt, a present from the lads in the station on my last birthday, and I caught a glimpse of a nipple pressing against the dark-blue material. The horizontal blinds cast hard shadows across her body. I'd seen much more of the nipple last night before falling into a dreamless sleep. Now, I felt refreshed and I watched Trish finishing a yogurt, the fat-free low-calorie variety that had the consistency of melted wine gums.

'It's Uncle Gino's sixty-fifth birthday in a month and there's a big family celebration. Cousins are flying in from Lucca and my mother has been full of the arrangements. She wants Dean to be there.'

Trish raised an eyebrow. 'So, tell me about the family.'

I swirled the dregs of my espresso around the cup. 'He's the eldest of the three boys and the one who still feels more Italian than the rest.'

She cupped a mug of tea and sat back.

'When *Nonno Marco* died he left the ice cream business to Papà, the café in Aberdare to Uncle Gino and a lump of money to Uncle Franco who started a rock group and toured the world. And there's the old place in Pontypridd.'

'Really, the Marco Empire.'

'Papà worked hard building the business – two ice cream parlours and a business that supplied supermarkets –

he even had a contract with the prison service. Uncle Gino is the lazy brother who spends his time serving toast and milky coffees to the people of Aberdare.'

'Does Uncle Gino still work?'

'Every day and all he does is pine for the old days that have disappeared. He still wants to be Italian, even though the number of Italian families and businesses left in South Wales is small. My father's worked really hard to get the business where it is. He mortgaged the house up to the limit when he was younger.'

'Does Uncle Gino have kids?'

I took another sip of the cold espresso. 'Mary and Jeremy.'

'Do they work in the business?'

'Jeremy does as little as humanly possible. He works in the café occasionally, but mostly sponges off a rich wife for a living.'

'And Mary?'

'She married an estate agent. Lives up in Whitchurch. Two kids.'

I looked down at the coffee cup and then glanced at my watch, realising that I didn't have the time for another.

I stood by the mirror in the hallway and Trish straightened the tie she had chosen for me, which matched the shirt with the light-blue stripe and single cuffs. She ran a dampened finger over my eyelashes, pushing the thick black hair into place. It was my best feature, she would say, although I reckoned I had at least one better. She kissed me on the cheek, lingering to smell the aftershave she'd bought, and I left the flat.

'What do we know so far?'

Cornock had miscued the gel on his hair that morning and a blob had landed at the back of his parting.

'Paddy says it was strangulation.'

He glanced over at the fish in the tank. 'Any forensics?'

'Nothing substantive, sir. Paddy says the tongue was cut out before death.'

Cornock made a look of revulsion before continuing. 'The second death has changed things of course.'

I nodded, uncertain what exactly he had on his mind.

'You'll need some additional resources.'

I could sense Dave Hobbs lurking in the background.

'I'll allocate two detectives from the Regional Crime Unit to assist.'

'Thank you, sir,' I said, pleased that Hobbs's name hadn't been mentioned.

'The press are going to be all over this like a rash, John.'

'No one has contacted me yet.'

'Good, then perhaps it's early days – I'll talk to the press office.'

I made to leave but Cornock had one last thing on his mind.

'I've had contact from the Polish embassy. They want to send someone to liaise on the case.'

'Liaise?'

'Home Office has been in touch with the ACC and then it got passed down to me.'

'That was quick work. How did they hear about Leon's murder?'

Cornock shrugged. 'All seems cloak and dagger. Just humour him and keep me informed.'

I'd taken a couple of mouthfuls of tea when the telephone rang.

'Marco.'

'Constable John Williams, sir. I don't know whether this is something for you but we had a complaint about a break-in at a health club last night. Thing is, sir, nothing seems to have been stolen but my boss saw in the system that you might have an interest in …'

'Where are you?'

'Radyr, sir.'

I listened as he gave me the details. 'And when did the call come in?'

'First thing.'

'Has the CSI team been called?'

'Yes, sir. But they haven't arrived.'

'And why the bloody hell not?' I was standing by the desk now. 'Don't touch anything and treat the place like a crime scene.'

I slammed the telephone down, shouted for Boyd and left the tea.

It was thirty minutes until we pulled into the car park of the Sunshine Sport and Social club in Radyr. It was part of one of those out-of-town developments that needed to be refreshed or simply knocked down. The building had an old door that needed a sharp tug to open it and wooden windows that were beginning to rot. A heavy smell of chlorine hung in the air.

A uniformed officer stopped talking to a woman behind a small counter when he saw us and walked over.

'DI Marco?' he said, introducing himself as the officer I'd spoken to earlier. 'It's through here,' he added, pointing to a door that said *Staff Only*.

Since the call on Sunday morning I'd become accustomed to seeing rooms that had been trashed and this locker room was no different. The doors had all been forced open and contents thrown all over the floor. I heard a noise behind me and, turning, saw a woman with long blond hair and a troubled look on her face.

'This is the manager,' Williams said.

'Maggie Furlong.' She blinked quickly.

'Who's been in here?' I asked, more sharply than I'd intended.

'It might take some time ...'

'Now. Please. And nobody leaves the building until I say so.'

She turned on her heels and left.

'Boyd, can you please find out where the CSIs have got to? And don't let them give you any shit about operational imperatives.'

'Yes, boss.'

The prospect that the crime scene had not been contaminated was remote and that meant the evidence could be questioned and challenged by even the most incompetent barrister. And if we ever got anyone in front of a court then we'd need a lot more than unreliable forensic evidence. I gave the door of the room a kick of despair as I left Constable Williams chewing his lip, with orders not to let anyone in until the CSI team arrived.

Maggie Furlong still displayed the worried look when I sat down beside her in a windowless room that passed as an office. She pulled her blond hair over her ears and I noticed her pronounced jaw line and thin figure. She was wearing a tracksuit on top of a pale-pink T-shirt.

'I'll need a full list of all your customers and a list of your employees. Everyone, including cleaners and part-time people employed here. And a list of everyone with a locker here – including their mobile numbers.'

She nodded.

'Do have any Eastern Europeans working here?'

'One or two. Why do ask?' There was a reluctance in her voice.

'I'll need all their details too.'

'They're good workers. No trouble at all. The girls, in particular, work hard.'

Furlong sounded guilty about employing Eastern Europeans, as though there was something wrong in doing so.

'Sergeant Boyd will stay until the crime scene investigators arrive. You can give him all the details.'

She nodded and turned to the computer on her desk.

I headed for the front door, motioning for Boyd to follow me. Outside, I found the cigarettes in my jacket pocket, and lit up. Lately I'd not been counting my daily consumption as carefully as I should have done, knowing that I had to justify to my mother that it really only was five a day. But that morning I was certain it was my second – I hadn't had time for any more.

'CSI team are on their way,' Boyd said.

'Have you heard anything from the BTP?'

'No, boss. Once they'd found Janek they were going to contact me.'

I drew on the dying embers of the cigarette and then ground it into the loose gravel under my feet.

Dagmara sat opposite me in the conference room on the

first floor we used for witnesses. When we had first met I was convinced she was telling the truth. I'd been doing this job a long time and I could tell when someone was lying. It was in the eyes, in the lips and in the way they held themselves. The experts called it body language. Then there were the hands and the listless answers. I'd done all the management courses on reading body language and knowing when a witness was lying or not. The first interview I'd done after the course was with a drug dealer who sat and stared at me without blinking, sitting on his hands. Watching me. I scribbled down the side of the interview plan whenever I thought he was lying and tried to drag out the interview with long silences. Later, I discovered he had a borderline personality disorder and that no amount of reading his body language would have worked. I went back to the old-fashioned way.

Trusting my instincts.

Dagmara had warm, green eyes and a pale complexion that suggested she needed sunshine. Her hair was jet black and it fell past her shoulders down her back. I guessed she was around twenty-five.

'Where do you work?'

'In agency helping immigrants with business set-up.'

She pushed a bilingual business card over the desk – Welsh and English with a sentence of what I took to be Polish on the back.

'How long have you been there?'

'Two years – since coming to Cardiff.'

'Do you like working in the UK?'

She nodded and then smiled at me. 'It is much better than Poland. The conditions are better. Back home it is bad.'

'Are you going to go back to Poland?'

'Maybe I stay here and marry an Englishman.'

'Or a Welshman?' I replied and she gave me another smile. 'Where had you been on the night of Leon's death?' I asked, looking at the initial notes of her evidence.

'I'd been staying with a friend. We go to Polish club. We have too much drinks.'

'Where does your friend live?'

She flicked back her hair and gave me the details.

'What time did you get back?'

'It was after half past four. I know for sure because I look at my watch.'

The eye contact was good and the body language relaxed. Unless Dagmara had been on the same management courses as me she was telling the truth. I noticed her high cheekbones that moved upwards when she smiled.

'Tell me what you saw.'

'It was still early.' She cradled a beaker of water on the desk in front of her before taking a sip. 'I saw two men leaving the house.'

'Did they see you?'

'I do not think so.'

'Can you describe them?'

I jotted down the descriptions she gave, occasionally stopping for her to clarify the details about height and weight and hair. There'd been nobody else around at that time of the morning.

'Would you recognise these men again?'

'Maybe. I was far away when I saw them.'

'And what about the car?'

Like most women she managed only a summary – it was big and blue with four doors. Dagmara didn't drive but she knew her father had an Opel and she thought the car was a BMW, maybe a Mercedes. She was pleased with herself and surprised me when she gave me the first four digits of the registration number.

'How well do you know Michal?'

She shrugged.

'Was he a friend of yours?'

Her eyes darted around the room. 'For sure he was friend. Not good friend but he was from Warsaw same as me. Same as Leon.'

'Who were Michal's friends?'

Another shrug before she replied. 'Leon was good friend of Michal and Pietrek and Gerek. They all work in the factory and clubs.'

I wrote down their full names and the little details that Dagmara knew.

'And Leon? Did you know him better?'

We spent the rest of the interview filling in the gaps, colouring in the background details. Dagmara laughed at my lame jokes, smiled at all the right places and occasionally threw me a sideways look with her eyes.

Boyd returned from Radyr, his tie loosened, just enough to be respectable without him looking dishevelled. He gave me a summary of the CSI feedback and complained that the uniformed officer had been awkward when he'd asked for a lift back to Queen Street.

'And did the CSIs find anything?' I said, knowing what the answer would be.

'Nothing, boss. There were prints all over every door and every surface. And they took away a pile of other material. But ...'

He slumped back in his chair and blew out his cheeks.

Before I could reply, the telephone rang.

'There's someone in reception for you.' The voice

sounded tired. More tired than I felt and more jaded than Boyd at that moment in time.

'Who is it?'

'Bloke with a foreign-sounding name. Kam … something or other. One of them East European names.'

She made it sound exotic as though it was unusual instead of commonplace, now that the EU extended into Eastern Europe.

'Put him into the interview room.'

'Okay.'

'And give him some tea.'

Boyd straightened his tie, sat up in the chair and looked interested now that we had some real policing to do. It was a short walk to the interview room and when we opened the door Kamil was blowing on the surface of a plastic cup he was clutching in one hand.

'Have you found anything?' he said.

He stopped blowing and started chewing the nails of the fingers of his right hand while he looked at me.

'It bad. I am scared.' He broke off a piece of nail and spat it into his palm.

'We're doing everything we can,' I said.

'Has anything happened?' Boyd asked.

Kamil shrugged. 'Nothing, but I need to know what happening. What you are doing.'

'We're doing what we always do,' I said.

'Have you found who killed Michal?'

I crossed my arms and sat back, thinking this was a waste of time.

'Look Kamil, this sort of case takes time. And we don't know enough yet.'

'You not understand.' He raised his voice.

'What do you mean?'

'There are bad things happen.'

'What are you talking about?'

He leant forward, his eyes wide open. 'It is not safe for me.'

'Why not?'

Kamil was on his feet now. 'You need to keep me safe.'

'We can't do that,' I explained.

'You have witness protection. I can help with case. You must help,' Kamil shouted.

'It doesn't work that way.'

'You don't know what going on.'

'I haven't got time for this,' I said, pushing the chair away, glancing at my watch and knowing I was late for the post mortem.

'Come back when you want to cooperate.'

Every senior investigating officer had to attend the post mortem in a murder inquiry, and the exhibits officer should have been with me, but he'd been called to a fatal road traffic accident on the motorway so Boyd had to deputise. He stood by my side making no attempt to hide his discomfort. Blood and guts obviously disagree with a man who has to shag on demand in the hope of leaving his mark on society.

'It's the Fourth Cycle of The Ring,' Paddy said.

'I prefer the Fifth,' I said.

Truth was, I didn't know the First from the Fifth Cycle, but I did know it was the music of Wagner thundering through the mortuary. It reminded me of Christopher Lee in *Lord of the Rings* on top of the tower, hair billowing, watching the massing hordes of Orcs attacking the good guys.

'Did you watch the City game against Chelsea?' he

asked, holding a saw in his right hand.

'Missed it. I had a ticket but the floater got in the way.'

'Bloody good game.'

The electric saw rattled and slowed as it cut through bone. Boyd put a hand to his mouth and coughed loudly.

Paddy began dictating into the microphone suspended from the ceiling and settled into a routine. Occasionally he called out some comment of interest.

'Much the same as the other one,' he said. 'Healthy and evidence of good muscle tone,' he added, lifting up the right arm.

'Forces?' I asked.

'Maybe.'

It would make sense to have ex-forces as bodyguards for the night clubs and for the protection that the massage parlour racket needed. Eastern Europeans guarding Eastern Europeans – neat. And Michal was gay so he wouldn't be tempted to dip his toe in the water.

By the time Paddy was finished he'd explained that a single knife wound from a right-handed assailant had killed Leon. His clothes had been stored to one side in a neat pile ready for the forensic lab.

Leon had fewer belongings than Michal. The contents of the bed-sit had been emptied and catalogued. Apart from his telephone and a television there was little of value. Some Polish paperwork and his payslips, and I had another Polish family to see and explain about their son.

Once the post mortem was finished I stepped out of the mortuary with Boyd and the fresh air hit us. Thick white clouds scuttled across the sky and we stood, letting the autumn chill refresh our faces. I could see how working in the mortuary could be a one-way ticket to the bar. What was the career progression in pathology? It was always the same: cutting up dead people.

Chapter 11

I saw Hobbs and Cornock talking privately, nodding to each other, exchanging confidences. Then Alvine Dix came in and smiled at me; she even showed some teeth. I heard the word *John* and *investigation.* I felt warm, as though a blanket had been thrown over me. I raised my hand but my arm was heavy.

Then I woke up.

The air in the bedroom was stale and dank. I ran a hand around my neck and felt the perspiration. I kicked off the sheet and blankets and stared over to look at the clock. Swinging my legs over the side of the bed, I sat up, stretching, rubbing my hands over my face.

The dream was still vivid and I pondered whether there was some hidden message from my subconscious. A Jungian analyst had offered to interpret my dreams a couple of years ago, but because I'd arrested her for kicking the shit out of a Freudian analyst when they had a disagreement outside a pub in St Mary Street I doubted her bona fides.

I ate toast and drank a cup of instant coffee, before showering, and then I found some clean clothes. My car still needed cleaning but listening to Elvis singing 'Johnnie B Goode' cast the dream into a dark corner. I reached Queen Street in good time and parked alongside Boyd's newly cleaned Fiesta.

At the office I sat by my desk, suppressing the desire to yawn violently. A message from the front desk told me that Kamil was back, sitting in reception.

Boyd looked smart and fresh when he walked into my room unannounced. He had the sleeves of his heavily striped shirt folded high up his arms and he chewed on an apple.

'Sleep well?' I asked, giving the apple an inquisitive look.

'Slept like a baby, no interruptions.' He almost sounded relieved. 'Mandy's idea,' he said, holding out the apple in his hand. 'Have to eat more fibre.'

'Kamil's back,' I said.

'He's turning into a time waster.'

I nodded. 'We'll give him ten minutes max.'

I pushed a plastic mug over the table towards Kamil. It had in it a rancid-looking liquid that passed for coffee. He had a pack of roll-your-own tobacco on the table by the side of a battered Nokia and a set of keys with various fobs, one of which was pink and fluffy. The dark-grey stubble around his face and the heavy bags under his eyes made him look older.

I sipped some water and Boyd, sitting by my side, was running his tongue around the inside of his cheek, a look of irritation on his face – he wasn't accustomed, I imagine, to pieces of apple lodging between his teeth.

'I told you yesterday; unless you can help us then you're wasting our time.'

He started chewing a nail and glancing up at me. 'It is no easy.'

'What are you frightened of?'

'I no sleep last night.'

'Did you know Leon?' I began.

He fidgeted with the tobacco pouch. I could feel the crumpled remains of the Marlboros in my shirt pocket – I got the feeling it was likely to be the sort of day during which my five-a-day would become ten.

'For sure.'

'What's the connection to Michal?'

He averted his eyes. 'They work together.'

I tried another tack.

'Stop pissing about. You're wasting my time. I've got a murderer to find and you're pulling my chain. Either you tell us what you know or you can leave now.'

He gave me a startled look and played with the lighter on the table. He let out a vague sort of cough and cleared his throat. 'You know Frankie Prince?'

I crossed my arms and lowered my head slightly.

'He is big gangster in Cardiff,' Kamil continued.

Tell me something I don't fucking know.

'He runs the Four Seasons,' I said.

'Michal and Leon worked for him in the club ...'

'Doing what?'

He looked up and gave me a surprised look. 'Security.'

'Where did they work?' I thought about the security checks for doormen but, being Polish, they had no record in the UK and that made them ideal candidates.

'In the clubs and all over Cardiff.'

Kamil averted his eyes – lying again.

'Doing what?' I raised my voice.

'I tell you. Security.'

'Why do I get the feeling you're not telling the truth?'

'I tell truth.'

But he sounded unconvincing. Boyd and I sat and stared at him.

'I think we're finished,' I said, pushing my chair backwards.

He straightened in his chair and put the lighter down by the side of the tobacco pouch. 'He go work with the whores.' He spat out the last word.

It was my turn to straighten my posture and

concentrate. 'What do you mean?'

'He go work with Frankie Prince and Lech Balinski in Whitchurch and other places.'

We were making progress. Boyd scribbled notes as Kamil spoke.

'What do you mean, "whores"?'

'The massage parlours and other places.'

'What other places? Kamil, we're going to be here all day unless you give us the details.'

After half an hour, maybe a little more, Kamil slumped back in his chair. It was a neat arrangement. Frankie Prince ran massage parlours that doubled as brothels and recently he'd been bringing in girls from Eastern Europe. He operated from houses all over Cardiff and Michal and Leon were the hired help. They had a smattering of Hungarian and Latvian too, so paying for them to keep the girls in check made economic sense.

'They are slaves.' Kamil sounded angry.

'Is that where Michal was working on the night he was killed?'

He nodded.

'Do you know the addresses of the houses that Frankie uses?'

Kamil shook his head.

'So who is Lech Balinski?' I asked.

Kamil raised his head and I saw the fear crossing his eyes. 'He is gangster too. From Łódź. He kill many people for money.'

'He's an assassin?'

Kamil knotted his forehead.

'I mean – people pay him to kill other people,' I said.

'No. He give people money and if they no pay back, then bang. People fucked.'

'And Frankie Prince …?' I was beginning to get the

feeling I knew where he fitted in.

Kamil shrugged. There was the Aston and the club and the house in the Vale and the health club. And it had all happened in the last two years. Frankie Prince had gone up in the world very quickly.

The bacon sandwich I'd eaten for lunch was giving me heartburn by early afternoon and no amount of moving around or drinking more water was helping. I was expecting Superintendent Cornock to arrive with the two DCs assigned to the case, but I hadn't expected to see him in full uniform. His jacket looked newly dry-cleaned, the creases of his trousers were crisp, and the cap that he placed carefully on the desk was gleaming.

'Good afternoon, everyone.'

I recognised the two officers standing by his side.

I first knew Phil Woods from my time in Pontypridd when he transferred from traffic to CID and was keen to make his mark, but I knew within a week that he'd take a long time to succeed. I nodded at Joe Lawson, trying to conceal my opinion that he should have retired long ago. He was a good two stone overweight, his chin hung over his collar and crimson blotches were developing at the end of his nose.

'This is Phil Woods and Joe Lawson. I'm sure they need no introductions. I can't stress how important it is to get a result here. The Chief Constable is taking a personal interest in the progress of the case. With the second murder to investigate we mustn't leave anything to chance. If the Polish community is under threat in any way then we need to find the killer fast.'

He pulled back his jacket sleeve to look at his watch.

'I'll leave you in the hands of Detective Inspector

Marco. I've got a meeting in headquarters with the Chief Constable.'

Cornock picked up his cap in one hand and brushed an imaginary piece of dust from its peak, before putting it onto his head. He gave me a nod that said get-on-with-it and I nodded back.

Woods and Lawson relaxed once Cornock had left.

I moved a couple of paces into the space where Cornock had stood and looked at the team. 'We've got two Poles in the mortuary, one with his tongue amputated, and two human tongues. One of which is from a body we haven't found – assuming that the person is dead. Then we've got a shed-load of animal tongues that we have to assume are a warning to the Polish community not to talk to us. Phil, Joe, both of you need to call on all the Polish shops in Cardiff and dig around. Boyd and I are going to the factory where Leon and Michal worked.'

The receptionist was still struggling with her English, as I tried to get her to understand that I had to see somebody in authority.

'Manager away,' she said.

'I know, I saw. Him. The day. He left,' I said, as though she were deaf.

'What you want?'

'Boss,' I said.

She picked up the telephone without breaking eye contact and spoke quickly. Soon enough a thin woman with a large flowing skirt in flat shoes came through a door and introduced herself. I explained that I needed to interview the staff on Leon's shift

I could see her thinking. It seemed to be a taxing process, but eventually she led us through into a room in the middle of the building.

'We want to speak to Pietrek Nowak and Gerek Kalka.'

She gave me a blank, vacant look. 'They're not here.'

I felt a brief stab of worry.

'Are they late? When do you expect them to arrive?'

'I'll find the shift supervisor.'

It must have been less than ten minutes, but it felt like longer before she pushed open the door and a chubby-faced man with heavy glasses and a pronounced paunch followed her.

'This is Adam Bachar.'

'How can I help?' The accent was thick and heavy.

'We wanted to interview Pietrek and Gerek.'

Bachar hadn't shaved that morning and he kept rubbing his nose with the back of his hand, sniffing simultaneously.

'Gerek not here. Sick, for many days.'

I stopped making notes and looked at him, a grain of anxiety gathering in my mind.

'When did you see him last?'

'Few days. He rang, say that sick.' He opened his mouth wide and pushed his tongue out.

'Did you speak to him?'

'No. Message with girl in office.'

'And Pietrek – he should be working today. Has he made contact?'

'No. Manager very pissed.'

The answer heightened my unease. 'Did you know Leon Ostrowski?

'For sure, he work here.'

'Did you know of anyone who would want to kill

Leon?'

He leant forward. 'Leon was nice man and good friend.'

'Did he talk to you about everything?'

'What you mean?'

'Did he have any worries? Anything on his mind? Was he frightened of anything?'

He shrugged slowly. 'He was quiet last few months. He no go out too often. Usually Saturday night we get drunk, but not so much now. He had girlfriend maybe.'

'Who was she?' I sounded casual.

Another shrug and I sensed my irritation rising. 'Does anyone know her? Does Gerek know who she is?'

He made a scrawny smile, showing some yellow teeth. 'Leon, Gerek and Pietrek, good friends. Best mates, you say.'

A new fish swam around in the tank; it was a bright-orange colour with flashes of white and blue on its head, like an American Indian in a cowboy film. A stream of bubbles rose from a pipe connected to a pump and the glass was pristine and polished. Cornock dropped small quantities of food onto the surface of the water. The aquarium had arrived when his daughter first became an addict. It was a coping mechanism, something to distract him. Just as I'd convinced myself I wasn't a drunk by only drinking one glass from a bottle of wine and re-corking it, only to open another bottle later the same evening. What harm could one glass do?

Cornock glided a hand over the gel on his hair as he sat down. The paperwork on his desk was still a foot deep and I wondered if this was the fate that awaited me if I ever passed the interviews for promotion.

'So what does Dr Paddy say about the second death?' he said.

'Single knife wound to the heart.'

'Anything else, John?'

'Looks like there could be a connection to Frankie Prince and his flesh trade. They're bringing in girls from Eastern Europe. Maybe underage girls and Michal was a minder. He was Polish, spoke their language.'

Cornock raised an eyebrow and looked over at the aquarium. 'Be careful of Frankie Prince. He could make trouble.'

'I know, sir. We've also got the name of another Pole who's involved – a Lech Balinski. Could be nothing, but we'll look into it. Frankie Prince has got ahead very quickly and there's a suggestion this Pole could be the money.'

Cornock got up and bent over a pile of papers, sifting through them.

'There's a report in the middle of all this rubbish.'

I glanced over at the aquarium. A purple-nosed fish pushed its face from the door of a plastic castle and then rushed around the tank after the orange fish.

After a couple of minutes Cornock yanked out a glossy bound report and pushed it towards me.

'Better read this.'

Chapter 12

The following morning Boyd bowled into my office, holding the remains of a banana.

'I've had the result of the DVLA check on the car Dagmara saw,' he said, waving a printed sheet in his hand.

'And?'

'Car is owned by Ringtone Investments.'

I waited for all the details. Boyd continued. 'It's a company that runs a couple of garages, one in Pontypridd, the other in the Cowbridge. I did a directors search.'

'Get to the point, Boyd.'

'Frankie Prince,' he said simply. 'He owns the company.'

I'd opened the window a couple of inches when I'd arrived that morning, but the room was still muggy and I ran a finger around my collar. I motioned for him to sit down. It was the nearest we'd got to making any progress.

'Good,' I said, not quite certain if I knew where this piece of information would take us. 'We'll need more than circumstantial links to Frankie Prince.' I reached for the telephone and dialled Alvine's number.

'Dix,' Alvine answered, with an undercurrent of menace in her voice.

'Alvine. Anything in Leon's possessions?'

'John.' She sounded frustrated. 'You know it'll take days to get all the forensics done.'

'Anything at all?'

'Clothes, books and some paperwork and then fingerprints all over the room. It hadn't been cleaned for weeks, maybe months.'

Boyd sat listening as he finished the banana, then he tossed the skin into the bin. It landed on the rim, one side of the flesh hanging out.

'Boyd'll be over for the exhibits later,' I said, nodding to Boyd.

'I'm leaving early tonight,' Alvine replied.

'Another date?'

'Fuck off, Marco.'

I didn't get time for more pleasantries before the line went dead. Boyd looked over at me. 'Alvine has a date?'

I nodded. 'Mr Incredible.'

'What do you reckon?' Boyd said. 'Is he in there?'

I sat next to Boyd in an unmarked car looking up at a block of flats, trying to avoid the inquisitive glances from kids circling on their bikes. The address we had for Gerek Kalka was a flat in Grangetown and we'd parked alongside some bins by a row of garages.

'Let's find out,' I said, tugging at the car door.

Dog shit and empty beer cans littered the stairwell to the first floor landing and a nasty smell hung in the air. I thumped the front door, which badly needed painting, and stood back. I noticed the blinds in the adjacent flat moving slightly.

I heard a voice, muffled at first, behind the door, calling out to someone. Good chance Gerek was in then. I gave the door another couple of blows with my fist. After a few seconds – it felt longer – there was a scratching sound as a chain was drawn in place.

'Police,' I said, once the door opened enough for me to see a man's face on the other side. I pressed my warrant card to the gap to make certain he understood.

'What you want?'

'Can we come in?'

'Tell me why you come.'

I could see an unshaven face, a mass of greasy hair

and a dark T-shirt.

'Is Gerek in?'

'Why ...?'

'Is he in or not?'

The door closed and the chain fell to one side. The temperature in the flat was tropical and I hesitated in the doorway. I walked around the pile of unwashed clothes that were responsible for the tacky, heavy smell in the tiny hallway.

We followed the man into the kitchen and he filled a kettle before folding his arms and pulling them towards his chest tightly.

'Does Gerek live here?'

'He is away.'

The accent was Eastern European and he spoke quickly, telling us his name was Aleksy.

'Has he been ill?'

He shrugged and looked at the kettle.

'How many people live here?'

'Four.'

'Who else lives here?'

'Nobody.'

'I heard you talking to someone.'

He gave me a surly look and then shouted something in Polish or Hungarian or Latvian. The girl with the short skirt from the factory reception came out of the bedroom down the corridor and gave me a blank stare. I stared back; so did Boyd: she was only wearing a thin bra and knickers.

I said to Aleksy, 'When did you see Gerek last?'

'A week, maybe more. He is away.'

'Where do you work?'

'In abattoir.'

The smell of dead animals must have stuck to his

clothes and then clung to the wallpaper, curtains, carpets and every surface in the flat. The kettle boiled. He opened a cupboard door and reached for a jar of coffee.

'Where is Gerek's room?'

'It is locked and I no have key,' he said, without turning his head.

'Which room?'

He pointed his head towards the hall and the stairs to the first floor. 'Number 4.'

At the top of the stairs were two rooms, each with a number screwed to the door, and there was another odd smell coming from the bathroom. I stared at the number four and tried the handle. I rattled it a couple of times.

'We need to see inside,' I said.

'We haven't got a warrant,' Boyd said.

'We've got reasonable grounds ...'

'Reasonable grounds for what?'

'To believe he might be implicated in a double murder.'

'Stretching it, boss.'

'That his life might be in danger.'

Boyd gave a look of disbelief. Whatever flak might come my way, I could deal with it later. Now I needed to find out where Gerek might be. I slipped a credit card between the Yale latch and the frame and pushed hard. The door was thin and it gave way easily under my weight.

The room was hot and humid; the curtains were drawn but narrow shards of light skirted the edges. I left the door open and walked over to the windows, moving the curtains to one side before pushing at the casement latch to allow fresh air to flood into the room. It made a change to look at a bed-sit that was tidy. A bright, red duvet covered a single bed, which was pushed against a wall; the furniture was old but clean.

It didn't take us long to work our way through a chest of drawers, a wardrobe and an old bedside cabinet, its drawers broken and loose. We spread the results of our search on the bed – Polish driving licence, some loose change, and bankcards.

'Can't have gone far without these,' I said.

Back at Queen Street I pondered. Do I make it a priority to look for Gerek when there might be an innocent explanation for his disappearance? The return of Woods and Lawson, raised voices, moving chairs and cans of soft drinks cracking open, all interrupted me.

'There's no sign of Pietrek,' Woods began.

'We got into his flat,' Lawson said. 'Legally I mean,' he added.

I ignored Boyd's stare.

'There was a girl in his flat who had a key and she's been worried that he's disappeared without telling anyone where he's gone.' Lawson again.

Woods took a large mouthful of soft drink before adding, 'We've been around the shops and some of the pubs the Eastern Europeans use. There's something up, sir.'

Lawson had a super-large bag of crisps on his desk and a sandwich to match but he found time before his lunch to add to the conversation. 'I'd say they were frightened.'

Woods nodded.

'What do you mean?'

'We couldn't get any response. Everyone was evasive. Didn't want to talk to us. No banter. The owners of the shops kept saying they've never seen anything like it.'

Lawson took an enormous bite from the sandwich and chewed vigorously. I was getting hungry watching him.

I had an hour to kill before meeting Terry so I decided on some fresh air. Trish said I never did any exercise, usually while sitting on the sofa watching TV.

I needed some lunch and time to think. I left the stuffy atmosphere of the station, cut through the side streets and back entrances of the chain stores, and walked up Queen Street. I took a right towards Boulevard De Nantes and then waited by a pedestrian crossing for the lights to turn green.

I found a quiet table in the café at the National Gallery, away from the bustle of the office workers and teachers on trips with school children. I thought about Michal and Leon. There had to be a thread that was linking them altogether. It just couldn't be random. I blocked out the noise from the café and tried to concentrate. And then there was Dagmara; she had caught a glimpse of Leon's murderers and she would make a good witness, but even so, something niggled at the memory of her interview.

After I'd finished the Americano and brushed the crumbs of the almond croissant from my tie I walked back to the foyer and then turned left into the first gallery. I never missed it. It was too good to miss. I sat down and looked at *Running Away with the Hairdresser*. A man and a girl were running along a street somewhere in the south of France. I tried to work out who was the hairdresser – it didn't matter really. It was such a wonderful painting. Then it struck me that I knew why Dagmara had niggled me.

She'd recognised the men that night.

A cool draught from the air-conditioning feathered my

cheeks as I entered court two at the justice centre. I slipped into a seat at the back, after the usher gave me a wary look. Terry was sitting in the dock wearing a suit, looking suitably contrite. I raised my eyebrows when he turned to look at me and for a moment he lost the careful look of humility and a flash of worry passed over his eyes. The prosecutor finished outlining the facts of the case.

On a night out around the clubs of the city, Terry's girlfriend's honour had been tarnished so it had to be salvaged, by a head-butt. The problem Terry faced was the CCTV cameras that had recorded the incident, which made a denial pointless.

Glanville Tront stood up. He was tall and wore his hair in long strands pulled back from his forehead, giving him a look of an actor from a period drama.

'This is a classic case of a man driven to the extremes of provocation,' he began.

He cleared his throat and addressed the magistrates, occasionally fluttering his hands in the air, emphasising some point or other. He tugged at the heartstrings — Terry loved his girlfriend and they'd been celebrating their engagement on the night of the assault. I looked around, half-expecting to see members of the public dabbing handkerchiefs to their eyes.

The magistrates made notes and occasionally glanced at Terry. I was certain I saw his chin wobble. Once GTi had finished, the Chair announced that they would retire to consider their verdict and we all stood up as they filed out. Terry gave me an angry look as I walked over to the dock.

'Brought a toothbrush?' I said.

'Piss off.'

'Six months, you know.' I reminded him of the maximum sentence for common assault.

'GTi's got them sussed. What do you want?'

'Our chat.'

He glanced around furtively and hissed. 'Not here. I told you to meet me at Leftie's.'

It didn't take the magistrates long and Glanville Tront had certainly worked his magic again. The court accepted the degree of provocation, but scolded Terry and told him they were going to be lenient – this time it would be community service. Terry gave them a puppy-dog look. The suit and tie must have helped.

When the magistrates left Terry quickly undid the tie and took off the jacket.

'Good result,' I said to Glanville Tront.

'Another day, another dollar.'

'I need a pint,' Terry said impatiently.

I left the courtroom with him. The foyer was empty. The last of the defendants had left the building.

'Any progress?'

'Not here. I can't be seen with you.'

'Don't get so jumpy. You're in court. It's a good place.'

Terry wasn't convinced and he hurried off to Leftie's, but I dawdled around the court building. An usher gave me another wary look before I passed through security, into the early autumn sunshine that tingled my skin after the coolness of the air-conditioning. I strode over the wide carriageway towards the middle of the city where the solicitors and accountants had their offices. On the opposite side of the road I took a lane that led me to Leftie's Lounge. When Alex Leftrowski had arrived from Russia and opened his bar nobody could pronounce his name so he became Leftie. The lounge came later, when he put in some leather chesterfields in one corner and began offering coffee and tea.

The smell of slops hit me as soon as I walked through the door.

Stale lager and the dregs of Brains beer. Years ago I would have welcomed the smell, particularly at the end of a long day. In fact it didn't need to be at the end of a day: it could be pretty much any time.

There was girl standing behind the bar wearing a thin cotton sleeveless dress and a push–up bra that made the most of her natural assets. She gave me a smile and her face lit up. Mine must have too because her cheeks puckered and the smile widened. I asked for a tap water, ice but no lemon and she looked disappointed, as though my order was faintly unnatural.

Terry was sitting on one of the chesterfields, his jacket draped over the armrest. He had a pint of Brains and a whisky chaser in a glass with lots of ice; a packet of cigarettes sat neatly alongside the smartphone on the low table in front of him.

I sank into the chesterfield opposite him.

'Good result,' I said.

'GTi's fucking good. The best.'

He sipped on the beer. It had been over a year since I'd last had a drop of Brains pass my lips and when I looked at Terry I could still taste the bitter sensation in my mouth.

'You'll be painting the house for some old dear. Or cutting grass and mending fences.'

'I can do gardening,' he said, not sounding convincing.

I got down to business. 'Frankie Prince,' I said. Terry's eyes narrowed and he shushed me, even though the place was practically empty.

'Look Marco. Frankie Prince is bad enough but I've heard that he's in with some heavy-duty gangsters from Russia. Fucking Mafia ... and they don't take any prisoners.

Anybody they don't like …' He imitated firing a gun with his hand.

'Anything concrete?'

Terry blew out his cheeks.

'Look, I owe you. But this is different. When I asked around about Frankie Prince it was as though he'd been promoted to being the fucking prime minister or something. Things have changed. Frankie's got really big-time and there's a Polish gangster called Lech Balinski involved.'

'Any details?'

'For fuck's sake, Marco.'

'Come on. There must be something.'

'Lot of money into the clubs and lots of girls brought in. Really young too. I might have more for you in a couple of days.'

He took another sip of the beer and chased it down with the whisky.

'And this Lech character?'

'He's the money. All from Russia. They're fucking taking over the world. On holiday last year in Costa Blanca – place full of fucking Russians.'

'I don't want to hear about your holidays.'

'Stay clear of this Lech. Know his speciality?'

I raised my eyebrows.

'Cutting out tongues.'

Chapter 13

A week had passed since Michal's body had been washed up in the Taff and despite feeling that I should be in the Incident Room working I had taken time off. I paid little attention to Trish's conversation on the journey to my parents' house. It passed in a blur, my mind trying to make some sense of how I could make progress. Lech Balinski was emerging from the shadows, Frankie Prince was turning himself from a Cardiff gangster into something more sinister, and there was the report from Cornock that I couldn't avoid reading any longer. Trish complained that I had to switch off from work; a fresh mind was always better, she said. I heard her say something about work-life balance as I pulled into the drive of my parents' home and killed the engine.

'I must tell you about the arrangements for the party,' my mother said as we sat at the table. My father rolled his eyes as I glanced over at him. 'Uncle Gino has bought a new suit.'

'John doesn't want to hear about Gino's clothes,' my father said.

'Of course he does,' she replied. 'It's family.'

And my mother continued, giving us the minutiae of the arrangements for the party.

'Are you going to buy a new suit?' she asked.

'No, I haven't …'

'I'll take him to buy a new suit,' Trish said with a half-smile.

My mother looked pleased. 'It must be good quality. It's good for you to listen to your mother once in a while,' she said, turning to Trish. 'Nothing cheap. And a new shirt too.'

My father sat silently, nodding occasionally.

I'd lost interest in the party by the time my mother had recited the details for the tenth time. I sat, San Pellegrino in hand, with my father who sipped a bottle of Peroni, while my mother insisted that Trish help her with the food. Trish sat down by my side as my mother placed a plate of antipasto on the table with a flourish.

'They look lovely, Mrs Marco.'

My father opened a bottle of Bardolino, sharing it with Trish. I'd become accustomed to eating on the move and grazing on takeaways, so taking my time over a meal was unusual. A niggle that I needed to be reading reports or reviewing evidence worked itself into my mind. My mother cleared the plates into the kitchen and returned with a dark-red casserole dish held between thick oven gloves.

My mother spooned the stew onto plates. 'It would be wonderful if Dean could be at the party,' she said, too casually, before passing a plate over to Trish.

'That would be good but Jackie wouldn't let him,' I said, wondering what my mother was up to.

'Smells wonderful, Mrs Marco.'

'One of my favourites,' my mother said.

'What is it?' Trish asked.

'Bollita.'

'What's in it?'

'Beef and veal tongue boiled very slowly.'

Suddenly, I felt a lump in my throat and I lost my appetite.

After lunch I sat with my father in the sitting room half-listening to my mother talking to Trish in the kitchen. My father had something on his mind and it was only a matter of time before he would tell me. I had taken a couple of sips of my double espresso before he cleared his throat.

'Gino wants to sell the property in Pontypridd'

The building was the first premises the family had owned and there was too much sentiment attached to ever consider selling the building.

'And do you want to?'

'No. I've told him straight.'

'Why does he want to sell? It's bringing in good rent.'

'From all accounts his business isn't doing too well and he needs the money.'

'Why doesn't Jez take it over?'

'Your cousin is bone idle, that's why.'

'The place is in your name – and Uncle Gino's name.'

'But there's some complex trust provisions contained in Nonno Marco's will that means you have to consent to the sale.'

'And Uncle Gino's in a fix.'

'He's tried everything. Being nice to me and then bullying me with suggestions that Nonno Marco would have been shocked with my behaviour.'

I sat back in the chair and finished the espresso.

'Gino's bound to tackle you about it at the party.'

I thought about my childhood when my father would take me to see the café and how my grandfather would make a fuss over me, make me weak coffee, and tell me how lucky I was to live in Wales. I could see why my father wouldn't want to sell the café. It was part of him, part of what made *us* as a family.

'It was delicious,' Trish said, for the fourth time during our journey back to Cardiff.

I forced a smile and I thought about the reports I

needed to read and the case review I needed to finish. And there was *Top Gear* on the television later, so I had to finish in good time.

Back at the flat, Trish made coffee and we sat at the table with papers open in front of us. I adjusted the blinds, blocking out the rays from the early-evening sunshine. I started at the executive summary of the report which had a lot of management-speak about *stakeholders* and *outcomes* and *objectives* and I skipped through the jargon until I found the substance. The human trafficking into South Wales was becoming a political issue. A committee of assembly members was going to report directly to a minister, but I knew it wasn't the sort of issue that would get them headlines in the press or votes in the next election. I could just see the politicians running a campaign on the evils of trafficking people around Europe, while paying minimum wage to girls from Poland to clean their apartments in the Bay.

There were pages of details about the numbers involved. It was the sort of report that went from one desk to another, bouncing around until it ran out of steam and then quietly shelved because of operational priorities or resource implications.

'They reckon there's four hundred and fifty girls trafficked into Wales every year,' I said.

Trish put down the coffee mug and looked up from her papers. 'Where from?'

'Eastern Europe mostly.'

There was a section from the Vice Squad about the activities of pimps and brothels in Cardiff, but nothing about the trafficking of girls into the city. I knew that the Vice Squad was under-resourced and lacked the motivation to do anything properly. It wasn't exactly the sort of career progression that most cops wanted. 'And Amnesty says it's modern-day slavery.'

The coffee in my mug was cold. I felt hungry again.

'It's the sort of thing we don't hear about,' Trish said.

'Nobody looks out for the women involved.'

I read more of the Amnesty section.

'Amnesty reckons families sell their daughters to the traffickers,' I said.

Trish put her biro down and looked up at me. 'That's awful. What sort of world is it …?'

Tomorrow we'd make progress. Real progress – there had to be some forensics. There had to be something on Lech and Frankie.

When *Top Gear* started I slumped into the sofa trying to insulate my mind from tongues and trafficking and reports from senior management. I watched Jeremy Clarkson walking around an Aston Martin parked next to a Porsche on the concourse of an airfield. Frankie probably liked *Top Gear*. He probably watched it on a massive screen. Tomorrow I would get a better picture of Lech. I needed to know who he was, where he came from. I wondered what sort of car he drove. Clarkson screamed around the track like a teenager, making grimaces to the camera. I felt hungry as the memory of the Bollita receded in my mind. I turned to Trish.

'Any chance of something to eat?'

I woke from a dreamless sleep and reached over to the alarm clock. My hand sent the clock flying off the table and I heard it crash against the skirting board, dislodging the battery that rolled under the bed. But the noise kept ringing and I fumbled for the mobile telephone.

Trish was making an odd grunting sound in her

sleep.

I pressed the receive button and stuck the handset to my ear. The voice from Area Control sounded wide-awake.

'There's a burglary on Rodium Crescent. The householder has reported a man with tattoos in his garden.'

I grabbed my watch and realised I'd been asleep for only an hour. I could feel the grit gathering in my eyes; I stammered something down the telephone, and the line went dead. I padded into the bathroom, threw cold water over my face, and brushed my teeth mechanically – Trish complained that my teeth could be rancid in the morning. After I'd dragged on some clothes, I bent over the bed, thinking about kissing Trish, but she turned over and drew the duvet over her head.

After pouring a glass of juice – no time for a coffee – I called Boyd.

'On my way, boss.'

I pulled the door behind me quietly and walked downstairs to the car park. The yellow glow from the streetlights shrouded the car with a soft neon haze. Everything looked still and quiet. A fox walked past the entrance and stopped to look at me, its bushy tail moving slowly. There was a noise from a car braking in the distance and the fox trotted away. I took out the cigarettes from the inside of my jacket and stuck one between my lips. My five–a-day rule was modified if I was working at night – it only seemed fair that I could have at least one or two more if I had to work long hours.

I powered the car through deserted streets towards town. Rodium Crescent was in Cyncoed on the northern side of Cardiff. A couple of coaches passed with *London* displayed in letters above the driver.

A Scientific Support Vehicle and a patrol car were

parked outside the house, so I drew the car into the kerb a couple of houses away. Boyd was standing by the front door holding a chocolate bar in one hand, a satisfied look on his face.

'I thought you were off the junk food?' I said to him, as he walked towards me, crumpling the wrapper in his hand.

'Christ's sake, boss. It's the middle of the night.'

The house was detached with two large bays and a drive leading to a double garage with electronic shutters. All the downstairs lights were blazing and I could hear voices from the rear of the house, as Boyd and I approached the back door. By a clean, well-polished table in the kitchen an elderly couple were sitting, two uniformed officers keeping them company. The man stood up and stretched to his full height. He had a thin white moustache hanging above narrow lips and his hair was short and cut almost flat on the top. His wife sat by the table nursing a glass that had a tired-looking slice of lemon floating in the final few centimetres of the clear liquid. She lifted her head in a slow, weary sort of way and then looked at me before taking another sip. Her skin looked tired too – it had an odd orange tint.

'I've got a photograph,' the man said defiantly, pointing at the mobile telephone on the table. 'Proper camera wouldn't work. Too damned complicated.'

'Gerald, don't be such an arse.' The accent was Home Counties, but the slurring was from a gin bottle.

'I can show the inspector the photograph,' he said.

'Wing Commander Bates caught the burglar in the act, sir,' said one of the uniforms with the faintest of smiles.

'I've been waiting up. Only a matter of time until he came around this street.'

'How ...?' I asked.

'Done Claudia Avenue. Every damn house – probably feeding some drug habit. Next street along. Stood to reason.'

'But there'd be no way of knowing …'

'I've seen it all before, Inspector. They don't know the meaning of respect and hard work.'

He sounded like an editorial from the *Daily Mail* so I stood up. 'Better show us where it happened.'

Bates led us through into a rear lounge that had expensive furniture and a large flat-screen television in full view of the French doors leading onto the patio area.

'I was at our neighbourhood watch meeting last night in the home of Judge Patricks. That's why I was awake. Half-expecting him tonight.'

'You were waiting up?' I asked.

'Good thing I was.'

I cast my eye around the room and saw the tripod with an expensive camera screwed to the top and a whisky bottle half hidden by the edge of a chair. I could see the headline – *Retired Wing Commander catches burglar red-handed*.

'We were all ready. Can't allow this sort of thing to happen. Not in this street.'

'What do you mean, ready?' I asked.

Bates leant forward and almost whispered. 'Prepared. The judge wanted us all to be ready.'

Judge Patricks was on a one-judge mission to lock up as many burglars as he could after his holiday home near Carmarthen had been broken into so many times he'd lost count.

I wondered if the thief knew where the judge lived and was going to avoid his house, since he'd also missed out the home of Glanville Tront in the next street. I peered out of the window into the garden but all I could make out were the vaguest shadows of the trees and the roof of a summerhouse.

I turned to Bates who was rocking slightly on the balls of his feet.

'Let me have a look at the telephone.'

We went back into the kitchen; he fumbled with the key pad, and his wife got more irate until she drank the final dregs, the lemon slice left sticking to the side of the glass.

A pleased and satisfied look crossed Bates's face as he passed me the telephone with an outstretched hand.

'There,' he said. 'First-hand evidence.'

I took the telephone in my hand and then laughed loudly. I was looking at the face of Robbie Williams, his smile wide, teeth gleaming.

Chapter 14

I heard Trish cursing as she dressed.

'Where's the fucking alarm.'

I grunted.

'I am *so* late.'

I opened an eyelid and looked for the alarm clock and remembered that the battery was somewhere under the bed. I turned over and dragged the duvet over my head. I couldn't function on two hours' sleep.

Trish crashed about in the kitchen, closing the cupboard doors with enough force to break the hinges before boiling a full kettle and then turning the volume of the radio up high. Eventually she slammed the front door and left. But I couldn't sleep and I tossed around the bed. I kept seeing the face of Robbie Williams every time I was dropping off to sleep.

After a shower and a double-double strength espresso I felt more awake. Outside it was another fresh, clear September morning; the wind ruffled the tops of the trees lining the half-empty car park.

I arrived at Queen Street at the same time as Boyd. The bags under his eyes were neat and clean and turning the colour of tepid coffee. He stared at me and gave me a feeble grin.

'Get any sleep?' I asked.

'I've done it twice. Once when I got in, then again this morning. I'm knackered.'

I thought about the grunt that Trish had given me when I slipped under the duvet at five in the morning and ran my hand up her leg. She'd pulled away into the warmth of the bedclothes as I'd lain there trying to remember when I last had a decent night's sleep.

I flicked through some of the paperwork on the

desk as a yawn gripped the back of my throat and I thrust my hand to my mouth. From the pile of paperwork I picked up the list of exhibits from Leon's flat. There was a long list of till receipts from his local supermarket, a loyalty card and some loose change. I read through the list until I noticed the restaurant receipt. I opened the plastic envelope and dragged out the flimsy piece of paper. I noticed the date – it was two days before Michal's death.

I shouted over at Boyd. 'Fancy lunch?'

Boyd started the car and we threaded our way slowly through the city traffic.

'Do you keep restaurant receipts?' I asked.

'Don't know, boss.'

'I throw them. Once I've checked the amounts. What's the point?'

Boyd was concentrating on trying to overtake a lorry that had *Keep Your Distance* in large letters on the rear tailgate. He grunted a reply.

I took out the receipt as Boyd pulled into the parking slot by the pavement near the Gaia Pizzeria. A small van covered in adverts for the best home-delivered pizza in Cardiff was parked in front of us. A young kid, no more than fourteen, was sweeping the rubbish off the pavements into the road and picking up discarded pizza boxes.

Inside, I searched for the face of authority. The girls cleaning the floors and washing glasses hardly gave me a second glance. I caught the eye of a man wearing thick-rimmed glasses and an angry expression.

'Yes?' he said, with as much enthusiasm as a man attending his own funeral.

'You the manager?' I flashed my card but it had no effect.

He nodded. 'What do you want?'

I fished out the receipt from a pocket. 'I need to

trace the people who paid for this meal.'

'What is this anyway?' He sounded defensive.

'We found the receipt on a dead man. We want to know who he was with on the night.'

After he'd scanned the receipt as intently as an invitation to a garden party at Buckingham Palace, he turned on his heels and walked through the restaurant. I nodded to Boyd and we followed him towards a large open-plan kitchen. He called out to a young girl who walked over.

'Lisa, did you serve this table?' He thrust the receipt towards her.

Lisa was very thin and the T-shirt she wore hung off her shoulders. She had eyes that seemed to float around in their sockets. She nodded without conviction.

'Do you remember who they were?' I asked.

She shook her head slowly before saying. 'He comes in a lot. Always has something cheap. He was foreign. Russian or maybe Polish or something.'

'Is this him?' I showed her Leon's Polish identity card, which I'd shoved into my jacket as we left the station.

'Yeh,' Lisa nodded. 'Is he all right?'

'No,' I said. 'He's dead and I was hoping you could remember who he was with that night.'

The colour drained from her cheeks and she clutched her hand to her mouth. 'That's awful.'

'Well?' I asked.

'It was a girl.'

'Can you describe her?'

Lisa trawled her memory and told us about the girl's hair colour and her face and how tall she was. It sounded like Lisa had a thing for Leon and once she'd seen him with a girl she'd paid lots of attention.

Once she'd finished I knew exactly who she'd described.

A Monday should have meant fresh minds after the weekend, but there hadn't been time to relax and I was back in the office, my mind losing its grip on the concentration it needed. Woods and Lawson were in the Incident Room with Boyd and I knew we had to make progress, but all I could think of was Dagmara and why we had come across her again in the investigation.

The telephone had rung out the first time I'd called and at the second attempt it cut into an answer machine. My mobile was sitting on the desk. I was looking at it, not wanting to call her a third time. I bit my lip, picked up the mobile and made the call. Another message. Another notch of worry tightened in my chest.

'Boss, BTP have called.'

I heard his voice but didn't listen.

'Boss, the British Transport Police ...'

I looked up and when he knew he had my concentration he stopped.

'What?' I said.

'Sergeant Parkes of the BTP has called. They can't find Janek. Wondering if we can help.'

'He's not at home?'

'No.'

'At work?'

'Not seen since last week.'

I sat back in my chair.

'Friends, girlfriends?' I said as Boyd shook his head. 'Boyfriends?' I added.

'Apparently his bed-sit has been cleaned out. Wiped down, clothes and belongings gone. He didn't tell anyone else.'

I made certain Boyd sent me Janek's details.

Tomorrow I had a meeting with someone who could help.

Chapter 15

Colonel Victor Laskus was dressed head-to-toe in a khaki-coloured uniform, the top of his breast pocket adorned with various coloured medals and the pips on his shoulders glistened in the artificial light. I offered tea and coffee. He shook his head. It was a large head to shake and he wore his hair in a style modelled by a blunt lawnmower. He shot out his hand, and when he shook mine I could feel my shoulder blade weakening. I stared blankly at the Polish letters on his business card until he suggested I look on the other side. It said *Diplomatic Liaison – Military*, which I took to mean he was a spook.

'How can I help?' I said.

'You are in charge?' He sounded like a villain from a *James Bond* movie.

I nodded.

'Michael Dąbek and Leon Ostrowski,' he announced. 'What can you tell me?'

'They were both murdered. Michal had is tongue cut out.' I watched the colonel but he barely flinched.

'Very bad. Russian criminals cut tongues out. It is …' he hesitated. 'Despicable.' He said the word carefully as though he'd learnt it on the train that morning.

'We don't know the motive yet. We know they'd been living in Wales for a couple of years. They seemed to be settled. What can you tell me about their background?'

He stared at me briefly, as though he were searching for the right answer.

'I understand they were in the Polish Special Forces.'

He raised his thick eyebrows and they almost met in the middle. It had been a guess but the surprise on the colonel's face had given me the confirmation I needed.

'Good men. Good soldiers.'

'Can you tell me about their service history? Were they in the same unit? Who were their friends?'

'Do you have suspects?'

I suspected that liaison for the Polish colonel meant me telling him everything without any reciprocal exchange of information. We spent another half an hour discussing the deaths of Michal and Leon and the only information he offered was the promise to check the records of the relevant army department.

'Do you have suspects?' he asked again.

'No,' I said.

'Do other Polish people help?'

'We have interviewed one of two.'

'Who are they? What are their names?'

'I'm sure, Colonel, you know that information is confidential.'

His lips twitched slightly and he gave me a dark stare. 'Good relations between our two countries is very important.'

'I need to trace a person of interest for us.'

The colonel narrowed his eyes as he looked at the photograph I'd pushed over the desk. Then I gave him a piece of paper with Janek's personal details – all we had was his date of birth and a witness who believed he was from the eastern suburbs of Warsaw.

'Can you help with tracing this person?'

'What has happened to him?'

'He's disappeared.'

The eyebrows rose again.

'Can you help? Will the police in Poland be able to help?'

'I'm sure that the Warsaw police can help.' It sounded like he wanted to avoid responsibility.

'Can you make the contacts for me? I want to report to the Assistant Chief Constable after our meeting – she'll be interested to hear how our liaison is developing.'

The colonel nodded.

'I will do what I can. I speak to Warsaw police.'

'Thanks. And could you ask them about these two men as well?' I said, finding another sheaf of paper in the folder on the desk with the names and bare details of Pietrek Nowak and Gerek Kalka. 'We need to speak to them urgently. If they've gone back to Poland then we need to know.'

The colonel stared at the images.

'Does the name Lech Balinski mean anything to you?' I asked.

A glimmer of recognition crossed his eyes, until the spook training cut in.

'I look into it for you,' he said, scribbling down the name.

He stared at me for a few seconds before checking the time and announcing that he had a train to catch. I opened the door and offered to arrange for a taxi to the station, but he shook his head.

'Walking is good.'

I watched him leave Queen Street and immediately he pulled out a mobile phone, which he pressed to his ear.

'I've had a complaint.'

Cornock was running a finger around the rim of a mug that had a large yellow dot on its side. The pile of papers on his desk was as thick as the last time I was in his room and the aquarium hummed silently in the background.

'Wing Commander Bates was on the telephone this morning,' he continued.

I waited for him to continue.

'You know the sort, John. Thinks he's still in charge. He wants to push people around.'

'What did he say?'

'He says you were rude and inconsiderate.'

I let out a long rasp of air and gathered my thoughts.

'He was pissed.'

Cornock raised his eyebrows. 'Wing Commander Bates name-dropped Judge Patricks and one of the ACCs, as though they were lifelong friends.'

I folded my arms before replying. 'His wife was pissed too.'

'This is Cyncoed, John. The residents need to be treated with respect and courtesy.'

And the people of Splott don't.

'The ACC needs a full report on the burglaries, soon as.'

I wondered how far Cornock lived from Rodium Crescent and whether it would be his street that would be hit next. I had to protest even though it was going to be a waste of time.

'The crime scene investigators were punctual. They went through the house and garden. Alvine Dix was in charge. Maybe she said something,' I said.

Cornock took a deep breath. 'I've agreed that we'll attend the next neighbourhood watch meeting.' He glanced over at the faded blue colour on my denim shirt. 'And you'll have to wear a suit.'

Boyd looked up from his desk as I entered the Incident Room. It smelt stale and humid and he stifled a yawn as he made eye contact. I raised my eyes and nodded towards my office, telling him to follow me.

'All right, boss?'

'You'll have to buy a new suit.'

Boyd gave me a puzzled look. 'Sorry?'

'Super wants us to attend the next neighbourhood watch meeting.'

'What good is that going to do?'

I shrugged. 'You know how it is. The residents of Rodium Crescent call the shots.'

'But it's not like we have nothing else to do.'

'Wing Commander Bates complained that I was rude and inconsiderate.'

'Did you tell the Super about the whisky bottle?'

I nodded.

'And did you tell the Super that the wife was pissed?'

I nodded again, vigorously, to emphasise the point.

'Apparently Bates knows one of the ACCs as well as Judge Patricks. Super's been on the telephone all morning.'

I shuffled papers around on my desk before glancing at my watch, realising that I was late for my appointment with Dagmara. Boyd had spoken to Alvine Dix on the telephone who'd told him that her report – she'd told Boyd to emphasise the word 'preliminary' – would be emailed later that day. I was half-listening and half-thinking about my meeting with Dagmara and her jet-black hair and pearl-like eyes. Boyd cleared his throat and succeeded in cutting short the scenarios developing in my mind.

'Do you want to meet the family?'

'Who?'

'Leon's family. They should be arriving later.'

I mumbled an acknowledgment. I glanced at my watch again, picked up the mobile telephone and composed a text to Dagmara.

'If I'm back in time, I'll see them.'

I could see Boyd beginning to form a question in his mind and, before he had the chance to take it any further, I put the mobile phone down and gave him a quick stare. 'I'll go and see Dagmara. I want you to get that report prepared for the ACC.'

I could see his enthusiasm deflate and he left my office tightening and straightening his tie as he did so. I finished the text to Dagmara, found my car keys in my desk drawer, and headed down towards the car park.

It took me longer than I expected to thread my way through the afternoon traffic towards one of the industrial estates on the west of the city. Eventually, I drew up alongside the offices of the anonymous-sounding agency where she worked.

I stood in the empty reception listening to a telephone ringing incessantly in an office down a hallway. A door leading off reception had been propped open with a wooden wedge. I pressed a button on the desk and within a minute I heard a door open down the hallway.

'Can I help?' asked the man who appeared.

'Dagmara is expecting me.'

He nodded and turned back on his heels. 'I'll take you through.'

I followed him into a corridor lined with photographs of smiling politicians, men in grey suits and women with severe haircuts and cheesy grins.

'Sorry we haven't got a receptionist. It's the cutbacks. We're just hanging on by the skin of our teeth.'

There was a sense of impending closure hanging around the place. I could imagine that an agency promoting welfare, education and business opportunities for various minority groups would have been high on the list for cutbacks. I was surprised that some politician had not yet called for its complete abolition. I could see their line – *British taxpayers support foreign jobs*. It would be a brave politician prepared to justify spending money on this agency.

'She's in there.' The man pointed at one of the doors further down the corridor.

I knocked and Dagmara called out a welcome. Her office was narrow with a window looking out over a paved area. Her desk had been pushed against the wall and I sat on a chair in the middle of the room.

'Mr Personality, your colleague,' I offered.

She gave a half-hearted smile. 'How can people work when they know their jobs might be gone next week?'

When she looked at me her eyes seemed to light up and she gave me a full smile.

'How can I help, John?'

The accent could have melted ice cream and I felt myself hesitating. 'How well did you know Leon?'

She blinked quickly, but kept the eye contact direct.

'Quite well. He was friends with Michal and we all share Howick Street. We were both – all of us – from Warsaw.'

'We found a restaurant receipt with Leon's possessions.' I saw the uncertainty in her eyes. 'We went to the restaurant. The waitress there was helpful. She gave a very good description of the person with Leon.'

Dagmara moved in her chair, waiting for me to continue.

'What did you talk about?' I asked.

She turned her head away.

'Lots of things. Many different things.'

'Such as?'

'Work. And about going back home. And how he wanted to leave Cardiff.'

'Was he unhappy?'

'For sure.'

'Why?'

She pulled her hair back behind her ear and then she crossed and uncrossed her legs. I leant forward in the chair and intertwined my fingers.

'Dagmara, why didn't you tell me this before?'

Then she gave me a frightened look.

'Were you and Leon ...?'

She didn't let me finish the question.

'No, no, never. I couldn't ... just friends.'

A part of me felt relieved, pleased even. I couldn't help but feel that Dagmara deserved better than a cheap bed-sit in Splott.

'How often did you socialise?'

'No, it was nothing regular.'

'Come on Dagmara, I'm trying to find who killed Michal and Leon. The day before Leon was killed you were with him in a restaurant. You want me to read the statement from the waitress?'

She shook her head.

'And when you saw the men outside the house, you knew who they were. So tell me – what's the connection?'

She fidgeted with some biros on the desk.

'Who are they, Dagmara? I need to know.'

'Did you know where Leon and Michal worked?'

'Tell me about the men first.'

She bowed her head. She paused as she spoke and I saw the fear in her eyes as she described the big man with a close haircut and enormous shoulders.

'Do you know him?'

Her eyes met mine.

'Is it Lech Balinski?'

She nodded then gave a hard stare until her jaw twitched. 'Evil man.'

'And the second?'

This time the fear had subsided – her voice confident as she described Janek's features.

'Michal and Leon work for him,' she said slowly.

'You mean Frankie Prince?'

She nodded. 'It was good money. At start it didn't matter to Michal or Leon what was going on.'

'You mean with the work in the brothels?'

'They were just paid to move the girls around. They do nothing else.'

'How old were the girls?'

She looked away. 'At first they did not know a thing.'

'Come on Dagmara. They were underage, weren't they? Just kids.'

'They both needed the money. It was cash and then they thought they could stop but—'

'It never did. Have you got any addresses?'

She shook her head. 'Michal never tell me.'

She was trying too hard to keep eye contact, but she was shifting uncomfortably in her seat.

'So what happened? What changed things?'

Dagmara hesitated. 'Leon wanted to tell the police. He fell in love with one of the girls. He was sick of doing work for them.'

'What was the name of the girl?'

'I don't know.'

'That's not much help.'

'I know she was in touch with Anna Best.'

'Who the hell is Anna Best?'

'Leon told me her name. She works for Amnesty.'

I drew both hands through my hair and let out an exasperated breath. At least I could put Lech Balinski at 14 Howick Street on the night of Leon's death. Now I had to find an anonymous call girl who knew the corpse in the mortuary and I had to deal with a do-gooder, all to make progress. And I still had to find the mysterious Lech and find out how he fitted into the jigsaw that seemed to gather more pieces at every step.

***

I got back to Queen Street late in the afternoon and Boyd looked relieved to see me as he told me about the family waiting downstairs.

'The mother and father are pretty cut up. There was a brother and an uncle but they left. The brother couldn't hack it – he was a bit simple – so the uncle took him back to their hotel.'

'Have they made the identification?'

'Yes.'

All we had to do was express condolences to people we had never met and didn't know and hope they could tell us something about the life of their son. The job never made it any easier and I often found myself wondering whether I could ever truly express grief and offer condolences when the time came for one of my family to die. I could remember my grandfather dying when I was young, but it was years ago and he was very old. Nobody seemed to be surprised and from what I remember he was happy. So I didn't feel sad. My father cried at the funeral and my mother held his arm tightly.

'Is there an interpreter?'

Boyd nodded. 'Same woman as before.'

Maybe she was good at condolences.

We straightened our ties and then took the stairs down to a conference room near the main entrance.

Leon's father looked worn out and his wife, a large rotund woman with straight grey hair that hadn't seen a decent hairdresser for years, had hollow eyes and dark shadows on her cheeks. I sat down and said how sorry we were at their sad loss.

Boyd kept up a frantic pace, scribbling down the replies as the interpreter gave the answers to my questions. The part where they talked about his time in the Polish Special Forces didn't come as a surprise. We got the details of his school and university and army career and his first girlfriend and the time he was sick all over the carpet and the time he drowned the cat in the water butt and his father thrashed him.

Leon's mother fumbled through a battered bag lying on her lap, found an envelope that she handed to Veronika and spoke a couple of sentences of Polish.

'Apparently he sent this photograph home,' Veronika said. 'He wanted his mother to see that he was making friends.'

She handed me the envelope and inside was a snap of Leon and Michal and Dagmara smiling broadly.

'Does she know anything about this?'

More translation and then the reply before Veronika shook her head.

'Did he have a bank account?' I asked.

I waited for the reply.

'Yes. Of course. He was a good boy and he send money back home.'

'Are there bank statements?' I asked.

Another silence.

'How much money is in the accounts?'

'They do not know,' the interpreter said.

There was a dull ache behind my forehead once we'd finished and I rubbed my temple in the hope it would disappear. Boyd was yawning as we walked back up to the Incident Room.

'Tired?' I said.

'I'm knackered.' But before he could begin a detailed explanation of his nocturnal activities we reached the Incident Room and saw the friendly face of Alvine Dix.

'Where have you been?' She sounded annoyed.

'Playing ten-pin bowling – where do you think?'

'All right, no need to get the hump.'

'Expressing our condolences and yours too, of course. Collectively on behalf of Southern Division of Wales Police Service, to another family from Poland.'

She forced a brief smirk. 'That's why I'm here.'

I nodded towards my office and once inside she sat down and pulled two plastic evidence pouches from the folder tucked under her arm.

'We found these sewn neatly into the hem of one of Leon's jackets.'

I leant over and examined the contents. The first bag had a SIM card for a mobile phone and the second a key. It must have opened a small door judging by its size and weight but behind it there had to be something very important.

Chapter 16

Boyd sat on the chair in my room, staring at the pile of papers he had dumped on my desk, the product of many hours of research, judging from the studious look on his face. He looked alert and fresh, presumably the result of a night's uninterrupted sleep.

'Where did you get the name from?' I said.

'What do you mean?'

'Boyd, the name Boyd. Bit unusual. I was just wondering where it came from. Family tradition?'

'My mother's American,' he said, as though that explained everything.

'Really.'

'She was a student in Cardiff when she met my father. Then she went back to the States but, you know, true love and all that, and she came back. She works for the council doing management work in the social services department.'

'Do you go to the States often?'

'Been a few times when I was younger.'

'So Boyd's an American name?'

'I suppose so, boss. Never thought about it much.'

I couldn't remember how Jackie and I chose Dean as a name. She probably decided when I was working or in the pub.

'We can put Lech and Janek in Howick Street on the night Leon was killed,' I said.

'Good. Is it—'

'Enough to arrest him? Don't think so. Not when he's connected to Frankie Prince.'

Boyd looked at his papers and the studious look came back.

'Alvine sent me the list of mobile telephone

numbers on Leon's SIM card. It's going to take us hundreds of man hours to go through them all,' Boyd said.

'And we might have another list from Michal's mobile.'

I knew that we didn't have hundreds of man hours to spare: only the grind of police work. I was deciding on how to divide the work between Woods and Lawson when the telephone rang.

'The lockers at the Royal House Hotel have been ransacked.' Cornock's voice had a sharp edge.

'When ...?'

'This morning. There's a CSI team on its way. John, are you any nearer to identifying what they're looking for?'

I drew breath for a moment, not wanting to admit too quickly that I was struggling, that I was waiting to see Dagmara again, hoping that Terry might come up with some intelligence and blocking out the reality that we still had a tongue-less body to find.

The staff room at the Royal House Hotel was a maze of separate rooms divided into various sections, each with a bench and some lockers screwed to the walls. I stepped over piles of clothes and magazines, discarded in the frantic search of the lockers. Doors had been prised open, their locks bent and buckled.

Alvine stood by the entrance door, arms crossed, a frown creasing her forehead.

'Do you have any idea what they're looking for?'

'No. But it must be important.'

'Then you'd better find it before they do.'

'Anything?'

'This place is a mess. And the realistic prospect is that there will be no DNA or fingerprints or anything else that will be of any interest. But who am I to say? I just do the forensics. It's for clever people like you to find out what's happening and why.'

Looking into the locker room I wasn't feeling very clever and I was getting angrier all the time.

'Inspector Marco.'

I turned and saw the personnel manager with the list of all the current and past employees.

'Thanks,' I said, and left.

Outside the main entrance, I found the battered packet of cigarettes in my jacket pocket and took a long drag as I walked over to my car at the far end of the car park.

I called Boyd and when he answered I gave him a summary before warning him to get Woods and Lawson ready for a long day and a long night.

I finished the cigarette and threw the butt-end into a fancy-looking hedge that lined the car park. My mobile rang as I searched for my car keys.

'We've had a report of another hotel break-in,' said the voice from Area Control.

Once I'd got the details I sat in the car, thinking that things had to get better. Isn't there a saying that things will likely get worse before they get better?

And then they did.

By the end of the day I'd stood in the locker rooms of another five hotels, each with anxious staff, teams of CSIs painstakingly working through each pile of discarded clothes. Exhaustion hit me at about ten, when I stopped talking to Boyd mid-sentence and my body seemed to shut down. In the old days it would have been an excuse for a pint and a whisky. It was gone midnight when I got home;

the flat was quiet and my mind was spinning, making sleep impossible. I clicked the television on and found an episode of *Top Gear*. I listened to Clarkson's voice in the background while pouring orange juice into a glass and putting a slice of bread into the toaster. I slumped into a chair.

Clarkson looked into the camera, pulled his face into an odd shape – an improvement really – and said something that made the audience laugh. I looked at the screen but my mind couldn't relax. I chewed on a mouthful of toast.

I woke an hour later; my drink had fallen, leaving a dark stain on the carpet and the toast was lying, butter side down, on the floor. The television was running a programme on the solar system. I staggered off to bed but when the alarm woke me in the morning a flash of panic went through my mind as I couldn't figure out which day it was.

I looked at the clothes hanging in my wardrobe before glancing through the window and deciding that the heavy clouds and the cooling September days justified a jacket. On the drive into town, I turned up the volume of the CD player and listened to Elvis singing 'Suspicious Minds'. I was still humming the tune as I walked into the Incident Room.

'You all right, boss?' Boyd said.

'Suspicious Minds.'

Boyd gave a puzzled look.

'Number one for Elvis in 1969.'

I wandered over to the kitchen and flicked the ageing kettle into life. My mobile beeped just as the kettle boiled. I pressed the handset to my ear with one hand and poured the boiling water into the cup with the other. I pushed the teabag down to the bottom and watched the water change colour.

'There's a visitor in reception.' The voice said the

words carefully.

'Who is it?'

'That Polish bloke who's been here before.'

Satisfied that the tea was a decent colour, I threw the teabag into a redundant ice cream tub on the worktop. I contemplated how long my patience would last with Kamil and decided that he'd get five minutes, maximum.

Kamil paced around the room, once again chewing his nails. His hair was longer and the artificial light in the room glistened on the three days of stubble clinging to his face.

'I must know what happening,' he said as I sat down.

Three minutes now: even less if he kept up his attitude. I blew on the hot tea and took a sip.

'We've got an ongoing investigation.'

'I work in hotels,' he said. 'I heard that lockers broken into. What is happening? What have you found out?'

I sat back in my chair.

'I can't tell you anything about the investigation—'

'But I am afraid.'

He'd stopped pacing and sat on a flimsy plastic chair.

'I know, but there's nothing—'

'I could be next. They kill me.'

'Who?'

He knitted his fingers together and averted his eye contact. 'Have you found anything from lockers?'

'It's too early to say if anything is missing yet.'

'Who else had lockers? I tell all my friends from Poland to come and ask you.'

I held up a hand. The last thing I wanted was hundreds of Polish people lining up in reception.

'We've got the names of everyone who had staff lockers so we'll contact them in due course.'

I stood up and walked to the door, which I held open for Kamil.

'I've got work to do.'

Woods and Lawson sat in the Incident Room, turning biros nervously through their fingers. Boyd had a hungry look in his eyes as he fiddled with an unopened bag of fruit.

I stood at the board that Boyd had been decorating with various photographs and names of victims and a list of hotels printed in a large font.

'Have you had the final list of all the lockers?' I said to Woods.

'Last one should be in later.'

'Divide it between you and Joe,' I said, nodding at Lawson. 'And then go after every name on the list.'

'Do you want us to go after the shops again?' Lawson said.

'After you've done the lists. And go and see that priest again. He might have more to tell us.'

Boyd started chewing on an apple.

'Any luck with digging into Frankie?' I said to Boyd.

He swallowed. 'It's taking longer than I thought.'

Everything about the investigation was taking longer than we had anticipated and with the paperwork and statements multiplying there was nothing I could do except wait. I finished the briefing and got back to my room as a woman wearing a powder-blue suit, perfect make-up and high heels, stood by the door.

'Inspector Marco. Sue Pennington from PR.' She walked into the room and held out her hand. 'I need to talk to you about the Polish murders. The press are going to run a piece and we need to prepare a statement.'

An hour passed with Sue who nodded occasionally, then narrowed her eyes as she concentrated on what I was telling her before scribbling notes on a large legal pad.

'So there's nothing we can say really that's very positive.'

'That's right,' I said, regretting that I somehow sounded complacent.

'Do you think there's any chance of catching the perpetrator?'

I hesitated, wanting to tell her that we'd catch the killer really soon and that they'd be behind bars, the public protected, the reputation of the Wales Police Service enhanced and those who questioned devolving police responsibility to Wales, silenced.

'It's slow progress.'

Dagmara's text had said three p.m.

But I arrived at Leftie's Lounge ten minutes early. She sat in a corner sipping a glass of juice and smiled when she saw me. I sank into the warm leather of the sofa by her side. She'd drawn her hair back and I followed the clear line of her jaw and saw a nervous twitch ripple the skin.

'She might not come,' she said slowly. 'She does not trust the police.'

I nodded. I knew from the Amnesty report that getting the girls to give evidence was the main obstacle to prosecution. The report had made depressing reading and, with resources scarce, the work of investigating human trafficking was a low priority. And even when there were girls willing to give evidence, the WPS didn't have the backup support, no safe-house, no counsellors and too few interpreters.

Dagmara kept alternating glances between the door and her watch. We were meeting the Amnesty worker and a girl from Romania who was willing to talk to me. Nothing more at this stage. The bar filled with women hauling designer shopping bags, ordering coffees from the newly installed machine and men in suits loosening ties and shirt buttons.

'Maybe she not come,' Dagmara said. She sat very still on the edge of her seat, her legs tucked against the leather.

'Let's give it some more time.'

Dagmara had a warm, open face that loved to smile. 'I love working here,' she said. 'It is better than back home. Do you have family?'

'A son. Dean – he lives with his mother and her new husband in Basingstoke.'

She frowned slightly.

'Basingstoke. Is that far? Do you see him very often?'

'Not as often as I should.'

'I would love to have children some day.'

'Do you have a boyfriend?'

She looked me straight in the eye, another smile. Then she shook her head. She laughed at my jokes and enjoyed hearing about my family. Occasionally, Dagmara touched my arm and I found myself thinking how I could spend more time with her.

'She is twenty minutes late?' she asked, looking at her watch. 'Do you think we should call her?'

'I suppose so.'

She drew her mobile out of her bag, and scrolled down the numbers in the memory, but as she did so it rang. She pressed the phone to one ear and her hand to the other to block out the noise in the bar. Once the call was finished she turned towards me.

'We have to go to another place,' she said, a serious tone to her voice.

'What's up?'

'Anna from Amnesty wants to see us somewhere else.'

We followed the narrow passage out into the main street; the traffic was building and the street was full of taxis and vans queuing by the traffic lights. She hurried to cross the road as the pedestrian lights changed to red.

'It's not far away,' she said.

Eventually we walked onto Newport Road and Dagmara increased her pace until she turned right, away from the main traffic into the terraces that marked the beginning of Splott. The houses were small and the pavements uneven.

'Not long. Not too far,' she said, flashing me a smile.

We rounded a corner and she slowed before turning into a side alley. Immediately we were standing before a small sandwich shop, its window damp with condensation.

Dagmara pushed open the glass door and a tall man with designer stubble, and wearing a full-length apron that once had stripes, gave her an inquisitive look as though he was surprised to see her. She ignored him, looked into the café, and saw Anna sitting in the far corner.

I put enough money for two coffees onto the glass top and the man nodded an acknowledgment, and told me he'd bring the drinks over.

I dropped into the seat across from Dagmara, who was sitting by Anna's side. Anna had a multi-coloured scarf tied in a bundle around her neck and a mass of curls falling over her shoulders. She cupped a mug of a clear liquid with a teabag floating on top that smelt like a mothball from my mother's old wardrobe.

'Anna,' I said. 'Thanks for seeing me. Is—'

'No. She's too afraid. Wanted me to meet you first.'

'She doesn't have to be afraid.'

Anna guffawed. 'Michal killed and his tongue cut out. And then Leon. Wouldn't you be scared?'

Dagmara had taken on a serious look and looked over at me as she gave out a sigh of agreement with Anna. The man from the counter put two chipped mugs onto the table.

'Will she see me?' I asked.

'Might do. I'll talk to her again, once I've spoken to you.'

I could sense the annoyance developing in my mind. This wasn't an interview and I wasn't going to seek approval from this woman to the way I was conducting the inquiry.

I made my voice heavy. 'When?'

'We'll see. She's lost weight and she's been ill. Hasn't gone down well.'

I furrowed my eyebrows and Anna continued. 'It doesn't do to have the girls losing weight. Punters don't like them too thin. And the bruises show up too easily.'

'Bruises?'

'Yeh. They get beaten if they fall out of line. Mostly on the back or the head. Somewhere where it's not too obvious.'

'I'll need to interview her,' I said forcefully.

'Sorry, Inspector. She doesn't have much faith in the Wales Police Service. That goes for me too, when it comes to trafficking human beings. Didn't they tell you at cop-school that slavery was outlawed a hundred and fifty years ago and that it's a crime to traffic people and enslave them?'

She picked up a spoon and poked the teabag.

141

'Look, I'm investigating two murders. But if there are people involved in trafficking I'll do everything to get them behind bars for a long time.'

'Come off it. The record of the WPS is pathetic when it comes to tackling the traffickers. Did you know that 85% of the prostitutes in the UK are non-UK nationals and that there are four thousand women trafficked into the UK every year? That's four thousand slaves.'

She spat out the last few words and lowered her head to look at the liquid in the mug.

'That's four thousand lives that have been destroyed,' Anna continued. 'Families torn apart. Have you got children, Inspector?'

I nodded.

'Then I'm sure you'd do everything to try and protect them and make certain they didn't come to any harm. So they could avoid living in the sort of half-light these girls inhabit.'

Now I felt resentment that she'd made me feel guilty. I hadn't seen Dean for … I couldn't remember. Was it a year? Maybe more. Was it that Christmas when it snowed and the car wouldn't start and I was late collecting him from Jackie's parents' home?

Anna voice broke into my train of thought. 'And they don't hear from them. Nothing: no letter or calls. This is the twenty-first century, John. The age of the mobile telephone.'

'How … I mean, what …?'

She opened her eyes slightly and stared at me intently with unblinking eyes.

'They're sold into slavery. Sometimes they're promised a better life. You know, the offer of work in a restaurant or hotel and great wages if you compare it to the pittance they can earn in their home countries. Then they arrive in the UK and are told they have to work to repay the debt they owe the trafficker for organising their travel.'

The Amnesty report that had languished at the bottom of the pile on Cornock's desk had mentioned the difficulties in measuring the extent of the problem, that a multi-agency approach was needed; extra resources allocated from central government and more joined-up thinking was needed. All the usual bullshit for inactivity.

'Amnesty has tracked women from as far as China. They arrive into the UK and then disappear,' Anna added. 'Into the backstreet brothels. And then they're moved from one town to another.'

'It's a matter of manpower.'

'Fuck that,' Anna said. 'What kind of society do we live in where women can be treated as slaves and we do nothing about it?'

'The WPS has budgets and objectives. It's a matter of priorities,' I said, sounding like an accountant.

Anna took a sip from her mug and placed it down on the table.

'Some of the families sell their daughters for money. It helps them make ends meet and pay the bills. Would you sell your child, John?'

She didn't wait for me to reply. There was a lump in my throat as I tried again to remember when I'd last spoken to Dean.

'Then when the girls resist, the traffickers tell them they'll kill their families. So they stay. And even if they could leave, where would they go? There are no safe houses and there's nobody interested in looking after them. So when they're picked up in a raid and taken to police stations most are too frightened to say anything and eventually they're back on the street.'

'So why are we here?' I wasn't going to listen to a

lecture for hours. I had a killer to find. 'Does this girl want to help or not? I've told you she can trust me and we'll look after her. You have my word on that.'

'Can you give her a guarantee that she won't be harmed or killed or that her family won't be killed or injured?'

'I'll do my best. Look, there's a murderer walking the streets of Cardiff and if we don't stop him there may be other deaths and maybe more of her friends will be killed or injured or maimed. She's got to trust someone.'

Anna gave me a surly look and downed the last of the liquid in her mug. Dagmara cleared her throat and made her first contribution.

'There's so much you don't know, John. There are lots of dangerous people. We've only just begun to find out who's involved.'

'Are you telling me that you've been trying to work out what's going on?'

Dagmara and Anna exchanged glances.

'Are you absolutely mad? Two men have been killed and you're running around like vigilantes in a Hollywood movie. It's not like that. Something really bad could happen.'

'We want to help,' Dagmara said.

'Best thing you can do is to get her talk to me so we can investigate. Leave it to us. You're mixing with some really dangerous people.'

'John. These are people on the edge. The traffickers don't give a shit about these girls. Somebody has to do something.'

'And that's got to be the police.'

Neither said anything, Dagmara wrapped her fingers around her empty mug and Anna tugged at her scarf.

'No more bullshit. I need to see her. Urgently.'

Chapter 17

I stood in the doorway of the cell, looking at the Scotsman arrested the night before. A dark-green plastic material covered a thin mattress and a grey blanket was heaped into one corner. The good citizens of the Heath and Cyncoed thought they could all sleep safely in their beds now that the burglar roaming their streets was behind bars. Cornock had left me a soothing message on my voicemail that combined a mixture of congratulation and relief.

No longer would he be harangued for daily reports from the ACC, or by insistent calls from Wing Commander Bates.

As I looked at the man sitting in front of me, I had my doubts. He was short and a couple of stone overweight. He had a good week's growth of stubble and his hair looked a greasy mess.

'Do you want anything?'

'Can of Special Brew,' he said, deadpan and serious.

He shuffled into the interview room and sat on one of the plastic chairs. I started with the usual details. Name – Jason Brown. Date of birth – made him thirty-five but he looked fifty. Did he know why he had been arrested? He nodded and gave me a wide-eyed look as though being interviewed by the police was a regular event. I noticed the tattoos on his neck; they matched barely the descriptions in the witness statements.

'What's your home address?'

'I live with friends.'

'What's the address?'

'Ah ... I can't remember.'

'Well, is it in Cardiff?'

He nodded again.

'What part of Cardiff?'

He shrugged. I decided to try another approach. 'Do you know that burglary is a serious matter?'

He parted his lips, exposing the stumps he had for teeth.

'Can I have some tea?'

'Jason. How do you get home?'

'I walk. Down by the Taff. I see bad fucking things all the time.'

Eventually Jason gave me the names of people to contact and directions to a house near a big pub with a bright-green sign, but our conversation was cut short when my mobile rang.

'Boss, there's a body,' Boyd said.

I had a dozen questions flashing through my mind and the ownership of the amputated tongue was high on the list.

Boyd stood by the desk in the custody suite, an edgy look on his face. 'Somebody saw the body floating in one of the docks first thing.'

'First thing?' I could hear the annoyance in my own voice. 'For Christ's sake, Boyd, why weren't we told earlier? I mean, for fuck's sake.' I strode out to the car park, Boyd behind me.

'Can't we tell those Muppets in Area Control that we've got a murder inquiry?'

'They wouldn't link it to our cases—'

'That's not the point; we've got a current case with a missing body.'

I shut the car door with a heavy thud and then I fired the engine into life, but the car stalled.

'Have they been able to identify if the tongue has been cut out?'

'Don't think so.'

'Did you ask?'

'No. I mean, it was—'

'Bloody hell ...' I started the engine again and accelerated the car into the traffic down towards the docks.

As every junction and set of lights delayed our journey the tension built in my mind. Eventually in the distance I saw the gantries that towered silently over the remains of the docks. Over towards the Bay the Millennium Centre dominated the skyline.

I braked hard near the Scientific Support Vehicle, left the car, doors open, and jogged over towards the CSIs. Alvine Dix stood over the body and by her side I noticed the familiar figure of Paddy MacVeigh.

'Morning John,' Alvine said. 'What kept you? I was half-expecting to see Dave Hobbs.'

I narrowed my eyes and pursed my lips. 'All right Alvine?'

I took a step towards Paddy and looked down at the body.

After days in the water the skin looked as though it had been shredded and the eye sockets were shrunken. Traces of blood and skin clung to the mouth.

I said, 'Has his tongue been cut out?'

Paddy pulled the mouth open with gloved hands. 'Yep. Same as before.'

Boyd, standing by my side, coughed loudly then moved away and spewed his guts up over the concrete.

Paddy continued. 'Only this one is ragged. Looks like he really put up a fight.'

'How long has he been in the water?'

I looked at the face again and wondered if it was the face of Gerek. And I wondered if there'd be another Polish family to see. But the post mortem might tell us more and before Paddy left we'd agreed a time to see him in the mortuary.

Boyd stood a few feet away, dabbing a handkerchief to his lips and looking pale.

'You're not eating enough,' I said. 'Need to keep your strength up in a job like this.'

He nodded slowly and I thought he might be sick again.

The message from the police at Bristol airport had been clear and it only meant more hassle. Janek had left for Poland on a flight from the airport and the British Transport Police were looking for someone to blame.

'An inspector from the BTP has been on the telephone,' Woods said. 'His head was so far up his backside he could see daylight.'

'And the details?' I asked, standing by the board and wondering why it had taken so long to find Janek.

'He wanted to know why we hadn't told them about the murders and the tongues.'

'He should check their emails,' I said.

'They're all knob-heads,' Lawson added.

Woods nodded vigorously with Lawson's assessment of the BTP.

'When did he leave?' I said.

'Day after the break-in at Cardiff Central, sir,' Lawson said.

'So they moved him out once they thought he was at risk.'

'And we'll never get an international warrant for a break-in at a railway station where the only evidence we have is a grainy CCTV film,' Boyd said.

I kicked the leg of the chair in front of me, feeling that I should be kicking something more important, like

Lech Balinski's bollocks. I thought about how we could get Janek to tell us what he knew, without the risk of his tongue being cut out, but it was as likely as the man on the moon texting me an invitation for tea.

But I did think of a man who might help. I walked over to my desk and dug out the telephone number of the colonel. After a couple of rings the switchboard in the embassy rang and the voice told me to wait before there was series of clicks and the colonel answered.

'There's been another murder.'

'This is bad.'

'I need your help,' I started, hoping a passive diplomatic tone might work. 'We know that Janek Symanski is in Warsaw. We need to speak to him urgently. And have the Warsaw police tracked the other two men we're looking for?'

He paused. 'The names again?'

'Pietrek Nowak and Gerek Kelka. Colonel. This is important.' It was all I could do not to shout down the telephone.

'I refer to police in Warsaw.'

The line went dead. Boyd stood in the door holding sheaves of paperwork in his hand.

'Lists from the hotels, boss.'

'The staff for each?'

He nodded.

'And?'

'There are at least ten common names. Leon, Michal, Gerek and seven girls, all with Polish-sounding names.'

I shouted through the open door for Woods and Lawson.

Paddy hummed a Wagner violin concerto as he prepared, or so he told me. For all I knew it could have been Mozart. The body on the slab was turning a nasty shade of dark green, the smell was fishy and behind me Boyd coughed loudly into a handkerchief. It had been impossible to be certain if the body on the slab was the man in Gerek's passport photograph.

'The colour suggests that the body has been in the water for longer than a week.'

'Can you be more precise than that?'

Paddy bobbed his head from side to side. 'Maybe. Forensic results might be able to tell us. You've got to remember that water can delay deterioration of the body because of the absence of air but the bloating is caused by the build-up of gases.'

He prodded the eye sockets and the lips that had disappeared, and then continued. 'The fish go after the soft tissue, the eyes and the lips. But then, do you see this waxy substance on the skin? It's called adipocere or mortuary wax. It prevents the body deteriorating too quickly.'

'Thanks for the lecture, Paddy. Any ID?'

Paddy moved to one side and started to examine the pile of clothes. He discarded a light-blue shirt quickly but a dark fleece tore easily as he pulled at the material, before starting an investigation of the trousers. The jeans were heavy but eventually he emptied various coins and sodden supermarket till receipts into a receptacle on the table. From a rear pocket he drew out a small plastic credit card.

'Is this what you're looking for?'

Chapter 18

It took me a couple of hours to finish my interview with Jason Brown, who denied any involvement in the burglaries while admitting stealing a handbag from a kitchen table. I bailed him and completed a dozen different forms.

By the time I arrived back in my office the temperature was still cold, despite the efforts of the ancient radiator that gurgled occasionally. I turned the credit card with Gerek's name embossed on it through my fingers and found myself hoping that family liaison would deal with his relatives. Boyd came into my room, balancing a pile of paperwork on his lap as he sat down. He had spent hours working through the records from Companies House and it looked like he was enjoying the whole experience. He'd been making comments about how similar it had been to studying for his final examinations at university. I couldn't imagine what that might be like, but if it involved wading through paperwork then I'd been fortunate to have missed the experience. Frankie Prince's activities created a lot of paperwork. At least that's what Boyd said and he had a degree, so he'd know.

'I've counted twenty companies where Frankie Prince is a director,' Boyd said. 'They all seemed to be linked together. One of the companies is Ember Vale Charitable Foundation. And you'll never guess who is one of the directors.'

'OK, Boyd. I give up.'

'Janet Helm,' he said, emphasising each word.

I could see the face of one of the leading opposition politicians at the National Assembly looking straight into the camera. A regular on the news broadcasts, she'd become accomplished at the Welsh way of tribal politics, always persuasive, comforting even.

'So why is Janet Helm involved with Frankie Prince?' I said out loud, not expecting an answer.

'Ember Vale was established five years ago and it takes disadvantaged children for holidays around the UK.' Boyd wasn't going to miss the opportunity to share all the details. 'Helm is the patron and one of the directors. At the time it was established Frankie got a lot of publicity. I've been trawling back through all the newspapers and he gets press coverage at least once a month.'

It came as no surprise that Frankie Prince would be arse-licking his way into the establishment. I wondered if Janet Helm had any inclination that the Ember Vale foundation was funded by prostitution.

'Frankie Prince has been able to get loads of important people to support the foundation,' Boyd added.

'He's buying insurance.'

'He's got lots of important friends. But you haven't seen the best yet.'

'Saved the best till last?'

'Something like that.'

'Okay.'

'Frankie Prince owns a company called FPL Properties. And guess what it does?'

'A wild guess says it buys and sells properties.'

'And, boss, more importantly, lets them out.' Boyd sat back and beamed. 'FPL Properties owns 14 Howick Street.'

'Really. And where does that take us?'

'It's another connection to the murders.'

'Owning the house?' I could sense Boyd disappointed with my reaction.

'Well. It's all part of the big picture.'

'Which is?'

Boyd hesitated; the smile had gone, replaced by the

matter-of-fact look that normally sets in when we're going round in circles.

I heard the sound of Hobbs in the Incident Room and I clenched my teeth. He'd recently taken to whistling as he walked through Queen Street and it was annoying me more than I realised. I wondered what he wanted and then his head appeared in my doorway.

'How are things going?'

Nothing was as simple or straightforward as Dave Hobbs asking after my welfare.

'Making good progress with the Polish cases? What's the latest?'

His eyes had that frosted look I'd seen in interviews when I was being lied to. There wasn't a flicker of emotion and it struck me then that if Hobbs ever made Chief Inspector my future in CID was going to be limited. He was probably the sort of officer that would make Chief Super dead quick. It wasn't a pleasant prospect.

The telephone on the desk rang before I could reply.

Hobbs's eyes still looked glacial as he left my room, but he managed a smirk as he turned his back and left.

'Marco,' I said.

'That Polish guy is back,' said the voice from the front desk.

Kamil was, as always, chewing what nails he had left on his right hand. He clutched his right wrist with his left hand, as though the exertion of eating his nails needed support for the work his teeth were doing.

'Gerek is dead,' he said.

'What do you know about him?'

'I knew him. Not too well.'

'Was he a friend of Michal?'

He blinked a couple of times. 'Michal had lot of friends. Have you found what the key opens?'

I hadn't finished talking about Gerek. 'When did you see Gerek last?'

'I don't know. Can't remember. Long time.'

'Where did you see him? Was it with Michal?'

More blinking and chewing of nails. I continued.

'Was it with Leon?'

'Bad things are happening. It is not safe for Polish people. Maybe I can help with keys.'

Boyd cleared his throat, and said, 'Were you friends with Gerek?'

Kamil shook his head. Boyd continued. 'What about Pietrek? Did you know him? Is he from Warsaw too?'

'I never like Pietrek. He was friend of Gerek only.'

'And Leon?' I said.

'Only Michal.'

Kamil started on the nails of his left hand.

'Have you been in contact with Michal's family?'

'No.' He sounded offended. 'His father ...'

'So what are your friends saying about the deaths?'

'Many people are frightened and I am scared because of Michal and me. I need to find what bad people are looking for. They must be stopped and I am worried that others killed. Or that I am next. It really bad.'

'What do you think they are looking for?'

Kamil squirmed in his chair, and then tilted his head as he gnawed at a stubborn piece of nail.

'I not know.'

I looked at Kamil, wishing I did.

Woods had an annoying habit of eating with his mouth

open and drinking at the same time. He bit off a chunk of banana and then took a mouthful of tea. He swallowed hard and then opened his mouth.

'Everyone is spooked,' Woods said.

The tea-infused banana chunks looked disgusting, so I glanced over at Lawson, but Woods continued.

'The priest looks like he's seen a ghost. He doesn't know what the fuck is going on.'

Lawson pitched in. 'And Social Services want to know whether there's anything they need to do.'

'What?'

'Watching their backs, I'd say, boss. You know. Deniability,' Lawson added.

'Deniability? That's just in the spy movies,' Boyd said. 'It doesn't happen that way in real life.'

'Don't you believe it,' Lawson said, sitting back in his chair and resting his hands on his stomach. 'When the shit hits the fan they can say, "We offered to help but the WPS declined." Makes them look good.'

Woods had finished the banana. 'Whatever. The Polish community doesn't know what's been happening. The buses back to Poland have been booked solid for the next two weeks.'

'Has anyone got anything substantive?' I said, loud enough to get the attention of the other three.

Woods had the banana in hand, but I gave him a discouraging look and he hesitated.

Boyd was the first to say anything. 'We're still waiting for the forensic results.'

I wasn't hopeful. Seawater can ruin crime scenes.

'We'll go to see Gerek's flat this afternoon. In the meantime Phil and Joe, you go and find Pietrek. He was Gerek's mate so he should tell us something about his friend.'

Chapter 19

A sudden shower of rain drenched the city's streets and overhead black clouds hung in a sullen mass. I darted into a shop doorway, watching as shoppers opened umbrellas and pulled collars up against the rain. The temperature had dropped too.

Arrangements had been finalised by my mother, behind my back, for Dean to be at the party in two weeks' time but Jackie had insisted we meet for lunch beforehand. Our telephone conversation had been short, tetchy and she'd said I needed to rebuild my relationship with Dean. As I stood watching the rain, all I could think of was Dagmara and then Michal and Leon and the thousands of Polish people who had come to Wales chasing the rainbow.

I should have been thinking about Uncle Gino's party. My mother had recounted the finer points of the arrangements over the telephone the night before, even though there was plenty of time until the family gathering. Who was picking up who, and from where. What I had to do and who I had to smile at and acknowledge. People I hadn't seen for months, years even, and probably wouldn't see again for a long time. Trish had been talking to my mother and my mother had been talking to Jackie. My father hadn't been talking to anyone, least of all his own brother. I wasn't asked for my opinion. I was told what was expected of me in tones that implied agreement would be good for me.

The rain stopped and plastic bags bumped against my legs as shoppers left the store, escaping from their temporary shelter. I stepped onto the pavement, avoiding pedestrians dodging around newly formed puddles. Passing the shop in the arcade where I'd bought my new suit, two shirts – Trish had insisted – and a new tie, the shop assistant, who'd been so keen to take my money, stared through me as he stood by the door.

I jogged over The Hayes, nodding a brief acknowledgment to the man behind the counter of the café. It was a good place for a milky sweet tea, the sort that reminded me of my childhood and where you could sit and nobody would pay you the slightest attention. It was like being invisible in the middle of the city.

By the time I'd reached High Street a light drizzle was falling and I was glad to reach the café Jackie had chosen for lunch. For once I was early and I found a table and flicked through the menu jammed into a metal stand.

It wasn't somewhere where Frankie Prince would visit and I caught myself thinking how he'd get on in prison. A bang-up jail would suit him fine, I concluded. Twenty hours a day in the same cell with a visit once a week to the library and one visiting order a month, until he'd earned privileges. His wife would get tired of course and after a couple of years of visiting once a fortnight, it would be once a month and then the letters would stop. And there'd be nothing Frankie could do about it. At the moment it felt that there was nothing I could do about it. We had no evidence to talk about and nothing to connect Frankie to the deaths.

'John. Sorry I'm late,' Jackie said, breaking my thought pattern.

She sat down and gave a nervous smile. Her blond hair was pulled back into a severe knot behind her head; her eyes were still a deep colour that made the iris indistinguishable from the pupil. Her scent ignited memories long forgotten, of a shared passion, of kissing her and feeling her skin next to mine.

'You keeping all right?' she began.

'Fine.'

'And Trish?'

'Good, too. How's Dean?'

She puckered her lips and hardened her eyes. 'How long has it been, John?'

I knew what she meant and last night I'd been trying to recall when I saw Dean last.

'I know …'

'Look, I'm only doing this for your mother,' she said firmly.

'It was last Christmas. When I couldn't start the car.'

She picked up the menu card and held open the stiff plastic as she scanned the contents.

'And since then, John?'

'I did remember his birthday,' I said, knowing that the year before I'd forgotten.

'But no calls. No visits.'

'It's been busy at work.'

She gave me a look that said it was an old excuse that wouldn't work any longer. A waitress arrived at the table and stood, without saying anything. She gave me a surly glance as I looked up. We ordered and then Jackie moved the conversation back to Dean until I felt like a stranger with my own son. I wondered if Michal and Leon had become strangers to their families. But Dean was seven and he lived in Basingstoke.

'I think you should get to know Dean before the party,' she said, as if I was choosing a pet dog. 'He … you … need to rebuild your relationship. I've spoken to Rosa and we both think—'

'How often do you speak to my mother?'

She paused and stared at me. 'She made contact with me. Told me she missed Dean and wished things could be different, and suggested he might go to the party with you. It might be an idea, just an idea, that you take him bowling. Get to know him. You need to rebuild your relationship with your son.'

The surly waitress came back, bringing with her the smell of second-hand tobacco and two plates with our food. We ate in silence, but there was noise all around us as the place filled with the sounds of lunchtime shoppers. After we finished, and Jackie had shaken her head at the prospect of a pudding, I thought about paying. I wondered if Leon had paid for Dagmara and I thought about what the waitress had said – that he always chose the cheapest food. What would I think if Dean went to live in a foreign country and found a bed-sit in a backstreet and a job that paid minimum wage?

'That's settled then,' Jackie said. 'Pick him up from my mother's place at tomorrow – go bowling and then back by eight.'

I walked back to Queen Street, surprised that I was annoyed with myself for being a lousy father.

The same tall, thin man opened the door, without ceremony, to Gerek's flat.

The temperature inside was still hot. The piles of clothes hadn't been moved. And Boyd looked disappointed when the Hungarian girl didn't appear.

The room was the same as we had left it last time but now nobody would complain when we entered, no protocols broken, no regulations breached. Boyd had made certain we had the landlord's written consent to enter Gerek's room. When I stripped back the curtains from the windows, light filled the room. The sound of children outside drifted in once I'd opened the latch.

I lost count of the T-shirts Gerek owned. They were hanging in neat rows, all ironed and clean.

After an hour we had the contents of Gerek's flat

neatly piled in various heaps: clothes in one corner, bedding in another and then the remains of his paperwork set out on the bed. There were bank statements from Poland and from one of the banks in the city. Boyd had assembled a stack of papers, no more than till receipts and as I sorted through them I wondered why Gerek would keep them.

Then it struck me that I'd seen them before, at least what was left after seawater had done its worst.

Boyd's laughter at some lame joke made blanking out the noise from the Incident Room impossible. There was a pile of paperwork on my desk that I had to read through, but instead of tackling statements and reports I dug through a drawer until I found a sheet of paper. I wrote the names of Michal and Leon in the middle and then Kamil, Gerek and Dagmara to the right hand side. I carefully drew a circle around their names and then lines to connect them to Michal and Leon. It looked pretty. I hoped it was going to work.

After spending a couple of hours on the exercise I was more confused than when I'd started. I had interconnecting black lines leading to the name of Frankie Prince whose photograph was next to a sheet with Lech's name printed in a large bold font.

The murder manuals and management directives couldn't help me now, so I decided to go back to the beginning and look again at Michal Dąbek. I cleared my desk and laid out Michal's personal belongings.

I fingered the photograph; it looked the sort of normal domestic scene that filled family albums. I put it down and reached over for the scraps of paper from

Michal's wallet. I struggled to read the faded sets of numbers and letters. Alongside them I put one of the slips of paper from Gerek's flat and I felt the first flush of success when the faint print matched.

From the box with Leon's personal possessions I took out the photograph and laid it alongside the one from Michal's wallet. Leon's had been taken in a bar, the background lights blurred against the flash, grinning faces tilted upwards towards the camera, half-empty glasses raised in salute.

I needed to know what the till receipts related to, so I picked up the telephone and punched in Kamil's number.

'Yes.' The voice sounded impatient.

'John Marco.'

'What you want?'

'I need to talk to you again. It's important.'

Another hour passed before Boyd and I sat opposite Kamil in the interview room. He was wearing a long face; the three days' growth on his chin was a reddish colour.

'I late for work,' he complained.

'Won't take long.'

I pushed across the scrap of paper in a plastic pouch.

'Any idea what this could be?'

He gave me an irritated look and glanced at his watch. 'It is paper from money transfer man.'

'Who?'

'Man in Polish shop. He send money home for Polish people. It is very cheap.'

After he gave me the address and telephone number I slid over the photograph from Michal's wallet.

'You show me this last time,' he complained.

'Where was it taken?'

He shrugged. 'I told you before. No idea.'

'What about this then?'

I showed him the image of Michal and Leon and Dagmara smiling at the camera. Kamil straightened in his chair, picked up the glossy image and opened his eyes a little wider.

'Where was it taken, Kamil?'

'Her again,' he said.

'What do you mean?'

'She's bad. No good for Michal.'

A momentary flash of worry crossed my mind.

'No good for Michal?' I tried to sound unfazed.

'She always interfere. Always making things difficult. She tried to help but only make things worse.'

'Were she and Michal lovers?' I got straight to what was on my mind.

Kamil looked up and gave me a wide-eyed, hurt stare. 'I know Michal had wife. And before that girlfriends. But he was happy with me. Maybe Dagmara years ago.' He shrugged. 'I not know. Michal kept secrets.'

'What did you mean, making things difficult?'

He sank back into his chair after tossing the photograph back at me. 'I saw them together.'

'When?'

'First time three weeks ago, maybe. Then I saw them again, always together. I followed Michal. He see her in restaurant.'

Before he finished I was scrolling my mobile for Dagmara's number.

Chapter 20

'Congratulations.'

I held my grip on the handset of the telephone as though my life depended on it. I thought I heard the muffled sound of another voice in the background and the movement of a hand over the mouthpiece.

'I'm sure you're very pleased,' Wing Commander Bates continued.

It wasn't the voice I'd have chosen to hear first thing that morning but at least he sounded sober.

'Yes, of course,' I said through clenched teeth.

'Everybody on the neighbourhood watch will be delighted.'

'Good.'

All I had was a Scotsman, who only had a passing resemblance to a human being, and the investigation into establishing his guilt had a long way to go.

Before Bates rang off I heard a female voice in the background reminding him to tell me about the neighbourhood watch meeting. I made an attempt at sounding interested and confirmed I'd be there.

Boyd stood by the door as I put the telephone back on the cradle. I waved at him, picked up my mobile, and scrolled the numbers, looking for Dagmara's details. She'd been blanking my calls since my conversation with Kamil and I was getting more annoyed with every message that I left asking her to contact me.

'Got the report you wanted,' Boyd said, thrusting a sheaf of papers over the desk.

I nodded and pressed the phone to my ear only to hear again the slow, warm tones of her voice inviting the caller to leave a message. Do Polish girls sound sexy to Polish men I wondered? Boyd had sat down and I decided against leaving a message.

One thing I hated was management paperwork. At my last appraisal Cornock used words like *team player* and *finding a balance* before he got to the subject of my inadequate paperwork.

'No point kicking against the system,' Cornock had said. 'You've got to get the paperwork done properly, John.'

But I never could and I looked at the report addressed to the ACC. I flicked through the pages and realised I needed an hour at least when I was in a better frame of mind.

'Well done,' I said to Boyd absently.

He gave a contented smile.

'Seems a good report. It's long enough … I'll read it through … But we've got things to do. Priorities, Boyd. We always need to prioritise …'

We drove down Bute Street into the docks, passing the rows of terraces stranded by the modernity of the high rises in the Bay beyond. We pulled into a parking space by the small arcade of shops. A young boy on a bicycle finished sipping from a straw and tipped the container into an overflowing bin that spilled it onto the street.

Boyd and I walked down the arcade, the boarded windows daubed with graffiti, an echo of the once-thriving shops. We passed a run-down Post Office with thick metal mesh covering the window and, high enough to be out of reach, a CCTV camera pointing downwards. An old man emerged from a newspaper shop and stepped into the adjacent betting office. The noise from the commentary inside faded to a dull thudding as the door closed behind him.

We rounded the corner and at the end of a row we saw a couple standing outside the Polish shop, talking and smoking.

A vinegary and salty smell hung heavily in the air when we entered. The aisles were stacked with bottles of gherkins of all shapes, packets of biscuits and dried goods that I'd never seen before.

We walked up to the counter and saw a man with dark stubble and high cheekbones sitting on a stool, watching the Polish channel on cable. He gave us a lazy, disinterested look and I thrust my warrant card under his nose.

'Detective Inspector Marco,' I said, before introducing Boyd.

He stared at the card and then looked up at me. 'What you want?'

'This your place?'

'Yes.'

'What's your name?'

'Stan.'

He turned to watch the television.

'Spell your full name please,' I asked.

'Stanislaw Verkanski,' he said slowly.

'Date of birth.' I guessed there'd be nothing on the Police National Computer. Boyd scribbled down the details.

'Who else works here?'

'Lots of people.'

'Anybody else here today?'

'Nobody. Just me.'

I produced the receipt from the folder under my arm and pushed it over the counter in front of him. The television programme had taped laughter and seemed to be a cross between *Big Brother* and *X Factor*.

'This yours?' I asked.

He barely moved his head from the television.

'Give it a good look, Stan,' I said forcefully.

He narrowed his eyes and peered down onto the paper. 'Sure.'

My mobile beeped and I fumbled in my pocket for the handset before reading the message for me to contact the station urgently. It could wait.

'Do you have records for the transaction?'

He shrugged.

'What sort of records do you keep?'

'Proper records, Mr Policeman.'

Big mistake.

I could feel the temperature rising around my collar.

'Well, Stan.' I counted to ten. 'You've got a choice. Either you cooperate now or I nick you for obstruction and we can talk about it in Queen Street police station. And turn that sound down.'

He pointed a remote at the television, heaved himself off the stool and stood by the counter.

'And either way, don't fucking call me Mr Policeman. It's Detective Inspector Marco.'

'What you want to know?'

'What's this receipt for?'

'Money transfer.'

I paused and looked at him. I needed more details and if we were going to have to extract every detail in slow motion it was going to be a long meeting.

'Let's have the details, Stan. Not just the highlights.' I stepped towards the counter. 'Who sent the money?'

He managed another shrug before telling me it would take time to get the computer working. He heaved his shoulders and made a sullen look when I asked about the business, explaining how the Polish population of Cardiff sent their money home through him.

'Why not use the banks?'

'They know me. Trust me. I give good rate.'

'So, how does it work?'

'Polish people give me money to send home. I give good rate better than banks.'

'How do you make money?'

'More money I have, better for me. I get better rate.'

I nodded. I could see how it worked and with a large Polish community there would be a regular source of customers for his service. He peered at the computer screen and then clicked the mouse a few times before uttering a sort of contented sigh.

'It was Michal Dąbek,' he said. 'I know him.'

I couldn't decide if he really didn't know about Michal or not.

'He's dead. Don't you read the newspapers or watch the television?'

Another shrug. The Polish language television was enough for them. They weren't staying in Wales long enough to get involved in the community or read the newspapers. I asked about Michal.

'He was from Warsaw,' Stan said. 'He was regular and buy lots of food.'

'Any friends?'

'How would I know?'

'You must know a lot about what's happening in the Polish community. You get lots of people coming into the shop. What are the favourite food Polish people miss living in Wales?'

'Sauerkraut. We sell lots in bottles. You like to try?'

I shook my head. 'Are there other Polish shops in Cardiff?'

'Sure. But nobody does money transfer like me. I

am number one.'

The mobile in my pocket beeped another message that I was needed urgently back at Queen Street so we left and headed back for the car.

'Shouldn't we get back?' Boyd gave me a strained look.

I flicked open the pages of a street finder. The spine had been broken in several places and once I'd found the right street I gave Boyd directions.

'Won't take long,' I replied eventually.

He didn't look convinced, but he followed my directions until we came to the first street where Jason Brown said he'd been living. It was a long terrace of houses with heavy net curtains on the front windows. I found the number Jason had given us and pressed the bell. There was a faint sound in the back of the property and I heard a yelp of a dog and a muffled shout.

A minute or so passed until the sound of the dog got nearer and I heard a hand struggling with the lock.

'Who is it?' the voice said, before the door opened.

'Walter Philips? It's the police,' Boyd said loudly.

There was no reply but the door opened and the face of a small man with a large beard and skin the colour of old pastry stood by the door.

Boyd pushed his warrant card into the man's face.

'I'm Detective Sergeant Pierce and this is DI Marco.'

'I haven't done anything,' the man said, holding onto a Jack Russell terrier that was straining at its collar.

'Are you Walter Philips?'

The man nodded.

'We need to talk to you about Jason Brown,' I said.

He let the door open and we walked through into a

small room at the front of the house.

'Do you live here alone?' Boyd asked.

'Yeh. Got Buster,' he said, patting the dog on the head.

'Does Jason live here?' I asked, rubbing my hand over the damp material of the chair.

'No. Why do you think that?'

Buster gave Boyd's trouser leg a hungry look and Walter tugged again at the leash.

'When did you see Jason last?' I asked.

'Dunno. Can't remember.'

Boyd tucked his legs to one side, away from Buster. 'Last week? Last month?' Boyd said, keeping an eye on the dog.

'Not last week. Must have been last month. No. Come to think of it, haven't seen him for months.'

'So he stayed with you a few months ago?'

'What? No. Down the pub. That's where I saw him.' He ruffled Buster's head. 'That's where I always see him. Down the pub.'

We left after it was clear Philips wasn't concentrating on our questions and Buster had begun to sniff around Boyd's shoes. There was another address on the list and we threaded our way through the backstreets of Butetown and Grangetown. He drew the car to a standstill outside the second address. We pushed an iron gate and took a couple of steps up to the front door. This time we gave the doorbell a loud ring and the sound of footsteps in the hallway followed.

We had our warrant cards ready. I did the introductions and Derek Jones nodded slowly before inviting us in. He was in his fifties and had a round, kindly face. We sat in a small lounge that smelt clean and declined an offer of tea.

'I know Jason. I work in the homeless shelter and I've seen him there. He followed me home one night. A couple of months back.'

We were making progress and Jason's story might just be adding up.

'He stayed here the one night.'

'One night only? Not regularly then?' I asked.

'No. We're not supposed to encourage them to be friendly with us.'

I gave him a quizzical look.

'In the shelter,' he explained.

'But he said you were friends.'

Jones shook his head.

'And that he stayed with you,' Boyd added.

'Jason's friends aren't the talkative sort.'

'What do you mean?'

'He alternates between a bench by the Taff near the Millennium Stadium and various graveyards. His only company are the gravestones and bottles of cider.'

'You're in shit so thick you can't move your arms.'

Dave Hobbs managed a smile that was a mixture of contempt and delight. His eyes sparkled and his teeth glistened as he grinned. He stood by the photocopying machine, waiting for it to finish spewing out reams of paper.

He'd got my attention and I waited, knowing he was willing me to ask a question. I turned to Boyd who had followed me up the stairs.

'Boyd, have you got those reports?' I said. 'DI Hobbs can do that photocopying for you.'

For a moment Boyd stood rooted to the spot, unable to decide how to react.

'Fuck off, Marco,' Dave Hobbs hissed.

On my desk there was an urgent message waiting, for me to see Cornock and as I passed Dave Hobbs he smirked again. By the time I was walking through the station I had the feeling that Boyd had been right about getting back to the station sooner.

I straightened my collar, regretted not wearing a tie and knocked on Cornock's door. There was a shout and I pushed it open.

Cornock had a china cup on his desk, full of tea, and a half-eaten biscuit sat on the saucer. Two other faces stared at me. The older man had a shaven head and a shirt one size too small for his ample neck and the other, sitting at the far end of Cornock's desk, sipped on a mug.

'John, do you know DCI Banks and DI Jacks from the Economic Crime Department?'

No hands were offered: just nods and blinked eyelids.

'The Superintendent tells me you've got the Polish murders,' Banks said, slowly putting down his coffee.

I nodded. A small fold of skin above the collar, underneath his earlobe, quivered.

'We have an interest in Stanislaw Verkanski,' he added flatly. 'Why were you there?'

I gave Cornock a quick look. He waited for me to reply.

'The floater had a receipt in his possessions.'

'We got the station to contact you. Why didn't you respond?'

I struggled for an answer.

'You could have seriously prejudiced our investigation, Inspector,' the voice slowed. 'We've had Stanislaw under investigation for money laundering for months and we don't take kindly to you putting your nose into our case. You could have cocked it up big time.'

I was struggling for the right thing to say.

'I was doing my job, following the evidence.'

'And your job is to answer urgent requests to respond.'

'I was in the middle of questioning him.'

'It was an urgent call.'

'I've got two bodies in the morgue and so far not a lot to go on. I need to go after everything.'

'Just do it right and don't tread on our toes.'

'But—'

'Did you get anything?'

'No. I'll need—'

'You won't go anywhere near him without talking to us. Understood?'

I nodded.

'And I want to be kept in the loop. Anything about Stan, you tell me first.'

'Anything I need to know?' I asked, remembering about the management training courses that emphasised inter-departmental cooperation and joined-up thinking.

Jacks had the oddest accent when he spoke: part Swansea, part Valleys. 'We were tipped off that he might be laundering money. Lots of small cash deposits going through his account that, once you added them all together, made a significant sum.'

'What happens then?'

Jacks continued. 'Money gets shifted to Poland and disappears.'

'Anything else?' I continued.

Banks looked at his watch and cut across me. 'No time now. DI Jacks can give you a complete briefing. You and your DS. We'll fix up a convenient time.' He was dismissing me and before I had a chance to think about

Michal's bank accounts he was by the door, shaking Cornock's hand and calling him by his first name.

Once they'd left, Cornock gave me a world-weary look. 'Sure you can handle this, John?'

'Yes, of course.'

'I can allocate the burglaries to Dave Hobbs, you know.'

'No, I can handle them.'

'John, just be careful and answer your bloody phone when it goes off.'

I slipped out of Queen Street, without going back past Dave Hobbs, and en route to Mario's I texted Boyd. He arrived just as a girl with long, brown hair down her back brought me a coffee. Boyd gave her his order and sat down.

'How'd it go, boss?'

'Economic Crime,' I said, hoping he could read my mind.

'What?'

'They've had Stanislaw Verkanski under surveillance for months.'

'And we fucked up their party.'

'That's about it.'

The same girl brought Boyd a coffee and a Chelsea bun covered in icing sugar that could have stopped his heart.

'I thought you'd stopped …'

'Starving. Need all the strength I can get.'

'How's …?'

'She's fine.'

'Any luck?'

'Not since the last time you asked.'

He took an enormous bite from the bun and chewed slowly, a contented look falling over his face. I pushed a spoon around my coffee.

Boyd continued. 'There's one thing we haven't followed up,' he said, licking some sugar from his lips. He pushed over a plastic pocket and I stared at the tickets for the Rumney library and leisure centre. Then I remembered I'd forgotten to call Dagmara again. I picked up the mobile, found her contact details and waited.

Another message. Another worry flashed across my mind. 'Fancy a trip down Rumney?'

Chapter 21

Through the open window I caught the smell of tarmac and oil through the air as the car crawled through the traffic. At the junction of Southern Way and Newport Road we passed a road repair team and Boyd took the overpass, slowing as the road narrowed.

I felt my mobile vibrating in my pocket before I heard it ring. I fumbled through my jacket, eventually retrieving it with two fingers. I recognised my mother's number.

'Mam.'

'John, how are you?'

I knew there was something on her mind.

'I just thought I would ring for a chat.'

Definitely something on her mind.

'Are you busy?'

'In the car.' I glanced over at Boyd.

'I won't keep you long.'

'Dad OK?'

'He's fine. Hope things go well tonight.'

For a moment my mind didn't connect. My mother continued. 'I know Dean is looking forward to seeing you. I've spoken to Jackie.'

It was like being a teenager again, my mother organising my life. *I've spoken to Jackie*. What she meant was that she had arranged everything behind my back, sorted everything, spoken to my ex-partner, and arranged the details of the visit for me to see Dean. One part of me wanted to tell her not to interfere: another knew that it would be pointless.

'Me too,' I said.

'Are you still going to the bowling?'

'And McDonald's.'

'You won't smoke when you're with him, will you?'

'Mam.' I used an exasperated tone.

'He's young and he needs a father.'

'He's got ...' I struggled with Jackie's husband's name.

'It's not the same. You're his father,' she said with authority.

Boyd parked in a slot outside the library, reserved for *Officials*.

'Look, Mam, got to go. I'll call you later.'

Boyd switched off the engine and gave me a sympathetic look. 'My mother's just the same. Always interfering. And Mandy's mother is much worse. In and out of the house. I keep thinking she'll catch us at it.'

'She probably wants grandchildren.'

'Talks about it all the time.'

I left the car before Boyd could continue. The entrance of the library had a selection of stands with various leaflets for local activities. In a far corner, behind the counter, a couple of pensioners were reading the newspapers and two men in their twenties with spiky hair ran their fingers over computer keyboards.

A woman behind the counter looked at me through thick glasses.

'Can I help you?'

I showed her my warrant card and nodded at Boyd. 'This is Detective Sergeant Pierce and I'm DI Marco. I wonder if you can help us?' I tried a smile but it had little effect. I gave her the ticket I'd pulled out of Michal's wallet.

'Can you tell me anything about it?'

She shrugged. 'There's no central record of who takes which book out. I can tell you if a book is late or overdue. Are you looking for any book in particular?'

'No, sorry. Do you get a lot of Eastern Europeans

coming in?' The men on the computers were raising their voices – it sounded Polish.

'Quite a few. Internet access is very cheap here. So many of them live in bed-sits and they can't afford computers.'

'Do they take out any books then?'

'Sometimes.'

'Do you know this man?' I showed her the photograph of Michal and a grainy photograph of Leon.

She squinted at the images and shook her head slowly.

I pulled out a packet of cigarettes as we made for the car. If I were to reach my five-a-day before seeing Dean I'd need to play catch up so I pushed the third of the day between my lips. Boyd pulled the car onto the main road while I opened the window and let the smoke drift out until the cigarette butt clung to my fingers and I threw it into the gutter.

Rumney Leisure Centre was a big concrete box, with doors that needed paint and windows covered in adverts for swimming lessons and keep-fit classes. The woman behind the glass counter was talking to a thin girl in a tracksuit. She must have seen Boyd and me standing by the counter, ties undone, without a sports bag between us.

'Police,' I said, running out of patience.

I pushed the photograph of Michal under the glass. 'Have you seen this man before?'

She gave it a quick glance. 'Only work part-time. Sorry, love.'

'Anyone else that might help?'

'Try the café. They might know him.' She nodded down a corridor.

We pushed open the door of the café, plastic tables and chairs strewn around the room; a girl with a nose ring and plaited hair leant against the counter at the far end. She straightened and stopped chewing the gum in her mouth when I produced my card. I showed her the photograph of Michal.

'Do you recognise this man?'

She looked at the face intensely. 'Sorry.'

Then I tried the image of Leon.

'Yeh,' she began. 'Been here a few times. Nice enough, mind. What's he done?'

'He's dead.'

'Fuck. That's bad.' She drew a hand over her mouth and threw out the gum.

'Can you tell me anything about him?'

'Nothing much. Dunno what he did. Swimming I think. How'd he die?'

'How often did he come in?'

'Every week. Was it murder? Like *CSI*?'

'Was he with anyone?'

'No, not much. But recently, yeh. Started coming with the same girl. Didn't seem his girlfriend mind.'

'Can you describe her?'

'She had this really black hair. And she was foreign too.'

My concentration sharpened.

'And last couple of times there was this other girl with them. She always had these long scarves. As though it was cold or something. And she came to the counter once – I could smell her. Really bad it was.'

Before Boyd had finished scribbling the details in his notepad I was reaching for my mobile.

Chapter 22

I strode over the car park, the mobile pressed to my ear, a sense of trepidation dominating my mind. As I reached the car the ringing stopped and I heard a tentative voice.

'John, I'm sorry.'

'Dagmara, where are you?'

'I need to see you.' There was a worried edge to her voice.

'What's wrong?'

'I've got Anna and Maria with me.'

My mind accelerated.

'Where are you?'

'In the Polish club.'

I reckoned it would take me ten, maybe fifteen, minutes to reach the Polish club, depending on traffic. I glanced at my watch and then at Boyd who was giving me an inquisitive look.

'Let's go,' I said.

'What's happening, boss?'

'We've got someone to see in the Polish club.'

I found myself looking forward to seeing Dagmara again. I tried to remember when I'd seen her last and found myself in a fog; the days seemed to merge together. I was pleased that I'd spoken to Dagmara but worried that she sounded troubled. We slowed and then stopped at a set of lights. The pulsing sound of the indicator broke the silence. Boyd cleared his throat.

'So. What's this all about?'

'Dagmara's in contact with one of the girls who's been trafficked.'

'Will she help?'

'Let's hope so.'

The traffic light changed and Boyd crunched the

gear stick into first and drove down towards the docks. It was another five minutes before we reached the Polish club. Dagmara walked over as we parked.

'John. Thank you.' She touched my sleeve. 'It's this way.'

We entered the building through a narrow door around the back and immediately a strong smell of stale alcohol fired all sorts of messages into my memory. Mostly the sort I wanted to forget. And none I wanted to relive.

Up a small flight of stairs, we passed a half-opened door leading to a storeroom and another to a stinking toilet. At the top of the stairs, Dagmara pushed open a door.

A window overlooking the rear yard was caked with dirt and grime and daylight filtered through in thin shards. I saw Anna sitting by the table, fiddling with a pack of roll-your-own tobacco. For a woman with large hands she was surprisingly nimble. By her side was a thin girl with a mop of blond hair, but in the half-light I couldn't tell whether it was natural or from a bottle.

'This is Maria,' Anna said.

Maria gave me a thin smile.

'Daggy say I must talk to you,' she said, glancing at Dagmara.

'I've told Maria she can trust you,' Dagmara said.

'You knew Michal and Leon?' I began

She looked away. Anna put the limp-looking cigarette to her lips, snapped a lighter in her other hand a couple of times and then drew deeply.

'Both my friends,' Maria said.

'Tell him about Leon,' Dagmara said.

Maria paused. 'We in love.'

Boyd, sitting behind me, took out his notebook with a movement that for a moment broke Maria's concentration. When Dagmara gave him a sharp glare, he raised his eyebrows as if to say that it was normal. Dagmara nodded a reassurance at Maria and then at Anna.

'They promise me job in London.'

'They?' I asked.

She lowered her head and then began her story in a low voice, almost a whisper. Her family ran a farm that had been devastated by a flood one winter and they'd lost everything. A man her father knew from the nearby town came to their village, speaking to all the families affected by the flooding. Maria stopped when she described him – her eyes alight with hatred.

'My father trust this man. He good before.'

Maria hesitated, looked down at her feet, then shook her head before restarting. From the kitchen she'd heard her father joking and reminiscing with the man about their days as young men when they drank too much and spewed into the gutters. Maria hesitated when she recounted how, after the man had left that first night, her father fetched the vodka bottle and drank in silence as her mother busied herself around the house.

'That night I hear Mama and Papa's voices. Talking. Very quiet.' She turned to Dagmara and muttered something in Polish.

'Whispering,' Dagmara said.

Maria nodded. 'Whispering for long time.'

'When was this?' I asked.

She shrugged. 'Three years ago. Maybe.'

'How old are you Maria?'

'Eighteen,' she said flatly. 'Then he came back.'

There was a dark edge to Maria's voice when she spoke about the man's second visit. He brought gifts for Maria's mother and money that her father had clenched tightly in his hands. Maria could remember the whites of her father's knuckles and the desperate look on his face.

The man took her father into town but he returned alone and drunk. Maria moved to the edge of her seat and tightened her hands into a ball on her knees.

'It was after one week when the man came back. On that day I come back from working with my sister; she married and had new farm. I came into house and my mother stared at me. She said nothing. I knew something wrong because my father there too. I stood by door and saw the ...'

Maria said something in Polish to Dagmara.

'Suitcase,' Dagmara said.

'My father tell me that it is for the best – that I will have better life. That family will be better. That they will have money and that I will have money. I will have nice place to live. I would have nice clothes to wear. That I have new friends. I saw my mother begin to cry. At first just a tear but then much crying – my father not look at me, he always look away. But he had big lump in the throat ...'

Maria raised her hand and stroked her neck.

'... that go up and down. And then he told me that man come that day to take me to England, that he look after me. I get good job in café or hotel. Then my sister arrive and my father tell her what is happening and she cries. Too much crying. Then my mother cries much. I do not remember when the man arrived but it dark and I remember I was hungry. We talked about family and about better life in England. And how I would have more money. When that man came he smiled at me. He had nice clothes and ...'

Another couple of words with Dagmara in Polish.

'A leather jacket.' Maria repeated Dagmara's translation. 'Then we left. My mother give me kiss. My father just stand, his head down. I hug my sister and man pick up my suitcase. He had big car with black windows and seats like his jacket. First we go Bucharest, for one week. Man said we get papers for passport. I met lots of other girls and often in the evening man would come back, very angry and shout and complain about papers.'

Maria fumbled through a small black bag by her feet and passed over a photograph of a group of smiling faces. It was difficult to make out the age of all the young girls but they were probably fifteen or sixteen, pouting to the camera. They all looked young and healthy.

'These my friends. After one week we travel to Warsaw. It is long journey; many hours in car.'

'How many of you were there?' I asked.

Maria scanned the faces of Anna and Dagmara as if the answer was a secret.

'Five. They my friends.'

'Where are they now?'

Maria shrugged; then a shroud fell over her eyes and she looked at the floor again.

'What happened in Warsaw?'

'We met bad man.'

'What was his name?'

She shrugged again. Dagmara and Anna had sat quietly, hardly moving, listening to Maria's description. I looked at Boyd once she'd finished. There had been an anger and a hatred in her description of Lech Balinski.

'Tell John how you came to England,' Anna said.

'It was many days later. More days in car. More travelling. I was tired. Then I was very sick on ship. Things change in London. After one week man take our mobile phones. He said we have to pay for money given to family. Then we start.'

A silence hung around the room and for a few moments nobody knew the right words to say. It was Anna who spoke first.

'We've got all the history documented, John. All the houses where she was taken and the dates as best she could remember them.'

'We'll need to get all this down in a statement,' I said.

'She was fifteen for fuck's sake, John. A child prostitute here in Cardiff and there are others. The ones with her in the photograph.'

'Tell me about Leon.'

Maria's eyes lit up when I mentioned Leon's name.

'We in love. We go back to Poland and start a farm and grow pigs and make children. Leon was good for me and he look after me.'

'What she means,' Anna said, 'is that Leon protected her from some of the worst specimens of mankind who want to rape young girls. He ran a risk protecting her.'

'Is that why he was killed?' I asked.

Anna exchanged a glance with Dagmara, as though they had to agree on giving me the next piece of information.

'He was trying to get Frankie Prince to let her go,' Anna said.

'And how was he hoping to do that?' I said, scarcely wanting to believe what I thought was coming next.

Dagmara now: 'Michal had helped Leon take photographs.'

My mouth had dried out and I struggled to ask my next question.

'Photographs of what exactly?'

'The men and the girls and the parties.' Anna again.

'And where are these photographs?'

'Michal kept them on his computer.' Anna's voice was almost a whisper.

'And it's missing, of course,' I said, realising what everyone was looking for.

They all nodded.

After the stench of the Polish club the salt in the air was a pleasant change. Once I'd checked the time – no way could I be late collecting Dean – I stood with Boyd and Dagmara by the car.

'So, how well did you know Michal?' I said.

'Very well. Good friends,' Dagmara replied.

'Why had you been seeing so much of Michal?'

Dagmara bowed her head. 'I … was trying to help.'

'Did he have any idea what he was doing?'

'He was very brave.'

Boyd wanted to know about the computer. 'Where was it kept?'

'He didn't keep it in the bed-sit or in the factory.'

'Did he give it to Leon?' I said.

Dagmara shrugged and then hesitated. 'There was more than just photographs. Michal was computer expert. He learnt about things like that in the army and he could do lots.'

'What do you mean?'

'He didn't tell me, but I think it was all about Frankie Prince.'

'All about Frankie?' I sounded angry. But not as angry as I wanted to sound. 'He must have been mad. Stark, raving, fucking mad to get involved with someone like Frankie Prince. And where is this computer?'

'He said it was in place where no one would think of looking.'

'Could his boyfriend Kamil know where it might be?'

'Boyfriend?' She sounded surprised.

My mobile purred with a text from Jackie, reminding me about Dean, and no sooner had I read it than another appeared on the screen from Trish. My life wasn't my own.

Chapter 23

I hesitated at the door of The Captain Scott; the warmth of the pub and the smell of beer slops and cheap clothes smothered me like an old blanket. It wasn't full and I walked up to the bar and stared at the optics. I had stood in the same place many times before, mostly waiting for a pint of beer in a straight glass and a whisky. I could remember the anticipation of seeing the drinks on the bar in front of me, of taking that first sip, of feeling the bitter liquid against my tongue and telling myself I'd only have a couple.

I ordered an orange juice and sat down. A couple of the regulars gave me brief nods of recognition before turning their attention to the Swansea versus Manchester City Premiership game on the television screen hanging on the wall.

Something had made me decide to call at the pub after taking Dean back to Jackie's mother's house. Something had wanted me to realise what I had left behind. Perhaps it was seeing Dean and realising that I didn't want him to be something I left behind.

Sometimes I needed to be on my own.

I put my mobile on the table by the side of the glass and looked at the screen, which reminded me I had two messages. I knew one would be from my mother and the second from Trish. I could have gone straight home. I should have been with Trish, drinking tea and eating toast and telling her about my evening with Dean and then telephoning my mother.

I thought about Maria sitting in the Polish club that afternoon, her hopes ripped to shreds and her future plans with Leon destroyed. I could see Anna turning the cigarette paper through her fingers with that hard-determined look in her eyes.

A shout, then a roar of approval, came from the bar and someone shouted at me that Swansea had scored and were in the lead. I was hoping that the reassurance of familiar surroundings and the comfort of strangers would help me think straight. Nothing was making sense. Cornock would want an update soon enough and I had Hobbs lurking in the background, hoping that I'd foul up so that he could take charge. But more than anything I had Dagmara and Anna running around like vigilantes.

I sipped the orange juice and played with my mobile, thinking that I should check the messages. Two girls came over, sat at the opposite end of the bench and gave me dark stares – the regulars of The Captain Scott could be jealous of their local pub, resentful of strangers they didn't recognise. But I felt like a local and ignored them.

Dagmara had touched my sleeve. I remembered that as though she was still sitting next to me. She'd given me a broad, open smile that had creased her cheeks, accentuating her wide cheekbones. I wondered about her life, who she was with, her lovers and family. Thinking about her crowded out the memories of Anna and Maria and I realised I should have been tougher. They couldn't interfere. It would be dangerous. I had to find out more about Lech so I picked up my mobile and, deliberately avoiding the texts, I tapped out a message to Terry. I finished the last of my orange juice and took the glass to the bar on my way out. Swansea scored a second and the place erupted with shouts of applause as I opened the door onto Bute Street. I stood for a moment and drew out a cigarette from the squashed pack in my jacket. I was pleased with myself for having succeeded in not smoking in front of Dean. I walked back to my car, enjoying the smoke filling my lungs.

Within ten minutes I was reversing into a parking

space before heading towards the flat. I could hear the sound of the late-night news programme once I'd opened the door to the apartment. Trish sat on the sofa, sipping a mug of herbal tea; a sweet fragrant smell hung in the air.

'Well, how did it go, John?'

'It was fine, I suppose.'

'How did you get on with Dean?'

'I think he enjoyed it. We went bowling for an hour or so. Then we had McDonald's.'

'What did you talk about?'

I suppressed the desire to shrug. 'Lots of things.'

'Like what?'

'Football. He supports Queens Park Rangers.'

'Maybe you could take him to see Cardiff playing. It will be a really good opportunity for you both to get to know each other.'

'The tickets would be hard to come by.'

'So what else happened? Was he nervous? Did you ask about school?'

'Ah ...'

'John, you really are hopeless.'

'It was fine. I enjoyed it. Dean enjoyed it.'

I got up, walked through to the kitchen and returned with an instant coffee. Trish was sitting square on the sofa, the empty mug standing on the table.

'Is Dean looking forward to the party?'

'Yes, we talked about that too,' I said. 'He's staying with his grandmother for the weekend. First time he's done that on his own.'

'Your mother's called. Said you haven't answered her text message. I think you'd better call her.'

I found my mobile and called my mother. Trish was looking at me intently.

'Tell me everything,' my mother said, striking a

friendly, threatening tone.

'Fine. Good,' I began and then I noticed Trish widening her eyes and rolling her hands telling me I had to be more effusive. I got the message and gathered pace, reassuring my mother that Dean had enjoyed his evening, had bowled better than me, had eaten a McDonald's with a strawberry milkshake and that he was looking forward to the party. Trish gave a satisfied nod as I finished.

'Make sure you remember everybody who's going to be there. I know you're hopeless with people's birthdays and names.'

I glanced over at Trish. Now it is my turn to roll my hands. Once my mother had finished I slumped back in the sofa, beginning to feel the effects of the long day. Then I clicked through to my messages and read the text from my mother.

'Did you text me earlier?' I said.

'I reminded you that I'm away tomorrow on that course up north.'

I'd forgotten, as usual. Since the WPS was created, officers from Southern Division seemed to spend more time than was necessary attending courses in Northern Division HQ or in dismal hotels in the middle of nowhere halfway between.

Before I could reply the handset lit up, the screen telling me I now had three unread messages. I read the one from Trish and then I scrolled down the screen expecting messages from Boyd or Terry. The first was from Boyd telling me he was making progress with identifying Lech. The second message was from Dagmara – *It was so good to see you this afternoon I hope we can fix everything together. Love x*

'Who was it?' Trish said.

'Just work.'

Chapter 24

It was late September, not yet autumn but cool enough to remind me that summer was over. The window behind me was firmly closed but I could hear the stifled shouts from the takeaway restaurants on the street below. I sipped from a coffee mug with multi-coloured stripes, trying to decide what needed my attention next. I should have listened to the management gurus, made a to-do list, and structured my morning carefully after checking my emails. Instead I put my feet up on the desk, chewed on a chocolate bar and then finished my coffee.

It had taken Boyd a couple of days to produce a pile of paperwork two feet thick linking Frankie Prince to the various properties in the Splott area occupied by the Eastern European immigrants. Boyd came to the door and I waved him into my room as I dislodged my shoes from the desk.

'I didn't think it was possible for one man to own so many properties,' Boyd said, making himself comfortable in one of the hard-backed chairs. 'Frankie's got thirty properties that I've been able to find so far. And that's only with one company. The properties have all been registered in the past three years. And I'm waiting for a search from Companies House that'll tell me if he's a director of other companies.'

'So where is all the money coming from?'

'I spoke to Didi Hawes in Economic Crime. She got all jittery when I spoke to her. Told me that I'd have to speak to her boss DCI Banks.'

The memory of the brief meeting with Banks was still raw in my mind. I had a murderer to catch and they wanted to bang on about a dishonest shopkeeper.

'I don't want to tread on anybody's toes, boss.'

'I suppose we had better talk to Banks.'

'I agree.' Boyd sounded relieved.

I picked up the telephone and, after a skirmish with Banks's secretary in which I had to insist that the matter was urgent enough to justify a meeting today, we arranged to see him after lunch. I turned back to Boyd.

'Lech Balinski,' I said out loud.

I'd had two conversations with the colonel and each time I knew he wasn't telling me everything he knew. Maybe it was the language or maybe cooperation for him was a one-way exercise. But something had been niggling me and I couldn't put my finger on it.

'Have you had anything from the Polish embassy?' Boyd said.

'Sorry,' I said, not paying Boyd any attention.

'Have you had any response from the colonel about Janek?'

Then it struck me what was wrong about the colonel and his reaction when I mentioned Janek. I hadn't told him that Janek lived in Warsaw and yet he was going to talk to the police there. I picked up the telephone and scrambled for the business card.

After patiently explaining who I was to a voice at the Polish embassy I was put through.

'Inspector Marco. I have news of Pietrek. He was not in Polish forces. He was two years in seminary and then go back to college to learn English and become a plumber.'

'And Janek?' I asked carefully. 'Have you made any progress with tracing Janek? Have you spoken to the police in Warsaw?'

'I have nothing to report, yet. The police in Warsaw have been looking for him. But, you know, Warsaw is big city. And the police department need more men.'

I paused and drew my tongue over my lips.

'I'm sure you get all the right information from your informants. But it didn't save Gerek, did it?'

'Good man,' he said.

'Was he in Polish forces as well?'

'Good soldier—'

'Now look, Colonel, I never told you where Janek lived. Either you get me the information I need or I'll go to my ACC and give her a full report about your cooperation.'

I could hear him breathing down the telephone.

'And another thing. I want you to tell me everything you know about Lech Balinski. And I mean everything.'

I was standing up now.

'I call back,' he said and the line went dead.

I sat back in my chair, drew my hands around my neck and blew out my cheeks. Chasing shadows was the hardest part of this sort of job. It was much easier when there was a crime scene with lots of forensics all pointing to one perpetrator that we could arrest, interview, and then charge.

Before I could start to think clearly, the telephone rang. I heard the clear voice of Cornock telling me that he needed to see me.

Cornock stood over his desk fidgeting with a silver ballpoint pen. It looked expensive, and he kept clicking the top. There was plopping sound from the aquarium, sitting down wasn't an option, so I stood.

'Have you heard of Janet Helm?' he said.

'She's an opposition assembly member.'

'Not just any AM. She makes a lot of noise. Gets a lot of attention.'

'An all-round pain in the backside then,' I said.

He gave me an almost sharp look and picked up

some papers on his desk.

'She's been able to blag her way into seeing the Assistant Chief Constable. Ostensibly to raise concerns about the lack of policing and the poor record of the Wales Police Service in dealing with people trafficking. Apparently she's got somebody from Amnesty with her.'

'Who?' I said.

'Why?'

'I've met Anna from Amnesty as part of the investigation.'

'It could be her. I don't know. What I do know is that I don't want this politician making life difficult.'

'She's just out to get publicity.'

Another sharp look. 'I don't like people interfering, John. This is police work.'

'So when is this meeting?'

Cornock looked at his watch. 'She's arriving in ten minutes. So you'd better bring me up to date.'

Janet Helm wore a long skirt that accentuated the enormous girth of her hips. She was taller than I'd imagined and it was difficult to guess her age but I thought at least fifty-five, definitely under sixty. She strode into the conference room dragging Anna behind her, who gave me a defiant look as both women sat down.Cornock stretched out a hand and did the usual pleasantries.

'Let's get on Superintendent,' Helm said. 'I've got an important meeting at lunchtime.'

'How can we help, Mrs Helm?' Cornock intertwined his fingers and laid them carefully in front of him on the table. A young civilian came in with a tray of fancy cups and saucers and a plate of biscuits.

'I understand that you're in charge of the

investigation into the murders of the Polish citizens.'

'Yes, and Detective Inspector John Marco is in charge day-to-day.'

'Yes, I know that,' Helm said, glancing over at me. 'I want to know what progress you're making. The Assistant Chief Constable tells me that you hope forensics will help.

I noticed that Helm had surprisingly small, narrow fingers as she lifted a cup to her lips and slurped on the tea.

'Well, it's difficult to be specific—'

'Don't try and throw sand in my eyes, Superintendent.'

'I wouldn't dream of—'

'Oh, come now. We both know that investigating this sort of incident isn't exactly top priority.'

Cornock unthreaded his fingers and fisted one hand, drumming the fingers of the other on the table.

'Mrs Helm, I want you to understand that murder always has top priority.'

For a moment it stopped Helm in her tracks. She blinked and fiddled with her teacup.

'I understand there is a link to organised people trafficking.'

Cornock squinted at her, but said nothing.

'Everybody has human rights, Superintendent. And these girls have a right to be protected. As a society we must take steps to ensure that anybody involved in this heinous crime is brought to book. I know that my colleagues in the European Parliament are equally concerned about human trafficking. We've got an appalling record in Wales for dealing with these criminals. We haven't got the support network in place; we haven't got enough facilities.'

'We're doing everything we can to find those responsible.' Cornock ran out of platitudes and I could see the irritation building in Helm.

'I have been working closely with the Polish community,' I said. 'And also with Anna, so that I can try and get a better picture of what is happening.'

Anna moved uncomfortably and avoided eye contact. If she had got Helm involved then things might be getting out of control. Anna was playing a dangerous game and now an ambitious politician had hijacked her.

'Anna has been very helpful in assisting me with the enquiries.' I tried flattery.

Anna unwound the scarf draped around her neck and then cleared her throat. Her voice was quieter than before.

'There are so many of them involved. So many girls. So many families—'

Helm butted in. 'And that of course is exactly why the Wales Police Service must do more. Not only to find the murderers. But also to find the awful people who are trafficking in human beings. This really is white slavery. It's modern-day torture and we can't allow it to continue.'

'Mrs Helm, I can assure you that we will do everything to make progress with the investigation,' Cornock added.

'I'm going to be raising this at the highest levels. It's the sort of thing that the assembly committee should be discussing. Now that we have policing devolved from Westminster I want to be able to see that policing priorities are in the right place.'

Helm sounded like a party political broadcast. I could see her on the television smiling to the camera, making acerbic comments about the failure of the Wales Police Service. This was a win-win situation for her. It was publicity all the way, attention from the press and no downside. People trafficking wasn't going to go away. We might lock up the occasional trafficker and send some of the unfortunate girls home, but from past experience they were usually back on the street within a few days. Helm knew that it wasn't really our problem, given that the likes of Lech Balinski could prey on impoverished families.

'Do you have any suspects?' Helm continued.

'You must know that I can't discuss the operational side of the investigation,' Cornock said.

Helm gave him an exasperated look.

'Is it too much to ask for a little cooperation? I'm here as a representative of the people. I was elected to do a job of work. These people are my constituents; they expect me to ask awkward questions.'

'And it's our job, Mrs Helm, to investigate crime.'

It was difficult resisting the temptation to ask her if she knew Frankie Prince. Did she know the sort of person that she was associated with? Did she think about the massage parlours and the two-to-a-room bed-sits in Splott when she shook Frankie's hand and drank his cocktails at fancy receptions attended by dignitaries?

'Are there any specific things you would like us to address? Perhaps areas of new evidence that you think we should be investigating. Things that would be constructive for the development of our investigation.'

Now it was my turn to feel surprised. I turned to look at Cornock. He was beginning to sound like a politician, turning out one cliché after another. Helm stared at him briefly.

'I expect the attitude of the Wales Police Service to change. I'd like to be kept fully informed.'

'Of course, we'd be delighted to arrange another meeting once we've made further progress,' Cornock said, getting up.

Helm left in a cloud of tacky perfume that matched her Crimplene clothes. Anna gave me a furtive glance as she followed Helm out of the door. I turned to Cornock who was picking up his papers.

'Be careful, John. That fucking bitch is dangerous.'

Chapter 25

'How did it go, boss?'

The sound of the radio was playing in the background and the café was filling with lunchtime customers.

'Helm is like any other politician. She wants to get as much publicity as possible. Useless bloody waste of time.'

'What did the Super think?'

'He told us to be careful. So now we have to be careful of the politicians, as well as Lech Balinski and Frankie Prince.'

'Was that Anna woman with her?'

I nodded as I ate a chunk of my tuna baguette. After swallowing a mouthful I looked at Boyd.

'She's pulling our chain. She's playing a really dangerous game. Once she's got the politicians involved, the likes of Helm will piss all over her. Trample her underfoot to get the publicity they want.'

'She must know that,' Boyd said, sipping his Diet Coke.

I wanted to think that Anna had the best motives but she was mixing with some dangerous people. And I was getting more and more annoyed, knowing that she was trying to manipulate the investigation.

Finishing my lunch I threw the napkin on the table.

'Maybe DCI Banks and DI Jacks will be easier to deal with.'

Boyd drove out to headquarters in one of the pool cars from Queen Street while I tapped out a message to Dagmara on my mobile. I avoided saying anything about the meeting with Anna and Janet Helm. If Dagmara was talking to Anna it was a racing certainty she knew about the meeting, and if Maria was talking to Dagmara and Anna then I was the only person who didn't know what was happening. I felt like a piece on a chessboard being moved by different players. It was about time that I moved the pieces around the board. My second text was a reminder to Terry.

Boyd slowed the car as we rattled over speed bumps on entering the car park. The massive electronic aerials and dishes screwed to the roof were the only way of telling that the building wasn't the headquarters of an insurance company. There was an enormous new sign advising every visitor, bilingually of course, that they had to report at reception. Boyd was the first to sign in, and as he finished my mobile beeped. I read the brief text from Terry – *rugby game tonight Arms Park, don't miss it*. I smiled to myself; at least he was keeping in touch.

We passed the smart leather sofas lining the walls at reception, the smell of freshly cut flowers lingered in the air. We threaded our way down to the Economic Crime Department and eventually pushed open the doors into a bright air-conditioned suite of offices. The computers hummed quietly in the background and I stopped momentarily, just to admire the clean carpet tiles. Maybe I should apply for a transfer, I thought to myself.

A young woman detective constable with high heels and a smart red jacket pointed us towards Banks's office. I knocked and then walked straight in.

Banks pointed to the chairs and we sat down, squinting against the sunlight pouring through the Venetian blinds covering the large window behind. He reached over to close the slats.

'So what's the big panic about, Marco?'

'Your man Stan and the money laundering. I need to know what's going on, sir.'

'Why?'

'Michael Dąbek had £40,000 in his bank account that his family knows nothing about. We fish another Pole, without a tongue, from the docks and a third is bent in half in his flat. And the obvious connection is Frankie Prince, who incidentally owns the house where two of them lived. Then I keep hearing about Lech Balinski, whose favourite Transylvanian sport is amputating tongues. So if there is anything I need to know that would help the murder investigation I want to be told.'

Banks hesitated for a moment and gave me an intense stare, 'Our man Stan, as you call him, is a small player. He just moves the money around. The Polish community trust him to repatriate funds for them to Poland. He offers the Polish community a better interest rate than the major banks and he makes a margin. The result is that everyone is happy. Apart from us, of course.'

'Sounds simple enough.'

'We had a tip-off once the amounts involved began to increase. Problem we've got is that hundreds of people visit Stanislaw every week. Some of them take him a hundred quid. Some will take him five hundred. Some will take him a thousand. Some are legit. Some, well, most, are not.'

'Do you think this money is proceeds of crime?'

'What do you think, Inspector? With the average Pole working for minimum wage, it stretches the imagination to think that they can save the sort of money that we're seeing going through Stanislaw's account. Our investigation is taking hundreds of man hours. We've only just begun to cooperate with the police in Poland. And we got the Serious Organised Crime Agency looking over our shoulders just waiting for the opportunity to take the case.'

Banks propped his chin on steepled arms and gave

me another cold, hard look.

'I don't want you interfering. Do I make myself clear?'

'Yes, sir.'

'You fuck up my inquiry and you'll be issuing speeding tickets on the M4.'

I spent the rest of the afternoon reviewing the forensic reports from Alvine Dix and nursing my hurt pride. They had all the usual references to their standard procedures, but the result was the same for all the reports. Nothing of substance. After I'd read that the tongues at the factory all belonged to dogs I'd delegated Woods and Lawson to call, until eventually they complained that the receptionist at the factory thought they were pranksters.

There was still no message from Dagmara and I picked up my mobile a couple of times during the afternoon, thinking about composing a text before replacing it on a pile of papers.

Tonight, I would definitely send her another text. Tomorrow, I'd would go and see her.

Boyd picked up his jacket as I left for the day.

'You all right, boss?'

Boyd hadn't said anything on the journey back from headquarters. And he hadn't complained when I had two of my five-a-day in the car. Banks had succeeded in stretching my daily limit of cigarettes and limiting Boyd's conversation.

'Fancy coming to the Blues game tonight?' I surprised myself with the invitation.

Boyd gave me a pained look. 'Sorry boss. Mother-in-law is coming to tea.' He let out a deep sigh.

'How are things?'

'If Mandy gets pregnant her mother will have to

help.'

'So, keeping in with mother-in-law. How's Mandy?'

'She felt sick one morning last week and got really excited. She was convincing herself she was pregnant. She wants to have a child so badly you wouldn't believe it.'

'How will you manage after Mandy gives up work?'

He cast his face into a weary gaze over my shoulder.

'Mandy will have to get back to work. Otherwise we could only manage to pay the mortgage for maybe a year. But you know how it is.'

I wasn't sure I did. My income paid the mortgage on the flat where I lived. It'd always been in my name and when I was living with Jackie we hadn't planned on Dean; he just sort of happened. I was fumbling for the right thing to say, various different alternatives swimming around in my mind.

'I'm sure things will work out,' I said, immediately knowing I wasn't sounding convincing.

The late afternoon traffic meant I was late getting to the Arms Park stadium. I paid for a ticket and a programme and made my way up towards the stand. It had been several years since I'd been to a rugby game and I climbed the concrete steps and found my way through the thin crowd towards the middle of a row of seats.

The Blues's fly-half kicked the ball hard and it landed at the bottom of the stand and the players ran to gather for a lineout. Cameramen with mobile units strapped on their shoulders ran down the touchline and shouts of encouragement reverberated from the crowd below me.

'Don't turn around.'

The voice behind me was harsh, but I knew it was Terry. I twitched my head.

'Don't.'

'This is a bit Jason Bourne isn't it?'

'You have *no* fucking idea.'

'So tell me.'

'Lech Balinski. That's his name.'

'I know his name, Terry. You will need to do better than that.'

'Fuck off, Marco.'

'So what else?'

'Anybody who gets in his way has a habit of winding up dead. All the money is coming from the Mafia in Russia. And Lech Balinski is your man. He scared the shit out of so many people nobody is talking.'

'Is that all?'

There was a pause and then Terry whispered an address.

'You going to the bar afterwards?' Terry said.

'Are you going to buy me a drink?'

'No, but Lech Balinski might.'

I heard a noise behind me as the plastic seat closed and when I turned my head I saw Terry walking away, the collar of his jacket tucked against his face.

The game had too much kicking, too little inspiration and the crowd booed. One of the forwards threw a fist when he thought the linesman wouldn't notice, then his opposite number retaliated and the game descended into pushing and shoving as an edgy crowd taunted the players until the referee's whistle finally cooled tempers.

The Blues didn't deserve to win but it was points on the board and they were second from the top of the league table. I streamed out of the stadium and walked around to the bar area, uncertain what exactly I was doing. I kept thinking about Michal and Leon and how their young lives had been ended, and if Lech was responsible I wanted him locked up. The smooth, reasonable tones of Cornock's voice as he spoke to Helm that morning came to mind and I wondered what he might say. But what harm could it do? Frankie Prince knew I was in charge of the investigation.

Two bouncers in dark suits, white shirts and black ties were standing by the doors to the bar with the curled wires from their earpieces straddling their collars. I stopped and adjusted my tie. I brushed away a faint dusting of dust and dirt from my trousers and checked my brogues. They were my second-best pair and I made a mental note that I needed to clean them properly.

I walked slowly through the cavernous bar, mingling through the rugby fans who had gathered for a drink after the game. Girls tottered on high heels with fancy make-up and hair extensions. I tried to look above the crowd. Maybe Terry was wrong. It was hot and sticky and I was thirsty, but I wasn't going to carry a glass of water around. I wasn't looking where I was going and I banged into a man who spilled the top of his beer on his shoes and cursed me. I gave him a dull look and shrugged an apology. I spent ten minutes circling the room, looking for Frankie Prince and anybody who might match the description of Lech.

I stood by a group of men with beer bellies hanging comfortably over their waistbands. I listened to the Scottish accents from the supporters travelling with the Glasgow team and then I stood on tiptoe trying to spot Frankie Prince. I heard a voice behind me calling my name.

I saw Paddy MacVeigh walking over to me. His drink was almost finished and by the colour of his cheeks I guessed he had stopped counting.

'John, let me buy you a drink,' he slurred.

I hesitated. It'd been a long day and I didn't want to prop up the bar with a drunken pathologist.

'You're on the wagon aren't you?' he said.

I looked around, bobbing my head up and down, and then at Paddy.

'What?'

'What are you going to have to drink? Orange juice?' he said, finishing his beer and turning to the bar.

'Yes. Thanks,' I said.

Paddy pushed his way through the crowd towards the bar and I stood on tiptoe again. Away in the distance at the other end of the bar I caught a glimpse of Frankie talking, gesticulating with his hands. Then I noticed the broad shoulders of a man who must have been six-four with a square head and no neck.

I had to see Lech, look him in the eyes.

I left Paddy and pushed my way through the crowd. I crashed into shoulders and bumped shins, ignoring the complaints but this time I didn't shrug or offer an apology. I just carried on. When I got close I could see the smart white shirt and expensive suit and then I recognised the familiar face of a television personality standing by Frankie's side.

There was no going back now. If there was flak I would deal with it. If Cornock complained, it was simply a matter of priorities.

I thrust my way towards Frankie. He was still sipping from a champagne glass when I barged into his shoulder.

'What the fuck are you ...' he said, as he spilled the champagne on his trousers.

'I didn't know you were rugby fan, Mr Prince?' I said feigning surprise.

I looked up at Lech. The hair was cut short, the suit a deep-brown colour with lapels from a Philip Marlowe movie. His hand, holding a champagne glass, was twice the size of mine. His eyes were as black as finely polished anthracite. There was no flicker of emotion; he just stood there and looked me. I turned to Frankie.

'Aren't you going to introduce me?'

Chapter 26

'You did what?'

Boyd sounded more surprised than I'd expected. He leant against the door into my office and let out gasp of air, as he thought of something else to say.

'Does the Super know?'

I shook my head.

'Are you going to tell him?'

'Of course.'

He gave me a suspicious glance, but before he could challenge me Lawson and Woods came into the Incident Room and I tuned into their conversations about the latest transfer rumours at Cardiff City, who needed to add a striker if we were going to stay in the Premiership. After Swansea's success in the previous season all the talk in Cardiff was about how much the club would have to spend to get the right players.

'You going to the Liberty next weekend?' Lawson said, referring to the home ground of Swansea City.

'We'll see how things go,' I said, mindful of the money I'd already wasted on the home game against Chelsea.

'I remember when we could get in for nothing,' Lawson said, leaning back in his chair, arms folded behind his head. 'When both teams were in the Championship. That was …'

'Hate to break up the reminiscing,' I said. 'We've got work to do.'

I stood before the board in the Incident Room and looked over the notes and photographs pinned in place, hoping that we could find the evidence we needed. The best images we had of Michal and Leon were pictures from the mortuary, eyes closed and pallid skin with a deathly pallor. We'd been luckier with Gerek, as the Human Resources Department at the factory where he'd worked dug out a small passport-style photograph that we'd stuck below the face of Leon. All in a row down one side of the board and I wondered whether there'd be more to add to the list.

Lawson cracked open a bottle of cola that fizzed some of its contents over his papers.

'Joe, I need you to cross-reference all the factory workers who are common to the lists from the hotels.'

He mopped the papers with a handkerchief while glancing up at me. 'Yes, boss.'

'Three of those names are dead so we need to trace the others.'

'Of course. Yes.'

'And I want it done quickly. Today, Joe. Now.'

He stopped mopping and nodded.

Woods looked more focused when I turned to him. 'Phil, I need to know about Leon and Gerek's bank accounts back in Poland.'

His mouth opened slightly, a troubled look crossed his face.

'Get that translator ...'

'Veronika,' Boyd added.

'Yes. She'll help,' I said.

'Boyd. Let's go and talk to our Hungarian receptionist friend.'

As we pulled out of Queen Street it occurred to me that we should take a detour.

'Go down Grangetown first.'

'But I thought ...'

'We need to see the priest again.'

This time Father Podolak wasn't expecting us and the surprise on his face as he opened the door to us lasted long enough to justify the visit. He sat behind a desk in the study, a Bible and some textbooks in a pile to one side. An old telephone was perched on the opposite corner.

'You've heard about Gerek,' I said.

'Yes, of course.'

'Did you know him?'

'No. I mean I knew about him through others.'

'Who exactly?'

'Others in the Polish community.'

'It is important that if you know anything or anyone with information then they should come forward.'

'Of course.'

I could sense the puzzled look on Boyd's face.

'Do you know Pietrek Nowak?'

'Who?'

Evasion, always a bad sign.

'He was a good friend of Gerek.'

'I see.'

'And he spent two years in a seminary.'

Father Podolak didn't say anything.

'And if he knows something about the killings he should come forward before there are more deaths.'

The priest nodded his head.

'After all, the Christian faith is about the sanctity of life and the forgiveness of sins. What greater sin is there than to take a man's life? Or indeed fail to prevent another.'

Father Podolak composed himself and adjusted his dark jacket. 'Pietrek Nowak, you say?'

'Yes.'

'I'll be sure to remember the name.'

Boyd hadn't said a word until we were in the car park outside the church. He bleeped the car and we got in.

'What was that all about?'

'The good Father Podolak knows Pietrek. Written all over his face. I wonder where Pietrek might be?' I pitched my head and looked through the windscreen at the presbytery.

Boyd drove and I hummed another Elvis song on the journey that should have taken us twenty minutes, but the morning traffic choking the streets of Cardiff meant we took over half an hour.

'How did you know she's Hungarian?' Boyd asked, as he yanked up the handbrake once we'd parked outside the factory.

'She doesn't sound Polish.'

I pushed open the door to reception and found her sitting by the desk, her legs encased in skin-tight jeans. There was only the vaguest hint of recognition when she looked at Boyd and me.

'I need to ask you some questions. What's your name?'

'Adelina. It very busy now.'

'It can't wait.'

'I no leave.'

I smiled. 'I'm sure you can find someone to cover for you. It won't take long.' I always said that but I never meant it.

She spoke into the telephone, more guttural tones and within a couple of minutes a girl walked into reception and they exchanged a few words. I thought I heard the name Gerek.

'There is coffee place,' she said, nodding towards the car park.

Within five minutes we were sitting by a table waiting for three coffees. Adelina folded her left leg over her right knee, a languid look on her face despite the glances at her watch.

'Where are you from?'

'My father is from Estonia and my mother is Russian. It is legal for me to be here.'

So not Hungarian after all.

'How well did you know Michal Dąbek?'

'He work in same place and I know him, yes.'

'And you shared a flat with Gerek. Did he know Michal?'

She looked away and swapped her legs around.

'I was friends with Gerek. He and Michal, they were together the night Michal killed.'

'What were they doing?'

She shrugged. 'They were shouting in the bedroom.'

'Did you hear what they were talking about?'

'No,' she said, as though the answer was obvious. 'My Polish no good.'

'So what happened?'

'Gerek say later that they go to Four Seasons. He say something about a new person Michal no like. He big man.' She spread her arms wide and opened her eyes. 'Gerek was frightened for sure. And then he call Frankie Prince on mobile.'

I could sense Boyd tensing up by my side.

'How do you know it was Frankie Prince?' he said.

'Gerek say his name.'

Another part of the jigsaw: my pulse was telling me this was going to help.

The autumn sunshine was waning and by the time we were back in the station the radiator was hot and my office was too warm. I started to feel that we'd reached the stage where we needed another discussion with Frankie Prince.

But it was the sort of conversation that would need some careful attention so I arranged a meeting with Cornock, put the telephone down and my mobile beeped.

'John, it is me.' Dagmara spoke slowly and then hesitated. 'I am worried about Maria. I cannot get hold of her. It is not like her.'

'You've tried her mobile?'

'No reply and I have texted her.'

'She's probably out of signal or her battery's died.' As soon as I'd said this I knew it sounded lame.

'I call you later.'

I stared at the screen for a few seconds, making sense of my emotions and wondering if the worry turning in my mind might change to real fear.

I spent longer than I'd planned reviewing the paperwork and deciding how exactly I could persuade Cornock that I needed to interview Frankie Prince and Lech Balinski. I built another mind map, and I stared at the interconnecting lines. The Home Office murder manual spewed out a dozen reports that I should have read carefully, reviewed and ticked off in a box to confirm that I'd read them and that action would be undertaken on each and the follow-through monitored. I walked around my office and then through the Incident Room, passing quizzical gazes and odd stares, clutching the mind map and rehearsing the arguments.

I found myself hesitating outside Cornock's door. Boyd gave me an uncertain look before I raised my hand.

'Strength in numbers, John?' Cornock said as we sat down.

'Something like that,' I said, clearing my throat. 'I want to question Frankie Prince about these murders.'

Cornock sat back. He threw his biro onto the desk and squinted at me. 'This had better be good.'

'Everything points to Frankie Prince and Lech Balinski.'

'But you haven't got the evidence.'

'We can put Gerek and Michal together in Frankie's club on the night Michal was killed and we know that Gerek's time of death fits in with him being killed at about the same time.'

'So they go and see Frankie – they work for him.'

'They're bouncers in a club. Hardly someone he's going to call or go down the pub with for a quick drink. And we've got Leon's mobile with a dozen-plus calls to Frankie's mobile.'

Cornock rolled his eyes, unconvinced.

'That's so circumstantial it's not circumstantial.'

Boyd let out a faint laugh and an appreciative smile brushed Cornock's lips.

'And we've got Michal's boyfriend telling us that Michal worked with the escorts in Frankie's flesh trade. And we know from the Amnesty report you gave me that trafficking is a major problem.'

Cornock stood up, walked over to the aquarium and dropped small piles of food onto the water.

'And we have a positive link to the house, sir. Frankie Prince owns the 14 Howick Street house through a company and a car owned by one of his companies was seen outside the house the night of Leon's death. But more importantly Lech Balinski was seen outside the house too.'

When Cornock stood up he'd managed to knot his brow so heavily that darks shadows fell over the ridges. He raised a hand.

'Do you know how well connected Frankie Prince is?' He stopped and stared at Boyd and me. We just sat there, saying nothing. 'He'd get the best lawyers that money can buy and once they'd be finished all you'd want to do would be watch daytime television for the rest of your life.'

And all I wanted to do was make sure that Frankie Prince had no choice but to watch daytime television from the comfort of a prison cell.

'We'll need direct evidence John. And after your stunt in the Arms Park he'll complain about police harassment.'

A silence fell on the room as we exchanged stares.

'I'm waiting to hear from the colonel about Janek's whereabouts,' I said. 'We could always apply for an extradition for the criminal damage to the lockers in Central Station.'

Cornock raised his eyebrows. 'I'll talk to the CPS.'

'And I'm seeing the Maria girl again tonight. She may have more information that we need.'

'Be careful. Don't tread on the toes of the Vice Squad. You're in trouble with the Economic Crime Department as it is.'

He leant over the desk and looked directly at Boyd and me.

'We need irrefutable, cast iron, bomb-proof evidence for a case against Frankie Prince. Let's hope this Maria girl and Janek will give you what you want.'

During my last conversation with the colonel I had been uncharacteristically diplomatic: a trait that I had to convince myself was worth maintaining. I doubted that in the absence of useful information being forthcoming I would be able to maintain my even temper. The door from my office to the Incident Room had been firmly shut, I had to think clearly but I failed, allowing my mind to develop jumbled thoughts. I was pleased when Boyd interrupted the little constructive work I had been able to do after lunchtime by placing on my desk a coffee mug with *Keep Calm I'm a Cardiff Fan* printed on the outside.

'Heard from the colonel yet, sir?'

I had the mug at my lips as Boyd spoke, so I shook my head briefly before slurping on the coffee.

'It's time I did some liaising,' I said, fumbling for the colonel's business card from the bottom of my desk drawer. It took me a few minutes to persuade the receptionists at the Polish embassy that I really had to speak to Colonel Laskus and after several loud clicks I heard his familiar voice.

'What you want?'

'Good afternoon Colonel,' I said, gathering my thoughts. 'Have you been able to trace Janek? We need to know because we are looking at the possibility of extradition proceedings against him. It's quite a complicated process. The lawyers for the Crown Prosecution Service have told us that court proceedings will be necessary, and that the magistrate will have to consider all the evidence. There might be publicity of course, but we'd try and minimise that if we possibly could. You know, have the case heard in the afternoon. Hope the press wouldn't be interested.'

I looked over at Boyd and I could see that he was impressed. In fact I was quite impressed myself.

I could hear the colonel breathing heavily on the other end of the telephone. I imagined him sitting by a large desk in a room with a high ceiling and walls covered with photographs and paintings of Polish officers and politicians.

'It is difficult.'

'What?'

'The situation.'

My confidence in my initial bravado started to ebb. I listened to another long sigh then what sounded like tapping on a keyboard and the clicking of a mouse.

'We have surveillance.'

I hesitated, uncertain what exactly the colonel meant. He continued. 'Janek is in home. In Warsaw.'

'You mean you have him under surveillance? You know where he is?'

There was another silence, this time with papers rustling.

'Have the police spoken to him yet?' I said, trying to curb my rising anger.

'Situation is very complicated, Inspector Marco.'

'Murder cases usually are,' I said, getting to my feet. 'How long have you known where Janek was?'

'It is difficult. You must understand that much going on—'

'My Assistant Chief Constable is not going to be pleased when I tell her that the liaison has been meaningless.' I was getting more and more annoyed.

'You must understand—'

'No. You understand, Colonel. I'm investigating the death of three of your countrymen here in Cardiff. You're supposed to be cooperating, but you're not helping my inquiry at all.'

'We will do more.'

'I should hope so. Just tell me if Janek moves.'

I put the phone down hard; there was a crack, sounding like plastic splitting from the force at which I replaced the handset. Perhaps I should be travelling to London to confront the colonel, and demanding to be told what he knew. Or maybe I should be booking a flight to Warsaw. Before I could think of how to discuss either of these options with Cornock my mobile rang.

'John, it is me.' Dagmara's voice sounded warm and friendly after the colonel's harsh tones. 'I still cannot find Maria.'

Now the pleasure of talking to Dagmara changed to a worry.

'I'm sure she's all right.'

'I'm worried. Really worried.'

I could hear her voice breaking, the hint of a sob.

'I'll meet you at Leftie's after work.'

She coughed briefly as though she was concealing her emotion.

'It'll be fine,' I added.

For the rest of the afternoon I tried to concentrate on the paperwork in hand, in between directing Boyd and listening to Woods and Lawson struggling to make progress. And all the time a dark cloud of worry was spreading through my mind.

Chapter 27

I sat in Leftie's, reading the *Western Mail*. After the sports pages I turned to the news section, and the smiling face of Janet Helm stared out at me. It's funny how people look different in newspaper photographs. She looked younger, leaner and I tried to imagine her in her twenties, like Dagmara, full of excitement and expectation. Then I read that she was presenting a cheque on behalf of some charity and all I could think of was Frankie Prince holding his champagne glass in the bar at the Arms Park stadium.

I saw the relief in Dagmara's eyes when she saw me, as she pushed her way through the crowd of early evening drinkers. She threw her arms over me and I felt her breasts pressing against my shirt and the warmth of her arms around my neck. She kissed me briefly on the cheek before sitting down.

'Thank you for coming, John.' She gave me a brief smile.

'So when did you last speak to Maria?'

'I'm so worried.'

'Do you have her mobile number?'

Dagmara nodded.

'Have you tried texting her?'

'Nothing. She always replies quickly.'

'Do you know where she lives?'

'I ...'

'Dagmara. You need to tell me what's been going on.'

'We were only doing our best.' She gave me a desperate look. 'We thought it was the right thing to do.'

'What do you mean?'

'Maria and Leon wanted to do the right thing. They wanted the trafficking to stop. They had the photographs.'

'Have you seen any of them?'

'It was going to be so simple.'

'So what happened?'

'Somehow, Maria met Anna.'

I drank from my water, the lemon slice caught on my lips and I thought about the first time I'd met Anna with her scarf draped around her neck.

'So what happened with Anna?'

I was beginning to believe that Anna was bad news.

'She was very forceful. She wanted Maria to be helping her. She wanted Maria to go public and appear at a press conference.'

My mouth must have dropped open because Dagmara gave me an odd look and then ran out of steam. All I could think of was the need to get Anna locked up for her own safety and the safety of others.

'Anna must be mad or stupid or ...'

Dagmara nodded. I continued, 'Does Anna know where Maria might be?'

Dagmara shrugged.

'She hasn't answered my calls and I've texted her twice. I am worried for Maria. She is not strong person. It was Leon that made her strong. They were so good together. Since Leon died it is like she shrivelled up like a dead flower, not wanting to live.'

'We will need to find her. Do you know where she lives?'

Dagmara nodded.

'What telephone numbers have you got for her?'

'Only her mobile.'

I finished the last of my water and I led Dagmara out of Leftie's as she made another call to Maria's number. She gave me a troubled look and then dialled again.

I braked hard and the car screeched to a halt by a set of traffic lights. I drummed my fingers on the steering wheel, silently cursing as traffic flowed past me. I was calculating how long it would take us to reach Maria's address – ten minutes if we were lucky but the evening traffic in Cardiff could be horrendous and the streets were beginning to choke up with taxis and minibuses – all keeping the pubs and nightclubs of the city busy.

Once the lights had changed to green I sped off, accelerating only to find myself caught behind three empty minibuses. I drummed my fingers on the wheel, and nudged the nose of the car out into the oncoming lane, trying to judge whether it was safe to overtake. Eventually I threaded my way through some narrow streets until Dagmara caught sight of a street name she recognised. I drew the car close to the kerb and killed the lights. I powered down my window a couple of inches and felt the cool autumn air chill my skin.

'It is number five,' Dagmara said.

I nodded. I looked over at the terraces running down both sides of the street. I caught the smell of chips and vinegar in the air.

'You try the front door,' I 'said. 'There's probably a lane at the back. I'll see what happens from there.'

Dagmara nodded.

I sat for a moment, watching her walking over the street, enjoying the sight of her curves through the tight denims. I found the narrow alley that ran down the back of the properties. Away from the streetlights the passageway was dark and there was a strong smell of urine and vomit.

I stopped at the back gate and took a couple of steps back. No shards of light seeped past the edges of the curtains drawn across the upstairs windows. The place looked deserted. I tried to imagine how many occupants each of the bedrooms might have – two, maybe three. There was a shout from a neighbouring house and a screech from what sounded like a cat, but nothing moved inside the house that I was looking at. I sent Dagmara a text – *anything?* My mobile lit up quickly enough – *nothing, no reply*. I turned on my heels, texted Dagmara a message and we met back at the car.

'I am worried, John.' Dagmara clasped the fingers of both hands together.

'Let's go and find Anna,' I said.

Through the back streets of Splott I listened to Dagmara's directions. I slowed the car by the Magic Roundabout, a well-known haunt for girls working the streets, and an area regularly patrolled by the Vice Squad. But I couldn't see any sign of Maria and I wasn't going to run the risk of being stopped or having my car number plates reported.

A light shower drenched the windscreen. After a couple of minutes the wipers squeaked so I switched them to an intermittent setting. Dagmara said nothing, and within twenty minutes I had reached Whitchurch and pulled the car to the edge of the pavement.

'So where does Anna live?'

She gave a shrug and stared out towards the newsagent and betting shop.

'I'm not sure. It is long time since my visit.'

'Can you remember the street name?'

Another shrug. 'There was a park, and maybe a church …'

I wanted to shout. I should have told her that lives were in danger and that she had to think clearly. Instead, I clenched my jaw and pulled the car away slowly from the kerb. We drove through a couple of the main streets of Whitchurch until Dagmara saw one of the old pubs that she recognised and then leant forward in her seat, directing me to a narrow street of semi-detached houses. I slowed, noticing the leaded glass in bow-shaped patterns in the front doors and the occasional neatly kept front garden.

When Dagmara recognised Anna's house she shouted and I braked. It looked like a typical street for a city suburb. Houses converted into flats, front gardens paved over and I hoped that Anna was home. Once we were out of the car Dagmara jogged over the road and headed down the side of the house. The property was in darkness; even the next-door house seemed empty.

She banged on the door to the rear garden and then fiddled with a latch before it burst open. I followed her seconds later and watched as she pressed her hooded eyes onto the window, peering into the darkness of a downstairs room. Then she rattled the rear door and called out Anna's name.

I reached over and put a hand on her shoulder. 'Place is empty.'

She turned and I saw the desperation in her eyes. 'What do we do, John?'

'You go back to the car. I'll ask a couple of neighbours.'

Dagmara nodded, but said nothing.

Twenty minutes later I was sitting in the car, having been reminded how anonymous living in the city can be. I'd spoken to three of Anna's neighbours. One had occasionally said good morning and smiled at her. The other two had no idea who I was talking about and two other households barely understood any English. Dagmara didn't seem interested; her head sagged and she kept folding the fingers of one hand through the other.

'Do you know any of her friends?' I said.

'No. I don't ...'

'What about family?'

'She never said anything.'

I buzzed down my window and lit a cigarette. 'She must've mentioned something, Dagmara. Work colleagues, anybody. Think.'

'I only met her ...'

'What about Maria? Where could she be?' It sounded an innocent enough question, but I knew the answer of course. And I wasn't going to march into the massage parlours of Cardiff demanding to speak to Maria. 'What about her friends?'

Dagmara said nothing.

'For Christ's sake, Dagmara. You must know something.'

'It is difficult, John. I can't remember.' She put her head in her hands. 'This is awful. I cannot think.'

And neither could I without something to eat and drink, so I retraced our steps to Whitchurch. The pub we'd passed earlier had a curry-and-pint night advertised on a billboard on the pavement. We found a quiet corner and tried to blank out the sound from the bar. Dagmara sipped slowly on a glass of cider, while I tapped out a reply to the text message from Trish that had arrived as I ordered drinks. I kept my message simple – *working, in Whitchurch, home late, how's mid Wales?*

I fished around in the bowl until I found four small pieces of chicken floating in the thick red sauce. The rice had been blasted in the microwave at a high heat for too long, making the grains dry and hard. Dagmara prodded the pieces of meat in her curry until she'd moved them around the bowl a dozen times.

'We'll try the Polish club,' I said.

Dagmara looked at me without emotion, before returning to prodding the curry with her fork.

'Maybe,' she said.

'We don't know that anything has happened to her.'

'Then why doesn't she reply to my messages?'

'Maybe her phone is dead.' I wasn't even convincing myself.

'She always replies to my messages.'

'Let's go down the docks,' I said, getting up.

As we left the pub Dagmara typed out another message before giving me a brief smile as she sat in the car. She had a smile that dimpled her cheeks in an old-fashioned way. But she said nothing on the journey down to the docks and when we parked outside the Polish club she touched my hand and I felt the warmth of her fingers and the caress of her skin.

'Thank you, John.'

I hesitated for a moment, then closed my fingers around hers.

She'd opened the door and left the car before I had a chance of saying anything. Dagmara hurried over the car park towards the Polish club and I followed her as she pushed open the door. Inside the heat and the smell of damp clothes hit me and she pushed her way towards the bar, scanning the customers in the process.

Dagmara had been talking with various people but the blank replies and occasional head shaking made it clear that our visit wasn't going to help. An hour had passed and I stood on the front steps drawing on a cigarette, hoping the rain would keep away and wondering if Dagmara was making any more progress inside the club. The door opened behind me, a blast of warm air brushed my face, and then Dagmara was standing by my side.

'Anything?' I said.

'Nothing. It is really bad.'

'Send her another text.'

Dagmara sent a message while I finished the cigarette and flicked the butt-end into the car park. I drew my jacket collar against my neck. Dagmara didn't seem to mind the cold.

'I'll take you home,' I said.

We drove away from the Polish club as a couple of taxis arrived and I heard muffled shouts as the club emptied. It was a short drive to Howick Street and I parked behind an Opel with Polish plates. There was still a heavy smell of boiled cabbage and vinegar in the house and a radio played in one of the upstairs bedrooms. Dagmara found the light switch that illuminated the dark hallway to her bed-sit.

'I'm sure everything will be fine,' I said.

Dagmara slumped onto the bed, and started crying softly. I sat by her side and drew my hand over her shoulder.

'We'll find her, I'm sure,' I said, wanting to sound reassuring.

She moved closer towards me. I could smell the embers of her perfume, see the gloss of her dark hair. Then her mobile beeped somewhere deep in the bag by her feet. She fumbled to pick it up and, opening it, she rummaged, cursing silently, until she found the mobile and read the message.

'Thank God. It is Maria.'

'What did she say?'

'She is busy. She will contact me tomorrow.'

Dagmara turned to look me in the eyes. There was warmth now where there had been fear. She leant over and kissed me. I reached my hand to her cheek, drew her face towards me and I kissed her back, really hard. Then I sensed

the warmth of her lips, and touch of her hand on my neck.
The bag fell onto the floor as I pushed her onto the bed.

Chapter 28

I kissed Dagmara's shoulder, lingering to sense the warmth of her body before I slipped out of her bed. She stirred but slept on and I left the bed-sit and drove home. The night sky was clear and yellow sodium lights bathed the empty city streets.

I woke twice in the middle of the night and each time I was thinking of Dagmara. It was six in the morning when I decided that sleep was going to elude me. I thought about Trish and a spasm of guilt lingered in my mind. After a couple of minutes of staring at the ceiling I got up and padded through to the kitchen. I could hear a shower running somewhere in the building. I made coffee and found some cereal whose death-by date had long passed. When I'd finished I stared at my mobile, thinking I should text Dagmara, but it was still early. I thought about the warmth of her body, the intensity of her kisses and the hunger in her passion and I knew it was something I didn't want to lose.

I sat in the lounge with a second double espresso and flicked through the morning television programmes, my mind turning over the night before. I closed my eyes and Dagmara's perfume lingered in my memory. I chose a cream shirt, a pair of navy trousers I hadn't worn for months and my second-best pair of brogues. My mother would approve. I even thought about a tie.

I was standing by the door when my mobile rang.

'Area Control, sir.' The voice was calm. 'We have a report of a body.'

I crunched the gears and swore when the lights of a pedestrian crossing turned red and a stream of young mothers pushing buggies crossed in front of me. I called Boyd's number as I raced down past the Millennium Centre towards Penarth Marina, shouting the details. Flashing my lights and sounding the horn helped to thin the traffic as I reached the exit towards Penarth.

Within a few minutes I was down by the entrance to the locks at the end of the barrage. Crime scene investigators were hauling their equipment from the Scientific Support Vehicle. Two uniformed cars blocked the entrance and behind me I saw Boyd leaving an unmarked car.

'Is there any identification on the body, boss?'

'Don't know.'

I knew who the body was going to be. I could probably make the identification. I stuck my hands deep into my pockets and I pulled up my jacket collar against the biting sea breeze.

Alvine Dix took a step away from the dockside when she saw me approaching.

'Is this your case then, John?'

'I got the call about half an hour ago.'

'Young girl. Early twenties I'd say.'

We watched as two police divers bobbed around in the water, securing the body, before they hauled it up onto the concrete staircase and then up to the concourse. I was praying that it wasn't Maria. Hoping that at least she might be able to go back to her home and buy a farm and raise a family.

Alvine leant down and moved the wet hair off the dead girl's face. A face I'd seen before and I knew well.

Sitting in the passenger seat of Boyd's car, watching him eating a banana from the bag of fruit on his lap, I wondered whether he managed five pieces of fruit and vegetables a day. I'd managed one of my own five-a-day with my espresso that morning and decided that the second was overdue. I buzzed down the window, lit a cigarette and found the smoke comforting.

'Does that Dagmara girl know?' Boyd said.

I shook my head. 'She hadn't been able to reach Maria for days.'

'Now we know why.'

There wasn't much for Alvine Dix and the CSI team to do and as soon as the undertakers had driven away with the body, they packed up and left. Boyd and I were sitting looking over the barrage.

'Are you going to tell her?' Boyd said, curling the banana skin into the bag.

I thought of Dagmara. I thought about the roundness of her breasts and her breath on my skin. I thought about anything except telling her.

'Sure thing. And we need to talk to Anna.'

Boyd gave an apple an inquisitive look. I drew the cigarette right down to the filter, then I threw the butt out of the window.

I dialled Amnesty's office number but there was an answer machine. Then I tried Anna's home but the telephone rang out. A voice answered my second attempt at the office number.

'I'm not expecting Anna in today,' the voice said, trying to sound helpful.

'Where can I reach her?'

'You can leave a message on her mobile.'

'I've done that.'

'Could you try tomorrow?'

'Get her to ring me: it's urgent.'

En route to Howick Street I left my car by the flat and set off in Boyd's, the hazard lights flashing, alarm wailing. I scrolled to Dagmara's number on my mobile but then hesitated. I had to tell her face to face, not on the telephone. Boyd parked outside the house and I jumped out and banged on the door. I waited but nobody came so I dialled Dagmara's number.

'I'm outside,' I said, when she answered.

'What's wrong?' she asked as I killed the call.

The seconds that passed before she opened the door felt like minutes. She stood for a moment and must have seen the look in my eyes.

'I'm sorry. Really sorry,' I said.

She threw her arms around me and I dragged her body towards me, the memories of the night before flooding back into my mind. I felt her tears against my skin as she sobbed gently.

'I should have done more to make it safe for her,' Dagmara said, between gulps for breath.

'There's nothing you could have done.'

We stood there for a couple of minutes. Boyd must have been staring at us but I didn't care what he thought.

'But last night, she sent text.'

'Probably someone else was using her mobile.'

She stepped back, a look of revulsion on her face at the thought of a stranger – a killer – using Maria's mobile.

'Let's go to Maria's place,' I said.

It took us half an hour to find the house where Maria lived. Boyd tucked the car in behind an old Toyota that had multi-coloured panels, and behind it an old Mazda with Latvian plates had a large crack in its windscreen.

It didn't look like a brothel, but then I had no idea

what one looked like. We ran over to the front door and I pounded it with a fist a couple of times. I sensed movement in the house and very soon the door opened and a face appeared.

The girl had hair tumbling over her face and she squinted at me.

'Who the fu—'

'Police.' I shoved my warrant card towards her. The door opened a little more and I could see the remains of make-up around the edges of her cheeks.

'What do you want? I've done nothing wrong.'

'Maria lives here.' I wasn't looking for confirmation as I stepped forward and the girl retreated.

'I don't know where she is. I haven't—'

'Maria's dead,' Dagmara said, standing by my side now.

The girl put a hand to her mouth. I stepped past her into the house, Boyd following Dagmara, as we went into a small lounge with a television and two sofas. The place was heavy with sweet perfume.

'Where is Maria's room?' I asked.

'First at the top of the stairs,' the girl replied. I left Dagmara sitting with her and jerked my hand at Boyd, telling him to follow me.

The door at the top of the stairs didn't have a lock so I pressed down the lever of the handle, pushed the door open and stepped in. Boyd was behind me and we both saw the chaos in the room.

'Fuck,' he said. 'Someone's beaten us to it.'

I walked around the piles of clothes and broken furniture.

'I wonder if they found whatever they were looking for?'

I moved some clothes with a shoe and then I kicked

the bedspread to one side, but it wasn't hiding anything except more clothes. There was a framed print on the wall of a Parisian scene advertising some fancy drink and a mass of perfume bottles and creams on the top of a cabinet. I wondered if this was the place where she brought her punters. Was this squalid room in a dingy house a brothel where Maria had dreamt of a normal life? A life cut short. Anger built up as I gathered my thoughts. 'That fucking Anna has a lot to answer for.'

'I'll call CSI,' Boyd said.

Back downstairs Dagmara was sitting by the side of the girl whose cheeks were scarred with tears. She looked young and I wondered where she was from and whether she had dreams like Maria.

'Has anyone been here?'

She shrugged.

'What's your name?'

'Zuzanna.'

I raised my voice. 'Somebody has been through her room. You must have seen something. Or heard something?'

She started crying and I turned to Dagmara. 'We need to find Anna urgently.'

Dagmara seemed reluctant to leave the girl.

'The CSI team will be here soon,' Boyd said.

'And we'll get officers to come and take a statement too,' I added.

We left the girl sitting on the sofa, sobbing. Boyd drove as I dictated instructions for Anna's address. Then I found my mobile and called Queen Street. Woods was eating something, I was certain, judging by the mumbling acknowledgments, as I dictated instructions for him and Lawson to take a statement from Zuzanna.

Boyd found the address easily enough and we sat

for a moment looking at Anna's house. The curtains open, the small front garden neat and tidy.

The front doorbell rang out and I pushed open the letterbox and shouted, but there was no movement. The gate to the rear garden had been left unlocked since our visit the day before and through the window of the back door I could see the pots and pans piled on the draining board. I tapped on one of the glass panes in the door a couple of times and then, with my back to the door, smashed the bottom pane with my elbow.

I didn't have time to think about not breaking the law.

'Get back to the car, Dagmara,' I said.

Dagmara nodded meekly, combining a look of surprise and fear. After she closed the gate behind her I turned to Boyd who gave me a resigned you've-got-me-in-the-shit-again look.

'You know the drill, Boyd,' I said. 'You go check the phone. Check out any messages. Then see if you can find any diaries, family calendars. Anything that might tell us where she could be.'

In the kitchen I opened the cupboards at random in the kitchen. Once I'd finished I found a laptop in a room at the rear of the house. As it booted up I flicked through some of the paperbacks on a small bookcase. I hadn't expected Anna to enjoy chick lit. There were contact names, addresses, phone numbers, files, and folders related to work with Amnesty. I made an executive decision, closed the laptop and tucked it under my arm.

We left the house and I pulled the door behind us. After we dropped Dagmara at Howick Street I caught a glimpse of her in the side mirror watching the car drive away, her arms folded tightly.

By early evening I was back in my office, having watched Dr Paddy MacVeigh humming along to the sound of a Mozart violin concerto. It was good to see a man happy in his work. I needed to know one thing from Paddy and after he'd prised open Maria's jaw he gave me a grim look.

Boyd had spent the afternoon telephoning names in Anna's address book and her laptop. I didn't know what Dagmara was doing but I guessed she wasn't sitting in her bed-sit at Howick Street twiddling her thumbs.

I was stretching one arm over my shoulder, trying to massage away a tired, dull ache when Boyd stood at the door.

'What did you do about Anna's house?'

'The usual. I told Operational Support there was a suspected gas leak.'

'But there wasn't—'

'Boyd. We've got a murder investigation. The door'll be fixed today.'

He gave me a stern head-masterly look. 'Anything from the post mortem?'

'She had her tongue cut out.'

Boyd flinched and loosened his tie as he sat down on one of the chairs. 'Nobody in her address book has heard from Anna recently. I should have the telephone records tomorrow.'

'Let's hope she turns up.'

'Inspector Hobbs was around the office earlier.'

I raised one eyebrow, knowing that Boyd had more to tell me.

'He kept saying things like – it must be a very heavy workload and how is John Marco? I told him we were doing just fine.'

A dull worry entered my mind about Hobbs. There

was always an ulterior motive to everything he did. He must be up to something I concluded.

Chapter 29

'Good morning, John.'

When Dave Hobbs was this polite I knew something was up.

I walked past the photocopier towards my office.

'The Superintendent wants to see you.'

It had the desired effect and I stopped.

'Seriously, check your messages,' he said with a grin.

I dipped into my jacket pocket and cursed when I discovered that my mobile was dead. I sat down heavily in my office chair and rummaged through the various drawers of my desk until I found a charger. I was kneeling by a socket when the phone on my desk rang.

'I've been trying to get hold of you,' Cornock said.

'Sorry sir. The battery—'

'Get over here now.'

I fiddled with my tie as I walked over to Cornock's office where he waved me to a chair. He had his usual white shirt but his standard dark-blue tie had red stars littered all over it.

'Good morning,' Cornock said.

'Sir.'

'There's been another burglary. It looks as though Jason Brown has been busy again.'

'What are the details?'

'An empty house on Rodium Crescent. The occupiers were out for dinner. Obviously, the burglar knew when to strike.'

'Is it the same MO?'

Cornock flicked through some of the papers on his desk.

'I'm going to assign Inspector Hobbs to lead the investigation of these burglaries.'

Now I could see why Hobbs was so polite.

'You've got a complex multiple murder inquiry and I don't want you distracted. So you'll need to cooperate with Inspector Hobbs. And you'll need to give him a full briefing.'

It made sense, of course. I could concentrate on the murders while another team investigated the burglary cases but I groaned at the prospect of having to work with Dave Hobbs. Cornock must have sensed my discomfort.

'John, I want you to work with Dave Hobbs.'

I scrolled down the messages on my mobile as it charged – there were two texts from Trish and yet another from my mother, all asking me to call. And I still had to deal with Dave Hobbs. I knew that any briefing with Hobbs would test my patience. He would screw up his piggy eyes, scratch his jaw and ask awkward questions that implied I was an idiot. Boyd would have to be present, just in case.

I dialled Dagmara's number but her standard message clicked on. Boyd stood by the door to my office as I finished the call.

He closed the door behind him and sat down. His tie was knotted carefully, a serious look in his eyes, the sort that made me realise I might be calling him 'sir' one day.

'We broke into her house last night, sir.'

'There was a smell of gas …'

He raised his eyebrows, stretched them really. 'If Anna complains—'

'She won't.'

'You can't be certain and then she could make life very awkward. For us all.'

'Maybe Dagmara had a key.'

'You broke the glass and entered illegally.'

'It was a fucking emergency, Boyd. I had reason to

believe that her life was in danger and I had to do something. And the lives of others. We'd only just pulled the body of Maria from the Bay, for Christ's sake.'

Boyd didn't reply immediately. He slid one hand over another, and avoided eye contact.

'We could be charged with misconduct in a public office,' he said.

'Don't be daft.'

'I did a study on that offence when I was at university,' he said, talking about me as though I was a subject in a test. 'Did you know the maximum penalty was life imprisonment?'

I sat back in my chair, realising it was the sort of offence that only someone with a law degree would mention. I continued.

'We've got someone loose on the streets of Cardiff amputating tongues. And if it's Lech Bal–fucking-inski, I want the bastard stopped.'

He gave me a sullen stare.

'We've got work to do. Did uniform call at Anna's house last night as we asked?'

'Twice, and nothing. Place in darkness all night.'

'Damn. Have you tried her mobile?'

'Three times this morning already.'

'Any luck from her telephone records?' He hesitated, probably still thinking about the possibility of imprisonment for the misconduct offence and worrying about his pension and his mortgage.

'Nothing. We've spoken to her parents. They live in Nottingham. She hardly speaks to them. Telephones a couple of times a month. Anna's an only child and there was no mention of a boyfriend or any other close friends.'

'Anything from the house?'

'A whole pile of books and paperwork on her work

with Amnesty.'

'Any contacts in her computer? Email addresses?'

'Forensics are working on the hard drive.'

I heard a rap on the door, which opened before I could say anything. Woods stepped in, reminding me about the briefing that was already late. Boyd and I left the office and stood in the Incident Room in front of the board, now with Maria's face pinned in one corner.

I paced the room, my mind a jumble.

'We'll need to go through her flat and find out where she was working,' I said to Woods and Lawson. 'Somebody must know. Talk to someone in the Vice Department. There must be intelligence on the houses where these girls work.'

I stopped pacing the floor for a moment.

'And then Frankie Prince and someone in the Four Seasons should know about her. It's time we had another visit to the club.'

I spent the rest of the day coordinating the house-to-house enquiries that the uniforms were undertaking in the flats and townhouses near the barrage. Two civilians from the Public Relations department sat behind desks in a Mobile Incident Room, handing out leaflets with broad, reassuring smiles.

I walked out over to the edge of the barrage, from where Maria's body had been dragged out of the water. I looked back towards the apartment blocks and the new cars parked neatly on driveways. If Maria's body had been dumped, then her killers had the audacity to bring her down to Penarth in full view of the surrounding households. I wondered if Anna had any idea what she was involved with. It was different somehow with Dagmara. She was more practical, more down-to-earth, realised the dangers but was still involved. But Anna just thought she was irrefutable. And she might just get herself killed because of it.

I could taste the salt on my lips after each gust of wind. I pulled up my jacket lapels and thought about a cigarette. It would be the third of the morning, or was it the second? I decided that I had to stop counting. I really needed to stop altogether. But it was only five a day.

One of the waterbuses bobbed up and down as it approached Penarth and drew up against the side of the quay. A handful of people jumped out and I counted six passengers going back to Cardiff. I wondered if Michal or Leon or Maria had ever taken the journey over the Bay. In the distance, I could see the tall masts of the yachts in the marina.

When I reached the Mobile Incident Room a crowd had gathered around a television crew and I heard the reporter saying that the Wales Police Service was no further forward in their investigation of the Polish murders. The cameraman panned around the Bay before making certain he included images of the nearby homes.

At lunchtime I sat with Boyd in a café, reading the menu, trying to decide whether I wanted a panini, a ciabatta or a baguette. I looked over at Boyd; he seemed to be slighter: perhaps the diet was working.

'How's Mandy?' I asked.

'Anxious.'

A waitress arrived at our table and she gave us a surprised look when we didn't take up her suggestion of a side order of fries.

'And what's made matters worse is that her sister

just announced that she's pregnant.'

'Mandy must have been pleased.'

'Pleased? She was angry, with me and with her sister. I don't get it.'

The waitress returned with two cappuccinos. Boyd continued with the family saga, as he stirred sugar into his coffee.

'You know how it is. Mothers and mothers-in-law. They all want to be in charge.'

I nodded, remembering guiltily that I still had to call my mother.

'Things will work out,' I said.

'Now Mandy's started talking about IVF through a private clinic if it doesn't work this month.'

'Isn't that expensive?'

Boyd rolled his eyes and stirred the coffee again.

'That's not going to stop Mandy. You can get it on the NHS but you have to wait a minimum of two years.'

The waitress arrived with the paninis that had criss-cross scorch marks on them, and a pile of salad in one corner. Boyd pushed some peppers around his plate.

'How's your family, boss?'

'There's a big party next weekend.'

'Sounds like fun.'

Now it was my turn to roll my eyes. Fun wasn't the right word to describe Uncle Gino's party.

I was chewing on a mouthful of panini when I thought I recognised a figure in a shop doorway on the opposite side of the street. I stopped eating and leant forward, but the man turned and stepped into the shop. I finished my lunch while casting the occasional glance over the road.

We crossed the road and a figure suddenly came out of the shop entrance and stood in front of me.

'I thought it was you,' I said, facing Kamil. He was wearing a dark jacket that he'd pulled up tight around his ears.

'It no good. Have you found who killed Maria?'

'And how do you know Maria?'

'I know friends and she was nice girl. Do you know where she work?'

I wasn't certain if it was a question or a statement.

'I can help,' he continued. 'I need to know where she work so I can help you with Polish people. I have lots of contacts.'

'It's too early in the investigation yet and we've got lots of work to do. And in fact that's where we're going now,' I said, moving past him.

'I have lots of Polish people tell me they know things. Polish people trust me and I can help.'

'We can't tell you where Maria worked.'

'But I can help. And I have very good contacts with Polish people. Ask Father Podolak.'

'Kamil, go home, go to work and leave us to ours.'

I got back to the station, realising that I had made no progress with Maria's death. I heaped two teaspoons of instant coffee into a mug and dribbled milk from a carton, until the liquid became a beige colour. Back at my desk I slurped the coffee and grimaced; there must be easier way to get a caffeine burst.

I logged onto my emails and found the formal request from Dave Hobbs for a briefing. It had all the right jargon, and looked important enough but instead I hit the delete key. If he asked, I'd play dumb.

I read the message from Paddy and tried to remember how to store the attached document when

Alvine Dix walked into my office holding a sheaf of papers. I left the email from the pathologist until later.

'Do you fancy a coffee, Alvine?'

She looked at the mug on my desk and turned up her nose.

'That looks disgusting. Have you seen the p.m. report?'

'No. I ... Has it been sent?'

'Paddy emailed it earlier. Are you sure you haven't had it?'

An inquisitive look now.

'You're useless with computers aren't you? So much for the modern man.'

'What do you want, Alvine?'

'I thought I would give you the benefit of my vast experience in helping you solve four murders. As you seem to have no idea where to look for the culprit.'

'Get to the point.'

She put the papers on my desk with a brief flurry.

'Well, if you haven't read it.' She gave the monitor of my computer a brief quizzical glance. 'Then you won't know what Paddy says about her.'

My irritation was rising. I had Anna, Dagmara and now Alvine trying to be clever. I picked up the report and began reading, waiting for her to find the right moment to share her profound wisdom with me. I'd reached the top of the second page when Alvine cleared her throat.

'It's at the bottom of page three,' she said. 'The lungs were full of seawater.'

I carried on reading, assuming there was more to come.

'And?'

'Come on, Marco, don't be stupid. She was alive when she went into the water.'

Then the realisation hit me.

'So she drowned outside the barrage.'

'Top of the class. Water inside is nice and fresh. So she must have been taken out into the Bristol Channel.'

'So how did that happen?'

'You're the detective. You work it out.'

Chapter 30

'We need to talk.'

Trish sounded like a troubled character from a daytime soap opera. She stood in the kitchen doorway, staring at me, arms folded, deep creases on her forehead.

'What's going on, John?'

Where to start? I had four murders to investigate, three of the bodies had had their tongues cut out, and I had a brace of do-gooders competing for a place in the shortlist of the next-to-die. Before I could think of how to reply Trish continued

'You don't answer my texts.'

I didn't answer my mother's texts.

'And I just feel that you're pushing me away.'

I pressed a switch on the Gaggia and watched the light flickering. Trish walked into the kitchen and sat down by the small table.

'Look Trish. I'm really busy,' I turned up the palms of my hands, hoping it would placate her.

'Too busy to send me a text.'

Now I folded my arms across my chest.

'Look, once this case is over things will get back to normal.'

'What is normal for you, John? You've got to find time for me. Or for us. It's never us, is it? It's always what you're doing. What you need to get finished. You're never thinking about what we could be doing. What our future might be.'

It was the sort of statement that had no simple reply. I didn't want things with Trish to be the same as they had been with Jackie and I was trying my best to find the right thing to say. But I kept thinking about Dagmara and Maria and Anna, their certainty and defiance infuriating me.

'Are you listening, John?'

'Yes, of course.'

'Then why don't you say something?'

'I'm in the middle of a murder inquiry. I haven't got time for this now.'

I reached for the coffee from a cupboard and after spooning the grounds into the cradle I snapped it into the machine. I flicked another switch.

'You didn't get back until after midnight last night. Surely you can spend some time with me this morning?'

I stood, leaning over the Gaggia, waiting for the hissing sound and the smell of fresh coffee.

'You know what it's like in a murder investigation. It's round-the-clock stuff. I can't simply decide to be late this morning.'

'That's typical of you. I know you've got to go to work. But sometimes why can't you just stop and make time for me?'

'There's the weekend and Uncle Gino's party. Why don't we do something with Dean?'

I took my coffee, sat down by the table, and touched Trish's hand but she pulled it away and glowered through tightly stretched lips.

'It's not the same John. All your family will be there.'

Trish was staring at the floor. Coffee started to dribble into a cup.

'It would be good for you to be there as well. With Dean and me.'

'I don't know, John.'

Trish got up, pushed back the chair and stopped at the doorway as she left the kitchen.

I listened to Trish rummaging in the bedroom, dropping shoes onto the floor, trying to find the right pair while I switched off the Gaggia and took the first sip of the espresso. Eventually, there was a silence and I guessed she was doing her face.

I was still sitting at the table when Trish paused at the doorway and narrowed her eyes.

'I'll text you later. Promise,' I said.

Her expression didn't change. 'Maybe I'll stay with Mum tonight. I haven't seen her for a while.'

And with that she turned and left. I tried to make sense of why I felt annoyed with myself and irritated with Trish. I didn't want to have a repeat of Jackie. Maybe I needed a transfer out of CID. What I probably needed was a long holiday.

I stifled a nagging feeling that I should have said something else to Trish, as I pulled my car into a vacant slot in the car park at the rear of Queen Street. I'd just locked the car as a text message came through. It was lucky for Boyd that the Wales Police Service didn't audit text messages; if they did he'd have some explaining to do about his warning that Detective Inspector Hobbs was waiting to see me.

I took the stairs up to the second floor at a leisurely pace and the words of Superintendent Cornock echoed in my mind, telling me that I had to cooperate with Dave Hobbs, something about the value of teamwork and corporate responsibility. I wondered how much teamwork had gone into killing Leon, dismembering Michal and drowning Maria. I reached the top of the stairs and before opening the doors to the Incident Room I stood for a moment, straightening my tie and buttoning my jacket. As I pushed open the door I thrust my mobile to my ear and started talking loudly. I marched through the Incident Room, making straight for my office at the far end and noticed Boyd glancing over his shoulder.

I stood behind my desk, the mobile still at my ear, as Dave Hobbs entered my room. I muffled the microphone with the palm of my hand and looked up at Hobbs.

'Super wants me to talk to you,' Hobbs said, drawing his tongue over his lips. 'About the burglaries and—'

'Will it take long, Dave? Only this is an important call.'

Hobbs walked forward and sat down, tugging at his trouser material before crossing one leg over the other.

'I'll need to call you back in five minutes,' I said.

I sat down and, looking at my desk, felt vaguely pleased that there was a semblance of order, with only two bits of paper cluttering the top.

'Coffee, Dave?'

Dave Hobbs narrowed his eyes until they became two black slits.

'I've read your file about the burglaries,' he said, measuring every word as though he had something important to add. 'Seems straightforward enough for me. Brown is in the frame. He'll go down, of course.'

'I don't think Jason Brown was involved.'

Hobbs jerked his head at me and blinked quickly a couple of times. I always enjoyed dropping something unexpected into conversations with Dave Hobbs. He had a mind that ran on straight lines, simple and uncomplicated.

'The Super wants me to review the whole file. From top to bottom, beginning to end. He wants me to do a complete reassessment of where we are. If, as you say, Jason Brown isn't responsible then we've been doing a lot of work for nothing. And there's a neighbourhood watch meeting.'

'Of course, Air Commodore Bates and his charming wife will be present.'

'You've got no idea, have you, Marco?' Hobbs pressed his lips together and made a narrow smile. 'You can't afford to antagonise people like that. And he's a Wing Commander.'

I picked up my mobile from the desk and turned it in my fingers. I wanted so much to slap Hobbs around the face that containing my irritation stretched my self-discipline.

'You've only got to talk to Brown to see what he's like. He's homeless, a drunk and he thrived on the attention being in the spotlight for burglaries in Cyncoed. He may be a sneak thief and perhaps he'll cough to pinching a handbag from a kitchen table through an open door but you put him to court for the sort of burglaries we're talking about and the likes of Glanville Tront will tear you apart.'

'That may be—'

'Guaranteed, Dave. I'm sure you wouldn't want the fallout from a prosecution that falls over in court. You know how it is. Who was the officer in charge? Why was the decision made to prosecute?'

Hobbs moved awkwardly in the chair, uncrossed and then recrossed his legs. But he kept staring at me; he was good at staring at people.

'The Super wants this case handled with care and precision. There are a lot of people involved and he wants to make sure that nobody could possibly feel that we hadn't given the case the most thorough attention. That's why he wants me to take the case, of course.'

'When's the neighbourhood watch meeting?'

Hobbs's eyes widened a little and he puckered his lips before I continued.

'I should be there. You know, Dave, to provide the logistical support and backup that you need, bearing in mind that I was the SIO at the house of Wing Commander

Bates.'

Hobbs tried smiling, but widening his lips proved too much of a strain and his mouth collapsed back into a tight, thin line.

'I don't think that will be necessary.'

I felt like telling Hobbs that I even had a suit for the occasion. Then I looked at his suit. A fine check pattern ran through the dark material and I noticed the row of buttons at the sleeve. His shirt was white and the tie a dark-blue – Cornock would approve.

'Least I can do.' I smiled at Hobbs, who didn't flinch.

I picked up the mobile and gave it a long hard look, as though I were willing it to ring.

Hobbs fingered the papers on his lap and flicked through the first few pages of statements before looking at me. 'We'll need to go through all the evidence and statements carefully.'

'Look, I've got to return a call. Can this wait until some other time?'

Hobbs managed a smile that said leave-it-to-me and then got up and left.

Seconds after Hobbs had left Boyd stood at my door and I waved him.

'Did you get my text, boss?'

I nodded as he sat down.

'He just appeared at my desk. Began asking questions about you. Why were you late? And how often were you late getting into work? And if things were going all right in the inquiry. Guy gives me the creeps.'

I was surprised when the inspector in me started composing a reminder to Boyd that Hobbs was his superior officer. But it soon passed.

'Hobbs is taking the burglaries as there's been another in Cyncoed. Super's instructions. He doesn't want us distracted from the murder investigations.'

Hobbs had left me nursing an attitude that wasn't good for my blood pressure, but then the telephone rang and when I heard the colonel's voice I knew that things weren't going to improve.

'I have news,' he said.

'OK, good news I hope.'

'Janek Symanski is home in Warsaw and police are going to speak to him about—'

'We really need to speak to him first. They can't possibly know what to ask him. And they might ask all the wrong questions.'

'We can try and help; that is all.'

'Who's dealing with it there?'

'I find name.'

'Just tell him to keep Janek under observation.'

'I do what I can.'

'And what about Lech Balinski?'

There was a pause and a wheezing sound like the chest of a heavy smoker.

'Lech Balinski is very dangerous man,' he said slowly. 'We have much to discuss with him if we have evidence. But no one will talk about him. If you have witnesses then we would be happy to see Lech in court.'

I drew a hand through my hair, then over my mouth and wondered when our luck would turn. Or whether it ever would.

'So why do you want to talk to Lech?'

'He is involved with Russia Mafia and then with many bad men who bring drugs into Poland and—'

'And they bring underage girls over as prostitutes.'

Another pause as his chest made a rasping sound.

'It is very sad.'

We spent the rest of the day working through the statements and reading the reports from forensics. The analysis of the tongues that had been amputated from the various animals didn't take the investigation any further. The evidence linked Frankie Prince to the house in Splott and then to another thirty properties full of Eastern Europeans working in the factories around Cardiff. I thought about Maria and the prospect of having to confront yet another Polish family with their loss. A sense of frustration was nagging at my mind that somebody on duty in the Bay must have remembered which boats had gone through the barrage. But the statements said simply that the barrage was opened every half an hour for boats and yachts to pass through. I walked out through into the Incident Room and stood over Boyd's desk.

'Was there CCTV at the barrage?'

'Don't know, boss.'

'Well, find out.'

The telephone rang in my office and I picked it up after the fourth ring and heard Cornock's exasperated voice at the other end.

'Get over here, now.'

Cornock had the door of his office open and I could hear the sound of the television blaring. He stood behind his desk, legs slightly apart, clutching a remote control in his right hand.

'Just look at this,' he said, pointing the remote at the television.

The sound increased and I watched the familiar face of a television reporter speaking to the camera. It looked like a hotel conference room with rows of seats facing a table.

'I've just had a call from the Public Relations department. Apparently Janet Helm is organising a press conference. She's going to be making some dramatic statement about the Polish murders. I knew she was bad news ...'

The reporter on the screen fumbled over his words, fidgeted with his earpiece, and then turned to look behind him as Janet Helm entered the room. As I watched Helm walking towards the table I didn't notice, at first, who was walking by her side. I took a step towards the television once I'd realised that I recognised the face and the tell-tale scarf, scarcely believing that Anna would be there with Helm.

'Who is that with her?' Cornock asked.

'That's Anna. She was with Helm when you met her.'

'Of course. Of course.'

'I've got a bad feeling about this.'

'One of the television stations asked if we wanted to be present.'

I stared at Cornock. 'Do you know what they're going to say, sir?'

Before Cornock could answer, the screen filled with the image of Janet Helm sitting at the table. Her hair was neat, her clothes sharp and she seemed slimmer than when I'd seen her face to face. The make-up was evident, but it couldn't hide the wrinkles around her eyes and above her mouth. The camera panned away and showed Anna loosening the scarf around her neck and I noticed the deep black bags under her eyes. Helm pulled a microphone towards her, then cleared her throat.

'Recent tragic events have only highlighted the

inadequacies of our policing service when it comes to dealing with human trafficking and what can only be described as modern-day slavery …'

Before Helm said much more the telephone rang on Cornock's desk. He almost knocked it over picking up the handset. He clenched his jaw as he listened to the message.

'Yes, sir. I am looking at the television.'

Cornock listened, occasionally confirming details. Once he'd finished he turned to me. 'That was the Chief Constable. He wants to see us.'

Chapter 31

Almost a week had passed since Janet Helm's press conference and the atmosphere in Queen Street had changed. Staff from Public Relations had been in Queen Street every day, poking their noses into every part of the investigation. When one of the tabloids ran an exclusive about the current state of the investigation, things got really bad. The rumours about leaks made everybody tense. Even Terry sent me a text telling me that things had 'gone to shit' and for me not to contact him. I wore a suit to work, not my best suit – that one I'd bought specially for Uncle Gino's party – but a cheap grey suit I'd bought years ago. It had a musty smell when I pulled it from the wardrobe, and had Trish been staying she'd probably have taken it to the dry cleaners first.

I'd spoken to Dagmara on the telephone and each time we stumbled over finding the right things to say. There were silences and she started but didn't finish sentences. Boyd gave me odd looks when I closed my office door to speak to her. Once the calls were over, all I could think of was seeing her again and watching her smile at me.

It had been barely a year since policing and justice had been devolved to the Welsh government and the Chief Constable had kept reminding us, during our meeting after Helm's press conference, that a lot of the right-wing press didn't think that Wales could run its police and justice system. Someone should tell them that small countries in Europe ran police forces without their bigger neighbours complaining.

I didn't much care for politicians. I knew Helm didn't really care about the murders and that all she really worried about was advancing her own career.

I had spent half an hour on the telephone the

previous evening listening to my mother telling me about the arrangements for Uncle Gino's party and getting me to confirm for her that I understood when and where everything was taking place.

My mobile was on the table with my half-finished breakfast bowl and I glanced over at it, thinking that I should call Trish. After our argument over breakfast she'd stayed with her mother for one night and then she'd gone back to her own flat. I'd been as good as my word and I'd sent her regular texts telling her what was happening. I scrolled through the phone for her number.

'Hello John.'

'How are things?' There was a pause and I continued. 'It's Uncle Gino's party tonight.'

'Of course. I remember. I was beginning to wonder if you'd forgotten.'

'You're joking; my mother has rung every night this week. Last night I was on the phone for half an hour. She asked after you.'

'And what did you say?'

'I told her you were all right. You know, looking forward to the party.'

'Yes, of course.'

'Do you want to come with me to collect Dean?'

She didn't sound enthusiastic. 'Yes. I suppose.'

We fixed a time to meet and then she cleared her throat. 'I hear things are a bit tense in Queen Street.'

I managed to get more aggression into my reply than I'd intended. 'What do you mean?'

'Well, that business with Janet Helm.'

'What have you heard about it?'

'No need to get defensive, John. Everyone knows how much pressure you're under to get a result.'

'What is everyone saying?'

I said it more sharply than I'd intended, sensing my anger developing.

'Forget it, John. I'll see you tonight.'

I threw the mobile on the table. Prodding the last of the cereal with my spoon I tipped the coffee cup to one side, disappointed that there was no espresso left. When I realised the time and, knowing I was late, I felt the tension building in my chest.

When I turned the corner by the front entrance of Queen Street police station that morning I almost fell over Kamil. He was carrying a super-size coffee, but his deathly complexion had lifted.

'I am in shit,' he said.

'What's wrong?'

'I must talk but not here.'

'What about?'

'Have you found where Maria worked?'

'Why do you want to know where she worked?'

He looked past me down the street, took a sip of the coffee and grimaced at the hot liquid.

'I can get Polish people to help. But you tell me where she worked so I find people who work same places.'

I stood and stared at him.

'There is no way I can tell you anything about the inquiry.'

Kamil pouted, said something about only wanting to help, and set off into town.

The leather sofa was smaller than the one in the Four Seasons. Boyd and I sat waiting for Janet Helm, my mind considering the alternative charges I could use as threats if she didn't cooperate. Her assistant had grey streaks running through her mass of dark hair that badly needed brushing. And cutting, too. Working for Helm had prematurely aged the girl who was probably no more than thirty-five.

Eventually, we were called through into Helm's office. The assistant looked pleased when we left. Helm had a smart office with a modern leather chair and a sleek desk. She had a supercilious look that professional politicians must practise for hours on end before a mirror.

'I need Anna's contact details,' I said.

'Tell me about the progress you're making in the inquiry.'

'We've been in touch with our counterparts in Poland through the Polish embassy and our principal suspect is known to them. And they've discovered that another suspect we want to interview in connection with the inquiry is back in Poland, so in due course we'll have officers interview him.'

I could feel myself getting into the swing of flattering Helm's ego.

'I must say that the cooperation we've had from our Europeans cousins has been very impressive. I'm sure the Welsh government would like to thank the Polish authorities in due course for their help.'

She nodded and gave a smile, but her eyes were cold, her mind working the angles.

'And the Polish community has been helpful of course, as much as they can. We've had officers visiting the shops and the churches.'

I was surprising myself. Boyd was relaxing by my side.

'But we are worried about Anna and her close association with Maria and we need to talk to her. She's not been at home and the house is empty. I was wondering if you could tell us where she's living?'

A report about Helm's movements the night before had landed on my desk before we left and I knew that Anna wasn't staying with her, although I was quite surprised about the age of a male visitor who left Helm's flat in the early hours.

'What makes you think I would know, Inspector?'

'Do you have a mobile number or contact details for her?'

'I don't think I could give them to you.'

'Not even if her life was in danger?'

She paused and her eyes narrowed slightly.

'What makes you think that?'

'She's created an awful lot of publicity for your campaign and those involved may think that she's become a danger to them. After all, Maria was killed after Anna met her with Sergeant Pierce and me. And then Maria was Leon's fiancée and Michal and Leon were good friends. It doesn't take a genius to work out that someone will pin the blame on Anna.'

I stood up.

'But I appreciate your predicament. If something does happen to Anna then I'm sure her family will understand your reluctance to help, once they'd heard your side of the argument.'

I pushed the chair back and turned to leave.

'Just a moment, Inspector.'

I sounded the car horn at least three times at incompetent drivers on my journey into Queen Street. I knew that I'd broken the speed limit and at one of the roundabouts I'd only just been able to stop in time behind a new BMW.

I took the stairs two at a time up to the Incident

Room and by the time I pushed open the doors my pulse was racing, the collar of my shirt was tightening uncomfortably around my neck and I could feel a small bead of sweat on my forehead.

'That was a load of fucking bollocks,' I said, falling into my chair so hard it careered across the floor.

'Didn't know you had it in you,' Boyd said. 'What next, boss?'

I didn't want to say that I had no idea. I was paid to have ideas and make a breakthrough. But sometimes cases don't get solved and sometimes the bad guys escape justice and sometimes the wrong guys get caught.

'Better find Anna now after all of that.'

Boyd got up.

'Try the Amnesty office again,' I said.

The telephone rang and I picked up the receiver.

'Inspector, call for you about that dead girl.'

There was a pause before the voice spoke.

'Inspector.' The voice sounded educated: Penarth not Pontypridd. 'I hope this won't waste your time. My son was sailing in the Bay last week and he was almost run over by a yacht that didn't give way to him. He had the right of way, as he was in his dinghy for the weekly race. It's a well-established routine.'

I sat up in my chair and reached for a notepad.

'What's your name?' I asked.

'James French and my son is Aaron. Well, as I said, Inspector, it may be nothing but it was the night before the body of that young woman was found. I was annoyed and at the end of the race we went to the protest officer, but he said there was nothing we could do, except maybe complain to the yacht club. My son went back to school and we left it until he was back last weekend and he mentioned the photographs.'

'What photographs?' I said, convinced my pulse had missed a beat.

'He took a photograph of the yacht on his mobile.'

I stood up now. 'Can I see these photographs?'

'Yes, of course. We can come in when convenient.'

'We'll come to you,' I said, before getting his details.

I picked up the car keys from the desk and threw them at Boyd. 'You drive.'

The French family lived in a smart detached house in one of the fashionable parts of Penarth. A silver BMW and a dark-blue Range Rover were parked in front of a garage with two grey automatic doors. Leaves from the sycamore growing in the front lawn cluttered the recently paved drive. The bell echoed behind the heavy front door, but it opened soon enough and a tall man with neatly clipped hair, wearing a navy shirt, appeared and stretched out his hand.

'Inspector Marco,' French said, his handshake firm.

We followed him into a large room at the front of the house, carefully laid out with immaculate sofas with bold blue stripes and matching scatter cushions – all very nautical.

'I hope we shan't waste your time, Inspector.'

The vowels were rounded and the voice authoritative.

'We sail a lot as a family, as you can probably tell,' he said, casting an eye on the painting hanging on the wall of a large racing yacht heeling over.

'You mentioned some photographs.'

Then a teenager came in clutching a smartphone and a large envelope. I guessed it was Aaron, maybe nineteen, tall and thin like his father.

James French was sitting now in one of the chairs

and cleared his throat.

'Aaron was sailing the night before they found the body of that poor girl by the barrage. It was the usual mid-week race. Something we do all the time. I was on the club launch and then this yacht was in the Bay. The yacht ignored all the rules of racing and the skipper tore around like a madman.'

'You've got some photographs?' I asked, again moving to the edge of my seat, raising my voice slightly.

'Yes, of course. Aaron, can you show the inspector?'

Aaron came to sit by my side and moved his fingers over the smooth face of the iPhone. After a few seconds he showed me the images. The faces were indistinct and blurred, but Lech Balinski still looked enormous in sailing gear. A can of beer was being crushed in one hand and alongside him was a young girl, and next to her the smiling face of Frankie Prince.

My lips were drying and I glanced over at Boyd who was staring down at the smartphone.

'Have you downloaded these?' Boyd asked.

Aaron nodded and pulled a photograph from the envelope. 'I blew them up so that I could complain. It was then that I saw the face of the young girl. It was the same as the picture in the paper.'

Chapter 32

'Have you found Anna?'

Trish braked at traffic lights. The seat belt cut into my shoulder. I waited for Boyd to reply.

'No sign, boss.'

The image of Maria on the yacht was fixed in my mind. When I thought that Dagmara might be next my pulse thundered in my neck.

'I've been to Howick Street already and—'

'Where have the uniform lads been?'

The fucking lights are stuck on red.

Anna or Dagmara or both might be next so I had to hope that Boyd, Woods or Lawson and the uniforms would find them before Lech did.

'And Dagmara ...' I could feel the tension dragging at my chest. 'Well, is she there?' I raised my voice.

Trish accelerated away from the traffic lights. A car blasted its horn and I glared at the driver before raising my middle finger.

'Nothing, boss. All her things are gone. The place was empty. The lock was broken.'

My heart missed a beat. I thought about the flowers and the photographs on the cabinet in her room. Trish was taking a wrong turn. I pointed my hand, holding the mobile, towards a junction.

'Down there. It's much quicker.'

'Don't be stupid, John. I know the way.'

I shouted. 'I drive here every day. You're going the wrong bloody way.'

'For Christ's sake, John, calm down.'

I put the mobile to my ear and barked at Boyd. 'Just bloody find them. Ring me on my mobile when you do.'

'I thought you were going to a family party,' Boyd

began.

'Just call me. The mobile will be on.'

The car cleared a bottleneck of traffic and the tension subsided a couple of notches. At least I didn't have the throbbing in my chest. I glanced at my watch and already we were late collecting Dean. My mother would be ringing me any minute. We left Cardiff and within a few minutes we were turning into the estate of houses where Dean's grandmother lived. I saw a new BMW parked on the drive – silver, of course, but no personalised plate: probably a lease car from the company where Jackie's husband worked.

I jumped out of the car and jogged up the path to the front door, pushing my arms into my jacket before straightening the tie that Trish had carefully ironed. The door opened without me having to knock and Jackie appeared. The sweet smell of potpourri lingered in the porch and Dean appeared behind her. I smiled.

'Ready?'

He nodded, but said nothing. I put my hand on his shoulder as we walked to the car. He stopped gazing at the floor when he heard Trish starting the car engine.

I asked about Queens Park Rangers but Dean sat in the back, not saying much, not saying anything at all really. I gave Trish a nervous glance and she puckered her lips in reassurance.

'What have you been doing today?' I asked.

'Nothing much,' Dean said, after a delay.

'Have you been out?'

'We went for a McDonald's at dinner and then I played on Xbox with Da... I mean Justin.'

The accountant with the BMW was Justin, of course. Right sort of name for an accountant. And he was probably a better father than I'd been or could be. But Dean was calling him 'Dad' and Jackie had no right, I thought. The spit in my mouth dried and I drew my tongue over my lips, reminding myself about Lech and wondering how his enormous hands could amputate a tongue. I wanted to turn back and go to Queen Street and direct the search for Dagmara. The tension bore down on my chest again.

Trish had more success with Dean and he told her about his school and his friends and where he lived. He even asked if she'd like to visit. When we turned into the car park of the hotel I got out and couldn't suppress the desire to call Boyd any longer. He answered after four rings.

'Where were you?' I hissed down the mobile, as I walked a short distance away from the car.

'I was in the toilet having a piss, if you must know.'

'OK. OK. Is there any progress?'

I could hear him draw breath. 'Nothing, boss.'

I wanted to shout at him. Scream down the mobile that Dagmara wasn't safe and that we had to find Anna.

'I've got everyone working on it. Place is like a fucking mad house.'

That was supposed to reassure me, but it only made me realise that I should be at the station, in charge.

'Don't worry, boss. We're doing everything we can.'

'I want everyone looking for them and keep me posted as and when you get anything positive.'

'Of course, boss.'

I killed the call and strode towards the entrance of the hotel. I noticed how cold it was and shivered. Then I saw Dean and Trish standing by the main door. When I was drinking, it was the sort of occasion when the justification for a skin-full came too easily – pressure of work; just one to relax.

Trish took me by the arm and whispered in my ear. 'You'll have to try and switch off tonight.'

I nodded without conviction. Trish continued, this time louder. 'Let's get Dean a drink, shall we?'

We walked through the entrance lobby, past a tall girl with long blond hair and rings on each finger, standing behind the reception desk. She smiled and said something in a heavy Eastern European accent. When it occurred to me to ask her if she knew where Anna and Dagmara were, I knew it was stupid and time for an orange juice.

The warmth from the crowded function room hit us and I looked around for my parents. In a corner a disc jockey was setting up his equipment. My mother sat by one of the circular tables – probably, in her opinion, the best table, and one she'd have taken great care in choosing, to be certain it was at the centre of everything.

She raised a hand and waved us over.

'Dean. This is so lovely.' She wrapped her arms around him and pulled him towards her. 'It's going to be a wonderful night. I thought you might be late,' she added, giving me a dark glance.

I saw my father making his way through the guests, carrying a tray of drinks, nodding occasionally and smiling at his friends. Trish had excused herself and was standing by the bar being chatted up by one of Uncle Gino's relatives. I had been so long, I couldn't remember his name.

My mother fussed over the tray my father laid on the table. He set down heavily and took a large swig from the Peroni bottle.

'Held up in traffic?' he said.

'Yeh. Bit busy at the moment.'

I thought I heard the mobile in my jacket and dipped my hand into the inside pocket, but the screen was blank.

'I want to introduce Dean to everyone,' my mother said, emphasising the last word. And she ushered him away towards the table where Uncle Gino was sitting.

'You mother was worried you were going to be late,' my father said, once she was out of earshot. 'You should remember that these things are important to her. Family and all that it means.'

I opened my mouth slightly, but anything I'd say would have sounded wrong. I furrowed my brow instead.

'The least you could do is be here on time.'

'I'm sorry. But the pace of things in the station is frantic at the moment.'

I wanted to tell him all about the case. Why I couldn't tell when I was going to finish. Why it was so hard to be on time.

'Haven't you got a sergeant or someone who can do the spade work?'

'Yes. But ...'

'You're the wrong side of thirty-five and you never see your son and your girlfriend wants to dump you.'

'No she doesn't,' I said indignantly.

'Well she bloody well should, the way you treat her.'

Very clever.

'You'll reach forty-five and realise that you've lost something you can't get back. Maybe you should have a holiday with your mother's family in Lucca.'

Trish arrived back with some drinks. My father stood up and kissed her, then sat down. I squeezed her arm and she gave me an inquisitive smile before handing me a glass of orange juice mixed with sparkling water.

'They've delayed serving the meal,' my father said, without enthusiasm.

I realised then that the staff had been waiting for me and Trish and Dean to arrive. I searched unsuccessfully for the accusing stares. I watched my mother with Dean and

Uncle Gino until the waiters came round with plates of soup and then she threaded past them and sat down.

'There are so many people you need to speak to,' she said, making it sound like a politician at an election rally.

I didn't get time to reply as a waiter leant over my shoulder and placed a bowl on the table in front of me. The waiters looked Eastern European too, and my mind went back immediately to thinking about Anna and Dagmara. The soup was a thick mass of vegetables and bits of pasta passing for minestrone. I spooned on some parmesan but the soup was still hot, so I dipped my hand again into my jacket which was hanging on the chair behind me and found my mobile. I almost cursed out loud when I saw the missed call. I pushed back the chair and walked out to the foyer.

Boyd answered after two rings.

'What's the latest?' I said.

'One of the uniforms has been talking to the staff from the agency where Dagmara works and they said she was very nervous the last couple of days.'

'What's that supposed to mean?'

'Just telling you what I was told.'

'Do they know where she might be?'

'Nothing yet.'

'For fuck's sake. Somebody must know where she is.'

I wanted to smoke but I'd left the cigarettes in my jacket.

'I'm going back to the factory and then down to Howick Street again,' Boyd said.

'Good. You've probably missed something.'

A woman in high heels tottered out through the front door and fumbled in her bag before lighting up and drawing deeply on the nicotine. I finished the call and went back inside. Waiters scurried back and forth with plates of chicken and bowls of vegetables.

'Where have you been?' Trish hissed as I sat down.

'Call I had to make.'

Trish looked over at Uncle Gino's table. 'Who is that with Gino?'

I glanced over. 'That's his son, Jeremy.'

'Looks very smart.'

'Looks can be deceiving.'

The parmesan had congealed on top of the minestrone and everyone around the table had finished their starters and were now glancing over in my direction. It was only then that I noticed the dark stare my father was giving me. I pushed the bowl to one side.

A waiter stretched over my shoulder and placed a plate with a large piece of chicken laid out in segments. He removed the soup bowl and another waiter left a dish of vegetables. I prodded the chicken. It felt rubbery and looked as though it had been sitting in a warming oven for hours. The first piece stuck to the top of my mouth and the vegetables were overcooked and tasteless.

I smiled at Dean and realised that I'd not spoken much to him. I couldn't think of anything to say to him and I remembered my father's comment earlier. I was relieved when the plates were cleared and the disc jockey mumbled into his microphone, telling us that the party would get started in fifteen minutes.

After a mouthful of the tiramisu I decided that a cigarette was the better alternative. The girl with high heels was back outside and she gave me a brief you-again nod before continuing the conversation on her mobile.

It was my fifth today, maybe even the sixth or seventh, I'd got to the stage that counting was pointless. I wasn't going to give up. I thought about Boyd and whether he'd made any progress. I heard my mobile ring and saw the

Superintendent's number on the screen.

'DI Marco,' I said, straightening my posture.

The girl by the door turned sharply towards me, drew her hair across her face, and went inside.

'John. DC Pierce tells me you're at a family party.'

'Yes, sir.'

I didn't know what to expect.

'What's the strategy?'

Catch the bad guys.

'We need to find Dagmara and Anna,' I added and, as an afterthought, 'And Kamil Holter. He was Michal's boyfriend. Dagmara knows more about what's happened, but she's frightened.'

'It feels like things are out of control. The Incident Room is like a mad house, so first thing in the morning I want to review.'

I lit a second cigarette but my hand trembled with tension. *Not what he seems.*

And then it struck me. The one thing I hadn't checked. I frantically fumbled again for my mobile and then scrolled down the numbers, praying that Paddy was at home and sober. The number rang and rang until I heard his voice.

'What do you want?' Paddy said.

'Michal Dąbek's post mortem.'

'What about it?'

'Do you remember that case a couple of years ago of the man who'd been raped violently?'

'Yes.'

'Was Michal gay?'

'There was no sign of any rectal trauma, John, if that's what you mean. Although you know that's not conclusive ...'

I killed the call even as I heard Paddy's voice starting

a detailed explanation. I called Boyd.

'Arrest the fucking bastard as soon as you can.'

'Who?'

'Kamil. Just find him.'

Trish was standing by my side now and pulled my arm.

'John. You need to come inside. Now.'

The room was full of noise and my mother was standing over a nearby table. Trish dragged me over to her side. Mam smiled briefly and turned to the woman sitting at the table.

'John. This is Aunt Lucia from Lucca. We stayed with her when you were young.'

I smiled briefly, but all I could remember of Lucca was cycling around the ancient walls and how hot it was. Lucia's English was poor and my Italian was worse and the music so loud that it made conversation impossible. My mother dragged me around other relatives and friends who had made the special effort to attend the party.

Eventually, I reached the table where Uncle Gino was sitting with his family. He had hairs growing profusely from his ears and wispy white hairs on his thick-set neck. His collar was open wide, his tie loosened.

'John, good to see you. I want to talk,' he said above the noise.

As if on cue the disc jockey played a slower song.

'I've been talking to your father about the building in Pontypridd.'

'He's mentioned it briefly.'

'We really have to sell the property, you know, John. But your father won't hear of it.'

'Look, this is something you need to discuss with my father.'

'But are you happy to sell the property?'

'Why do you ask?'

'The trust. Your grandfather made a trust and you have to consent too. Everyone else agrees.'

'Except my father.'

Uncle Gino narrowed his eyes into two small, dark balls.

Jeremy Marco moved his chair alongside his father and next to me. He had a nose that was too long and a chin so short his face disappeared into his neck. But he had an ugly attitude that small, ugly men seemed to develop. He was wearing an expensive suit with a pale tie on a shirt with fancy button-down collars. He crossed one foot over onto a knee so that I could admire the spotless cream loafers. No socks of course.

'Jez,' I said, holding out my hand.

By the way he narrowed his eyes I knew he hated me a little bit more for using the nickname he loathed. What sort of name is Jeremy for an Italian boy anyway?

'My father's a reasonable man,' he said, implying that somebody else wasn't – my father, I guessed.

Uncle Gino continued. 'The family want to move on now, John. It's time that there weren't any loose ends from the past.'

My father told it quite differently. Gino was up to his neck in bank loans and personal guarantees he'd given for Jeremy's business and they needed the money from the share of the property. But my father was happy with the income the rent provided and didn't want to sell the café. It was part sentiment, but I knew that it made good sense.

'This is family,' Jez continued. 'Your father owes us.'

'What do you mean?'

'Come on. We all know he got a better deal from Nonno Marco than we did. So now it's our time.'

This was beginning to feel like one more block on

the wall of tension building in my stomach and tightening all over my chest.

'My father's worked fucking hard on his business.'

'We know that,' Gino said, trying to mollify the situation.

'If you're using Nonno Marco's will as moral blackmail to help you out of the shit, then you can fuck right off.'

I felt the mobile beep in my pocket and saw the text from Boyd – *Call me*. I stood up.

'You can't leave now,' Jez said, his eyes narrowing.

'Some of us work for a living.'

I went through to the foyer, but Jez had followed me. I pressed the speed-dial button for Boyd.

Jez was standing beside me, legs astride, hands on hips.

'I told you we weren't finished.'

'And I told you I was working.'

'Know your trouble, John? You're a tall man with a small dick.'

I could hear Boyd's voice, but it was too late.

I drew my head back slowly and closed my eyes.

Chapter 33

Superintendent Cornock had his arms folded so tightly a sumo wrestler would have struggled to loosen them. He'd drawn his lips into a thin line, his eyes hooded and small.

'I've spoken to Jeremy Marco, John.'

I raised a hand to my nose and brushed a finger over the bruise under my eye where I'd collided with Jez's cheek as he tried to avoid my head-butt. I was going to find out if it had really been worthwhile. It certainly felt worthwhile when I saw Jez falling to the floor, grabbing his face, blood pouring from his nose.

'This could be serious,' Cornock continued.

He unfolded his arms, fiddled with his tie, and pumped the top of a ballpoint pen with his right hand.

'It was a heated atmosphere, sir.'

Cornock raised his eyebrows and kept them high.

'I was very stressed.'

Eyebrows still halfway up his forehead.

'Well. I'd say you're lucky. Jeremy doesn't want to press charges. I spoke at length with Mr Gino Marco and they understand how much pressure you've been under. So I think we can draw a line under this unpleasantness from last night.'

I let out a long, shallow breath.

'Having said that, John ...'

A bead of sweat dripped down my arm.

'I think we need to be clear that this is not the sort of behaviour we expect from serving police officers.'

His tone was getting more serious as he continued the reprimand.

'If the press were to hear about this then it could get very messy. I want you tell me, John, if you'd been drinking.'

I sat up and straightened in the chair. My throat felt dry.

'Not a drop, sir.'

Cornock nodded.

'I'm dry, sir. You can depend on that.'

'I hope so. I've gone out of my way to support you. I need you to be responsible. And there are others who won't be so generous.'

'Thank you, sir.'

'We need results here, John. This case is so high profile with all the press interest you cannot afford to have any problems.'

Cornock leant forward over the desk.

'We've got the Chief Constable and the Assistant Chief Constable, all taking an interest and then Janet Helm lurking in the background ready to take advantage of any opportunity for self promotion. God help us if she ever gets into power. So, having you head-butt a relative in a hotel is not what we need.'

I nodded in agreement. 'I need to interview Frankie Prince again.'

Cornock stared at me briefly. 'For Christ's sake, John.'

'We've got a photograph,' I said. 'We can link him to the death of Maria.'

When we were finished I stood outside the door of his office for a moment, relieved that I was still a police officer. Through the closed door I heard him ask for the Chief Constable.

Boyd strutted into my office wearing the look of a man satisfied with his sex-life and sat down.

'I heard about last night,' he began. He tilted his

head to one side and looked at my face. 'What happened?'

'Cousin Jez,' I said slowly, wafting a hand in the air as though the name itself explained everything.

'What did the Super want?'

'Words of wisdom and an update.'

'Is there anything happening about …?' Now Boyd held his hand up and pointed loosely at my face.

'No. Families, eh. We stick together in the end.'

Boyd gave me a puzzled look and settled back into the chair.

'We need to talk to Frankie Prince,' I said. 'And Lech.'

Boyd raised his eyebrows when he heard Frankie's name.

'Does the Super know?'

'Sure thing.'

'We went all over Cardiff looking for Anna and Dagmara and Kamil last night. I even had a couple of the uniform lads scan through the CCTV from Cardiff airport. But nothing yet.'

'Maybe Kamil left through Bristol airport or Birmingham or any of the other airports that have cheap flights to Warsaw.

'I've got the tapes from Bristol arriving later. I've got a DC on standby to look through them.'

I knew we didn't have time to look at the CCTV coverage from every airport with flights to Poland. Maybe we should try the police in Poland, I thought or perhaps my friend the colonel. I found his card and called the number in London.

A voice said something in Polish and then I asked for the colonel.

'And who is calling?'

'Detective Inspector Marco. The colonel is expecting

my call.'

'One moment, please.'

A couple of seconds passed before I heard the colonel's voice.

'Good morning,' he said without introduction. 'How are the cases going?'

I got straight to the point. 'Can you tell me anything more about Lech Balinski?'

The colonel paused.

'And have you heard of Kamil Holter? You must have done – you seem to know everyone from Warsaw involved in this case.'

'It bad idea to go after Lech. You speak to Under-Inspector Jorge Puławska of the Criminal Police Division in Warsaw.'

I scribbled down the number he read out.

'Please inform me when investigation is complete.'

'Colonel, I—' But the line was dead.

I wondered if Jorge Puławska spoke English. I slumped back in the chair, my mind wondering whether I could find Dagmara in time. I looked over at Boyd and, as if he was reading my mind, he told me about her.

'I called at Howick Street this morning. Dagmara's bed-sit has been trashed—'

'But last night?'

'I know, but since then someone took the place apart.'

My lips were drying; a dark realisation that I might never see her again started to prey on my mind. I thought about her room and the warmth of her skin and her breathing as I slipped out of her bed. Then I heard Boyd's voice.

'Then I called at that place where she works, but no luck. She can work from home and goes out to visit clients and stuff like that.'

'Joe, Phil,' I shouted and seconds later they both stood at the door. 'I want you two to find Dagmara and Anna and Kamil. Arrest them and bring them in.'

'Arrest them for what?' Lawson said.

I stared at the three of them standing in the doorway. 'Make it up as you go along,' I started, struggling for something to say. 'That Kamil bastard has been lying, so it's obstruction and Dagmara, well, for her own safety.'

'Where are you going, boss?'

'To see a man about a photograph.'

Jim White beckoned Boyd and me to sit down on one of the settees in the main bar area of the Four Seasons. He was wearing a grey suit with a white shirt and a narrow dark-blue tie full of creases. His shoes had a large plastic buckle over the top and thick soles, the sort old men wear for stability.

'I'm afraid Mr Prince isn't available today,' he said, running a finger around his collar.

'Where is he?'

He blinked a couple of times, too quickly.

'Mr Prince is away on business. And cannot be contacted.'

'Where exactly is he away on business?' I asked.

'Away.' Jim White was getting accustomed to lying.

'Do you know Lech Balinski?'

White did his best to keep eye contact but he still had to blink – working for Frankie Prince was making him an expert liar.

'Mr Prince knows him, of course.'

'Have you met him?'

'Once. Maybe a couple of times.' He turned one

hand through the other.

'Is Lech here in Cardiff?'

White shrugged. 'Sorry, can't help.' It was probably the first truthful answer.

We left the Four Seasons without having been offered a coffee or Danish or anything except the lies from Jim White. By the time we got to the car Boyd was eating an apple he'd found in his jacket pocket.

'What a toe-rag,' I said, fumbling for the keys after lighting my third of the day.

'Useless at lying wasn't he, boss?'

'Something's wrong. Where the hell is Frankie Prince? Everybody has fucking disappeared.'

'Maybe he's on his yacht?' Boyd said casually.

'Fancy a trip to the marina?'

I tossed the burning remains of the cigarette out of the window and headed down towards the yacht club. It was mid-morning and quiet. In the distance I could see the houses of Penarth peering down over the Bay and grey clouds were turning black at the edges.

It took us a few minutes and some raised voices to get the name and location of Frankie's yacht from the marina office. We walked over the pontoons, passing a motor boat with an inflatable hanging from the rear, just as my telephone rang.

'Mam,' I said, knowing a call from my mother was overdue.

'Your father's very upset,' she said, which meant he was seething. 'And your Uncle Gino's been on the telephone. Your father won't talk to him.'

'Look. I'm sorry.'

'And what do you think Dean made of all of this?'

I slowed my pace and let Boyd walk ahead.

'He needs a better example than this, John. Trish

looked after him last night. It was supposed to be your chance to be with him.'

I hadn't heard my mother like this before so I stopped. Boyd gave me a backward glance and I waved for him to carry on.

'I'll get him to stay. Once all this is finished.'

For the first time I heard exasperation in my mother's voice. 'We'll see.'

I noticed the pontoon swaying under my feet, the sound of water lapping underneath. Shrouds clattered against masts and an outboard fired up in the distance.

Eventually I caught up with Boyd and we found Frankie Prince's yacht. I knelt down and peered through one of the cabin windows at bottles of champagne and cans of beer standing on top of a table.

'Nobody here,' Boyd said.

'Let's get in,' I said.

'Don't be crazy, sir. You haven't got any reason to break in to the yacht. They'd throw the book at you.'

I wanted so badly to tear the cover off the boat, but Boyd was right. I'd get a warrant and do it properly. Until then we had two more places to visit in our search for Frankie Prince.

The art gallery his wife ran was the last place I'd expect to find him. There was a large sign hanging on the wall above the window with the word UN printed in large gold letters.

'It's Welsh for one,' Boyd explained, reminding me of long forgotten Welsh lessons.

'Is there going to be a two or three?'

'Looks closed,' Boyd continued, as we pushed open the door.

The first couple of exposed floorboards squeaked

noisily. A tall girl training to be a stick insect stood up from behind a desk. Her smile was tentative; she must have realised our bank balances wouldn't stretch to buying art.

'Good afternoon,' she said, her vowels rounded, her accent crisp and clean.

I flashed my warrant card. 'Is Mrs Prince here?'

'No, but she's expected back very shortly.'

'Mind if we look around?'

Boyd was already admiring a painting of a man crouching with his head in his hands, in what looked like a ruin in ancient Greece. Beside it were two others, both similar. Then on another wall was a canvas that was a mass of different colours with brushstrokes in no apparent order. I tilted my head first one way then another.

'Looks like a load of bollocks to me,' I said.

Boyd stepped back – forcing an intelligent looking frown. 'Modern art does take time to appreciate fully.'

The gallery was a long building divided into different areas, all hung with various canvasses. A small turtle sat on top of a pillar of roughly sawn timber.

'It's to represent the importance of time.' The tall girl stood beside me now.

'Of course,' I said, turning to look at the door on the opposite wall.

'What's through there?'

'Offices and the marketing suite.'

I walked over and pressed the handle.

'Shouldn't you have a warrant or something?' the girl said.

I ignored her and walked through into a small hallway that led to a flight of shallow stairs that I climbed two at a time. At the top there was a large room laid out with wine glasses and cartons of soft drinks. I walked around the room and glanced at the photographs of various celebrities, mouths stretched into cheesy grins for the camera. Photographs of various rugby players, government ministers and a couple of the Welsh millionaires, whose pictures had been in the *Sunday Times* rich list, covered one wall. I stopped by one photograph. A group of people were being served drinks by an attractive girl in a white uniform. Even I could recognise Maria.

I thought she must be staff. Then, I thought, there must be a staff room.

'When's the party?' I said to the girl who'd followed us upstairs, her face covered with a frown.

'You should be waiting downstairs.'

I ignored her and walked over to the door at the far end, guessing there were stairs to the second floor and hoping that Boyd would keep her talking. At the top there was a kitchen; it was neat and tidy – the air smelt faintly of bleach. There were two more rooms, both used as offices, and a desk with a computer in one of them. In the final room there were staff lockers, some open with various uniforms and clothes hanging inside. My mind raced and my pulse thumped in my neck. I didn't have warrant and any evidence would be inadmissible but I had a killer to find. I hoped that Boyd could keep her occupied downstairs.

I worked quickly through the first lockers, being careful not to disturb anything that might suggest I'd been rifling through the possessions. Three more were locked and I tried forcing the lock with my credit card without success. I looked around for something to prise the door from the lock.

'Are you all right? Mrs Prince should be here any minute,' the girl shouted up the stairs, before I heard Boyd asking her something about the latest exhibition.

'In the toilet,' I shouted back.

I opened every drawer and cupboard in the kitchen, looking for a knife or a spoon I could use to force open the doors, without thinking about the noise it might make. Then I walked as softly as I could into the office and opened the drawers in the desk.

My pulse was racing now and I was running short of time.

The first two drawers were full of pencils and felt pens. I found a letter opener in the second, but its metal was soft and it would fold in half under pressure. It was in the bottom drawer that I found the keys and relief surged through my body as I opened the three lockers in turn. On the inner face of the second door was a little notice on which was written 'Maria and Leon'. At the bottom, tucked neatly under a pile of clothes, I found a small digital camera which I picked up and slipped into my jacket pocket.

Hidden where no one would think of looking.

I heard a new voice downstairs. I didn't bother with the third locker and I quickly retraced my steps, before flushing the toilet.

As I was standing on the top step I could hear Boyd saying something about, *Inspector Marco not being well* and *having a touch of food poisoning*.

I made as much noise as I could walking down the stairs and when I entered the first floor Lucy Prince stood next to Boyd.

'What the hell is going on?'

'Detective Inspector Marco,' I said, holding out a hand.

'Do you have a warrant?'

'I'm sorry. I had to use the toilet. Bit of an emergency really. I think I ate something at lunch that didn't agree with me.'

Lucy Prince was wearing an expensive suit that

flattered her figure and high heels – not too high, just enough to make her legs look sensational. Her hair was immaculate and the perfume was delicate and hung in the air.

'And what do you want?' She didn't conceal the hard edge to her voice.

'We were hoping you could help us find your husband.'

She moved her weight from one leg to another – there wasn't a lot of weight to move and she had hard, determined eyes: obviously a woman accustomed to having her own way.

'Why do you want to speak to him?'

'Routine.'

Boyd added, 'It's part of the investigation into the murder of one of his employees.'

'He'll be at the club. Where he always is. Working.'

'He's not there.'

I caught a hint of uncertainty in her eyes.

'And we've tried the yacht – just on the off chance.'

Now I had my hands on my hips and waited.

'Then he must be on business somewhere. Jim will know where Frankie will be.'

I nodded. 'I understand Frankie will be here later for the reception. What time does it start?'

Boyd started the car and drove back towards Queen Street, but there was something nagging at the back of my mind. I stared out of the window, not saying anything. There were youngsters milling around shop doorways and the lights of an Aston Martin dealership shone brightly. My mobile buzzed and after reading the message I felt the first glimmer that I might get ahead of Frankie Prince and Lech Balinski.

'We need to make a detour,' I said.

'Where to?' Boyd asked without emotion; he was getting accustomed to unexplained actions.

'Grangetown.'

'Anywhere in particular?'

I rested my head against the restraint and shut my eyes. 'The priest wants to see us.'

I didn't sleep, despite the burning sensation behind my eyes. The car jolted at traffic lights and I heard the sound of an ambulance in the distance. Fifteen minutes must have passed before Boyd slowed the car to a halt and parked outside the imposing doors of the church.

After a couple of rings, an anxious-looking woman in her fifties opened the presbytery door.

'Father Podolak wants to see us.'

She didn't say anything or move her head. I heard a raised voice behind her. 'Come in. Come in.'

She eased open the door and Boyd and I walked in and over towards the staircase. Podolak stood on the half-landing and we exchanged greetings.

'What do you want?' I said, following him up the narrow flight of stairs to the first floor.

'Pietrek,' he said, once we were in the study where we had sat at our first meeting.

'Can I speak with him?'

Boyd turned sharply and stared at me.

The priest hesitated for a moment. 'How did you ...?'

'Police work,' I replied.

'You are right of course. He is here. Pietrek is very afraid for his life. He has seen much bad things.' He stood up and left the room, returning after a couple of minutes, Pietrek behind him.

His head was covered with the bristles of a few days' growth and he had large hands with long fingers. He spoke slowly at first.

'Father Podolak say I talk to you.' His coarse accent was heavy on my ears after the fluent tone of Podolak's. He looked at the father for reassurance.

'What can you tell us?' I said, as Boyd reached for his notepad.

'Night of Michal's murder I heard them talking.'

'Who?'

'Frankie Prince and Lech. They talk much. They shout and swear and …'

'Argue?'

'Yes. Much. They say that Michal and Leon have to be dead.'

Another ten minutes passed as Boyd scribbled down the details of the conversation Pietrek had heard. Lech had been telling Frankie how Michal had screamed out when his tongue had been cut out. Then Pietrek stopped and drew breath before clasping and unclasping his fingers.

'And I see them take Gerek.'

I moved forward in my chair. An overheard conversation wasn't evidence. We needed an eyewitness account.

'I meet Gerek one night. He no turn up. I go to Polish club and he no there. So I go to flat where he have girlfriend and then outside there was big car with fat men.' He spread out his arms in an exaggerated gesture. 'And then Lech come out with Gerek.' Pietrek looked away, paused, but his voice was breaking when he continued. 'I watch them kick him down onto ground and then they take him to empty factory in docks.'

'How do you know?'

'I follow him and see them.'

'Gerek much afraid.'

'Why didn't you call the police then?' I said.

He put his head into his hands and began crying softly.

Father Podolak answered for him. 'He is very afraid for his life and he blame himself for Gerek's death.'

I nodded. Boyd had stopped making notes.

'Can you show us the factory?'

Pietrek nodded.

By late in the evening sitting in the car had caused a cramp in my buttock to become a dull ache that had spread throughout my lower back. We watched the factory building as we waited for the Armed Response Unit to arrive, but nothing moved and the place was dark and lifeless.

The Scientific Support Vehicle was parked out of sight, waiting for us to clear the building. Boyd sat next to me chewing his lip. I could just make out the car driven by Woods parked in the shadows, waiting for the signal.

Once the ARU team arrived, things moved quickly. An enormous pair of pliers prised open the chain securing the door and we poured into the building. It took us an hour to find the room in the basement where the floor was tinted red and there had been signs of activity.

I left the CSIs to their work and stood outside in the cold of the autumn evening, smoking. Boyd shivered by my side.

'I want to start smoking on nights like this,' he said.

'It'll bugger up your sperm, probably.'

I threw the last of the cigarette onto the gravel by my feet and went home.

Chapter 34

I was back in the office before breakfast the following morning, already having spoken to Alvine Dix, who sounded fresh and alert even after a night working in the factory. Boyd was carrying one of those tall coffee mugs that I was convinced had more froth than coffee and he sat down in the plastic chair in my room.

'CSIs turn anything up?' he asked.

'Lots of blood and skin.'

He seemed to lose interest in his coffee.

'And I guess Frankie didn't show up last night?'

'Inspired guess,' I said. 'At least the uniformed lads we sent there enjoyed the canapés.'

I'd placed the camera in the middle of the desk. I sat back, wondering what we could do as Boyd cleared his throat.

'You'll never be able to use it.'

I didn't say anything.

'It's inadmissible and you've broken the law obtaining it.'

Boyd was right, of course.

There were images of middle-aged men at a party, enjoying themselves with girls as young as fifteen, maybe younger, unaware that they'd been photographed. I recognised Frankie Prince, who was shaking hands and featuring in most of the shots. I'd find out the names of the others soon enough but I did recognise one face immediately and I wondered what Mrs Bates would make of her Wing Commander husband attending private parties without her.

'This is why Maria was killed,' I said. 'She must have been using these photographs to blackmail Frankie for her family's freedom.'

Boyd nodded slowly without saying anything. There wasn't much either of us could say.

'Where has Frankie gone?' Boyd said.

'Lucy wasn't expecting Frankie to be away from the club and White was scared. Have you heard from the lads outside his house?'

Unmarked police cars had been sitting outside the detached house where Frankie lived. Uniform officers were visiting all the properties owned by Frankie, so it was only going to be a matter of time until we caught up with him.

Boyd shook his head. 'Nothing. Yet.'

There was noise from the Incident Room as Woods and Lawson appeared in the doorway of my room.

'We found Anna, boss,' Joe said, leaning against the door, sweat patches evident under his arms. 'Tracked her down to a flat in Whitchurch eventually. The place was stinking.'

'Really?'

'Dope and dirty clothes everywhere – all over the floor and every surface you could think of. There were more scarves than a charity shop.'

'So has she seen Dagmara?'

'Nope. Apparently Helm wants Dagmara to take part in a press conference.'

'For fuck's sake. What are these politicians going to do next?'

Woods cleared his throat, 'There was call earlier, sir, from Bristol airport. Kamil was on a flight to Poland yesterday.'

I didn't have time to respond before the telephone rang on my desk.

'Someone foreign for you,' the receptionist said.

'DI Marco.'

'John, it's me,' Dagmara said, as my pulse

quickened. 'I need to see you urgently.'

'Where are you?'

'Warsaw.'

I had a couple of hours to spare but I sped down the motorway to Bristol airport, just in case. After checking-in I walked around the concourse, bought a bacon sandwich and coffee and sat down, waiting for the flight.

Three hours later the plane was approaching Warsaw, but my neck was stiff after I'd slept in awkward position. Below us the flat industrial city sprawled out for miles without a hill or river in sight. I'd expected an old building, built in the Soviet era, but the terminal was a modern glass and steel construction with a vast expanse of roof. Rain drilled its way past the window of the plane and we landed with a thud and taxied.

I read Dagmara's instructions and I found the taxi rank without difficulty. A driver with a cigarette hanging from his lips nodded when I showed him the address.

'English?' he said, as he pulled onto the motorway and accelerated towards the city.

'Cardiff. In Wales.'

'Lots of Polish people in England,' he said. 'Money is better in England. Money shit in Poland.'

The driver had a cough that came from deep inside his chest.

'You come on business?' he said, once he'd stopped coughing.

I fumbled through my jacket for the cigarettes. I'd had one before arriving at Bristol airport and my second was overdue.

'I'm only staying a day.'

'I show you place for good time.' He looked in the mirror for my reaction. 'I take you there any time.'

'Sure thing,' I said, without conviction.

We passed rows of tall buildings, some with window boxes and others with towers, and bays hanging from their fronts. The tram cables strung over every street crackled and sparked when the trams passed. And my driver kept up a commentary on the city of Warsaw, telling me about the Old Town and the palaces and the heroes of the Second World War. But I was tired and hungry and I needed a shower.

We pulled up outside a large, old building and he pointed at the door. As I paid him he pressed a card into my hand, reminding me that he could take me to the best night clubs.

After pushing open the heavy door I saw a lift at the end of the hall. I'd memorised the instructions and found the right apartment at the end of the landing, panelled with dark, old wood. I couldn't place the smell until I remembered the odour of cabbage and sausage in Howick Street.

Dagmara opened the door before the bell had finished its chiming. She threw her hands around my neck and kissed me.

'Thank God you come.'

Suddenly she moved away from me, walked over to the window, and drew back the curtain slightly.

'Were you followed?' she asked, before moving to an old wooden-framed sofa and sitting down.

'What do you mean, Dagmara? What's this all about?'

She paused and leant forward in the chair, her hands clasped together tightly. 'I am frightened, John,' she said simply.

'You need to tell me what's happening.'

'We need to go and see someone who can help.'

We waited for the evening to draw in. I had a shower, she made coffee, and then I smoked without counting. She spoke about her life in Warsaw before she moved to Cardiff and the regulations and restrictions in Poland that made life in Wales easier. She explained about her schooling and how she'd gone to university to learn English. Her family lived in the city and when I suggested I meet them she gave me a kindly smile. We drank more coffee and ate stale sandwiches she'd kept in the refrigerator. Eventually we left from a rear entrance and drew our coats up against the rain that sheeted down. We hurried through the street towards the middle of town, until Dagmara decided we should catch a tram. We stood at the rear and she kept looking at every passenger that came on board. She dragged me off the first tram just as the doors closed and then boarded a second. After two more changes we found ourselves at the end of the line and the tram stopped in a turning circle.

I followed her as she marched off down a side street. The houses were smaller now and the roads narrower. The rain had abated and we could walk without the rain splashing on our shoes.

Dagmara suddenly stopped and pushed her shoulder against a doorway that led into a small alleyway, which was dark and damp. Water dripped down the wall on one side and she led me through to the rear. Another door led to a flight of stairs; we climbed to the top floor and I stood, catching my breath for a second.

'Down here,' Dagmara said, pointing down the landing.

Our footsteps echoed over the uncarpeted floorboards. She knocked gently on one of the doors and we heard movement from inside. The door opened against a chain, Dagmara whispered something in Polish and then the door closed as we heard the chain fall away.

Inside the floorboards were dark and creaked with every step we took. The air was heavy with cigarette smoke and we followed a man, no more than thirty, maybe less, into the main room of the flat. He had golden-coloured stubble, not thick – just wispy and unkempt – and deep sunken eyes that stared really hard.

'This is Tomas,' Dagmara said.

Tomas nodded. I nodded back; he seemed familiar.

Dagmara said something in Polish. Tomas replied, followed by a knock on the door. He turned his head and made a movement with his hand towards his jacket pocket.

'It's them,' Dagmara said. She opened the door and Michal's parents came into the flat. They sat down on the old sofa with flattened cushions and Mrs Dąbek let out a long exhausted sigh.

'My wife sick,' Antoniusz Dąbek said.

'I am dying,' his wife said slowly. Then she coughed and I watched her body heaving in pain. 'The cancer is all in my body.'

'Where is Markus?' Antoniusz said.

'He should be here by now,' Dagmara replied.

'I not stay long. My wife …'

Dagmara found her mobile and typed out a text. Tomas moved to the window and drew back the heavy curtain.

'He's good at replying to texts,' she said, looking at me for reassurance.

It was time I knew who we were waiting for. 'And who exactly is Markus?'

'Markus has been helping Antoniusz,' Dagmara said, looking over at Michal's father.

'I have nothing left. You must understand this Mr Marco,' Antoniusz said. 'Michal is gone and my wife, she ...' He tightened his jaw. 'Lech Balinski must ...' He drew a finger slowly across his neck, the hatred burning in his eyes.

Dagmara said something to him in Polish and he relaxed and sat back in the chair.

'Antoniusz has lost Michal and now his wife will be dead from cancer very soon. He has nothing to live for. When he talked to Markus about Michal he learnt about Lech Balinski. Markus is journalist who has been making research about this man. How the Mafia works in Poland and about the girls that they take to England. Antoniusz asks Markus for help. Michal had much money in his bank account and was moving money to Lech here in Warsaw.'

'Lech bad man,' Antoniusz said, his voice thick and rough. His skin was a dark-grey colour and the bags underneath his narrow eyes were tinged black. He had the look of a man out for revenge.

'Antoniusz has given Markus everything he knows about Lech. And when Michal was home one time he gave Markus some paper with a code on it with numbers and letters. Markus knows what the code is about.

'A code?'

I wanted to believe that this was the piece of the jigsaw I needed to complete the case. It had brought me halfway across Europe, into a flat in the suburbs of Warsaw with frightened Poles, so it had to mean something.

'Markus can tell you when he arrives,' Dagmara said.

Tomas hadn't moved since Antoniusz had arrived. He leant against a wall near the window, his eyes scanning the room. He'd pulled back the curtains a couple of times and peered out. Dagmara would look over and he'd shake his head slowly.

Antoniusz sat up and tried more faltering English until he gave up and Dagmara translated.

'He is proud man who was proud of his son for being in the army and for going to university. They had sacrificed a lot for Michal. They didn't want him to go to England and work for Lech.'

'Work for Lech?' I said. The shock was evident in my voice.

Antoniusz nodded.

'What was he doing? I mean how did he know? When did this start?'

Dagmara glanced at her watch and then at Tomas who shook his head again, more slowly this time.

'He was working for Lech in Cardiff ... how you say? Watching over Frankie Prince.'

'What, he was Lech's grass?' I said, with incredulity in my voice.

'Grass?' Dagmara asked.

'Informer. Working for someone else.'

Antoniusz nodded his head.

'Why was he doing that?' I said.

'It was good money.' Dagmara paused. 'Lech had much friends in Russian Mafia and they gave him money for him to give to Frankie Prince in Cardiff. Money from Frankie's clubs and girls and drugs go back to Poland. If Frankie did not pay Lech, then Lech did not pay Russians, and bad things happen to Lech.'

I imagined Lech's hands holding a pair of garden secateurs or pliers or scissors or whatever else he used to cut tongues out. I reckoned he could look after himself.

'I know it was stupid John, but Michal wanted to start business back in Poland in computers. It takes so much money to start and he had nothing, so ...'

'So he gets himself killed. What happened?'

'He became friends with Leon and then Maria and soon he wanted not to be involved with Lech and Frankie. He wanted to be free of them and what they were doing. He saw what they were doing to Maria and the other girls and their families. He knew all about Frankie's business and all the money.'

Michal would never have been free of Lech or Frankie Prince. Once he was in with them there was no way out. But it was too late for Michal and for his mother. His father hadn't moved in the chair and kept staring at me through dark lifeless eyes.

'Why didn't you tell me about this sooner?' I said, realising that Dagmara knew everything.

'We wanted to be certain ...'

'Certain? About how many people have been killed? You must be mad. Does Anna know all of this? Has she got something to do with it?' I could feel the anger building.

She bowed her head and stared at the floor for a moment. 'Michal was clever with computers and he knew about everything Frankie Prince was doing and about the club. He made a record of everything about the money. But Frankie found out and ...'

'It got him killed?'

Dagmara nodded.

'And where is the computer?' I asked, remembering the trashed flats, the hotel lockers and the left luggage storage at Cardiff railway station.

She shrugged and looked at Tomas. But he was looking out of the window.

'It's the computer that got him killed and Leon killed and Maria. Must be,' I said. It was a statement, not a question.

'He late.' It was the first thing Tomas had said.

Immediately Dagmara got up and paced around the

room.

'This is bad. He promised to be here. It was a time suggested by him we meet.'

Antoniusz sat impassively with his wife, who coughed again, bending her whole body forward.

'We go now,' Dagmara said. 'I speak to Markus and we see him tomorrow.'

We left Antoniusz and his wife and Tomas in the flat and retraced our steps to the tram stop. The rain had stopped but it was colder, and water was still lying in puddles on the pavement. A couple of cars passed, their radios blaring. On the journey through the city Dagmara stabbed out various texts on her mobile and then stared at the screen waiting for replies.

We stepped out of the final tram and as we walked to her flat she spoke for the first time since we left Antoniusz.

'I'm not happy, John. Markus should have replied and I text many other people about him – and nothing.'

'Where does he live?'

'Other side of town,' she said, without conviction.

The hallway of her apartment building was still dark and dismal when we pushed open the door and she hurried to the stairs. Inside the flat she made coffee and pulled some pastries from the fridge. She sat down heavily next to me on the sofa, cupping a mug of coffee. I wanted to pull her close and feel her next to me, but her mind was far away.

'Who is Tomas?' I said.

'A friend.'

'Why was he there?'

'He was in Special Forces of Poland with Michal and Leon.'

'Of course. That's why he was familiar. He was in

the photograph, the one in Michal's possessions. 'So what does he know?'

'I am frightened, John.'

She put the mug down on the table and put her hand on my leg. I could feel the warmth of her body and I put my hand on hers and pulled her close to me. She kissed me on the cheek, but she lingered. I could feel her breath on my skin and I could see the colour of her eyes. I ran my hand over her shoulder and down over her breast. She moved her lips close to mine and then I kissed her gently and I could feel her body relax as she kissed me back. I fumbled with her blouse as she pressed her hand against my trousers and then undid my belt.

We left the coffee unfinished and the pastries untouched.

Chapter 35

I woke with a start in a large bed under a heavy duvet. I reached out over the white sheet but the bed was empty. Then I heard the banging and realised that someone was at the door. It was still dark and I reached for my mobile – it was almost seven and I noticed the three unread messages. I dragged on my shirt and by the time I was at the front door the banging had turned to loud voices, saying something in Polish.

I opened the door and the colonel pushed past me. 'What you do in Warsaw?' he began, as another man in uniform walked in behind him. 'And where is Dagmara Sobczak?'

'She's not here,' I said.

'This is Under-Inspector Jorge Puławska. I told you to speak to him but instead you come here. This is very stupid.'

The under-inspector crossed his arms and gave me a defiant look.

'I had an urgent call from Dagmara,' I said.

The colonel walked around the room.

'What was urgent?'

The coffee mugs from the night before were still on the table and the pastries had dried even more overnight. I picked up the plates and took them through to the kitchen, buying time so that I could think clearly.

'I need to have some coffee,' I said.

I rubbed my face with both hands, chasing away the sleep and then I filled the coffee pot.

'Dagmara wanted to see me,' I said. 'Did you know that Michal Dąbek was working for Lech?'

I watched for the reaction, but neither man blinked. Not a quiver. So they knew and now I had the upper hand. I continued. 'What else should I know?'

'These are dangerous people and we have much work to do,' the colonel said.

'And I've got four murders back in Cardiff. Withholding evidence is a serious matter.'

'We have an ongoing investigation into Lech Balinski and his connections to the Russian Mafia,' Puławska said, an American twang to his accent. 'There are lot of different agencies involved. We liaise with your Serious Fraud Office in London. And we have our own sources of information.'

'Sources of information. That sounds grand,' I said. 'You mean informants.'

He nodded slowly.

'You need to go home this afternoon and not interfere any more.'

A strong smell of coffee filled the kitchen.

The colonel added, 'We send car for you later to take you to airport.'

Once both men had left I knew I had messages to pick up, but I needed a shower first. The bathroom was cold, and goose pimples raced over my body as I waited for the water to heat up. Afterwards I sat, drinking more coffee, before calling Dagmara, but the messaging service clicked in on the first ring.

I checked my voicemail and listened to a message from Boyd telling me to call Cornock and two messages from the Superintendent himself. I glanced at the time and, realising that Boyd would still be at home, I dialled his number.

After a couple of seconds I heard the muffled voice on the end of the line.

'Boyd,' I said.

'What's the time?' He sounded half-asleep and I could hear another voice in the background.

'Early. What did you want?'

'Cornock's after you. Superintendent Cornock I mean, and he's not pleased. I heard that Banks had been to see him again. When are you coming back?'

'Looks like later today. I've just had a visit from the colonel.'

'You need to call Superintendent Cornock,' he reminded me, before I finished the call.

Cracks of daylight appeared around the edges of the thick curtains hanging at the windows and I wondered where Dagmara might be. I thought about the warmth of her body and curve of her hips and the smoothness of her back. And then my mobile rang and I saw her number.

'Where are you?' I said. 'I've had a visit from a security services colonel who saw me in Cardiff and an under-inspector of police.'

'Who was the policeman?'

'Jorge something or other.'

She described Jorge to me. 'That's him,' I said. 'They're going to send a car for me this afternoon. Told me not to interfere.'

'I speak to my friend Markus. He was sorry about last night. He see us later this morning. I will collect you later and we go there.'

Before I could say anything else the line went dead. I paced around the flat, thinking about Frankie and Lech and Jorge's comments about the *Russian Mafia.* Frankie had acquired the house in the Vale, the health club, the tenanted properties and the art gallery very quickly. *Dangerous people* Puławska had said and I knew that Michal had lost his life meddling with them. Standing in the cold flat in the back streets of Warsaw I realised Markus was my best hope of securing the evidence to prosecute Lech and Frankie.

Cornock's answer machine clicked on when I called his number. I left a message telling him I was making progress and that I'd be back on the afternoon flight. I sent Trish a text and as I sent it I heard a key in the door. Dagmara walked in.

She kissed me on the lips.

'You left early this morning,' I said.

'I had to speak to Markus. He can see us later.'

She kicked off her shoes and slumped onto the sofa. She looked older, somehow, than when we first met.

'The colonel knew about Michal working for Lech.'

'Yes, I know.'

'You knew as well.'

'Don't sound surprised, John. Michal told me a lot of things. He didn't want to work for Lech in the end. He found out what Lech and Frankie were doing.'

'He must have known what they did before he started.'

'Michal was young and he wanted to make money to start computer business. Once he became friends with Leon and Maria things changed.'

'I need to know where this is going, Dagmara,' I said. 'What is Markus going to be able to tell me? I need evidence.

'He says he knows what the code from Michal means.

I realised that I hadn't started my daily fix, so I found my cigarettes and lit up. 'Has he got Michal's computer?'

She looked away.

'Dagmara?'

'He says he know where it could be. And ...'

'What?'

'There is much Markus believes will help you with

the case.'

'What has he told you?'

Her mobile buzzed and her face turned an icy colour as she stood up.

'There is something wrong. I go to see Markus on my own – you come when I call you.' She scribbled the address on a piece of paper.

'It's not safe, Dagmara. I'll come with you.'

'It is better I go alone.'

I wanted to grab her, hold on to her but she was out of the door before I could protest. The flat was empty without her and I felt a small part of my world leave with her. After half an hour of glancing at my watch I decided that I couldn't wait.

I scurried around the corner outside the block of flats and found a taxi. I told the driver I was late and he raced the car through the streets to the address I'd given him. We pulled up outside another dismal, grey building with rusting windows.

In the main hall were banks of letterboxes with names and numbers printed on them, all a dirty yellow colour, battered from years of use. I could hear the sounds of families arguing, children running in confined areas and the smell of more cabbage and onions and sausages.

The flat was at the far end of the landing. A single bare light was suspended from the ceiling and it cast a weak shadow along the corridor. I reached the door of Markus's flat and hesitated. It was ajar. I pushed it tentatively before going in.

A small chest of drawers was pushed against a wall and there was a coat stand heavy with various jackets and scarves. I strode quietly on tiptoe past the first door, my heart beating a little faster. The final door needed only a gentle push for it to open on soft hinges and I stepped in. I needn't have bothered being quiet because the dead body sitting upright on the chair wouldn't have minded.

There was mass of bruising all over his face. His neck was speckled red where the life had been squeezed from his body. I stepped over towards the chair.

I heard a noise behind me. Before I could see who it was I saw a shape coming through the air and then I felt a dull thud and a flash of pain.

Chapter 36

I knew I was alive because my head was pounding and my shoulders were stiff with pain. I was staring at a dirt floor when I woke up, and when I tried to free my hands I realised they were tied to the chair. There was a small light hanging in the centre of the room and I could hear voices in one corner.

I squinted and saw Lech leaning against a table, the top caving slightly under his weight. He still had the same wide-lapelled suit but now he smiled at me. It was when Kamil stepped out of the shadows and pulled up a chair that I really wasn't sure if I was alive.

'I think you friends,' Lech said. There was an edge like finely sharpened steel to his voice.

Kamil had shaved his head, had three days' stubble and a determined look in his eyes that I hadn't seen before. I could feel my anger rising and I screamed at him, but making myself heard through duct tape was hard. I even gave the chair a pathetic attempt at pulling my arms free.

'I like to protect my investment,' Lech said. 'And you make life hard. I have much money invested in Frankie. And it is important he make payback.'

Kamil laughed and turned his head towards the door. Another man came to stand alongside Lech. He had a large baseball bat in his hand that had ominous red streaks down its side.

Now I regretted coming to Warsaw.

'Michal was to be useful. But then Kamil keep check on him. When Michal decided that he no longer wanted to work for me and he went over ... how you say? ... To the dark side.' He laughed at his own joke, displaying an array of yellow teeth. Kamil laughed along and baseball-bat man just stood impassively.

'Michal had to die.' It sounded matter-of-fact, routine. 'And of course, Leon. Frankie tell me about Leon and Maria wanting money.'

Then I thought of Dagmara and my eyes opened wide. I tugged at the chair again and it scuffled along the floor. The baseball-bat man tapped the bat in his hand and tried to smile.

'I suppose you are worried about your little Polish whore,' Lech added. 'For now she is safe for sure. But we will find her. There is nothing you can do Mr Policeman from England. There will be an investigation. Some of the police here will go looking for you but in the end, nothing. Nobody will remember you in few months' time.'

The sweat was running down my arms and I wanted to piss really badly, but I wasn't going to let them see me go to pieces. My breathing was heavy and I wanted to throw myself at Kamil and beat the shit out of him.

'I hope that you enjoy your stay in Poland, Mr Marco,' Lech said, as he stood up, straightened his lapels and then spoke to Kamil, who looked me straight in the eye before they both left.

Baseball-bat man took off his jacket and folded it slowly before placing it on the table that Lech had leant on. He looked at me and another smile nudged his mouth. He had small hands that he ran along the baseball bat like a masseur on the back of a client. He put the baseball bat down on the table and came over to me. He loosened his tie. Bad sign.

Then he kicked the chair from beneath me and I crashed to the floor. He gave a laugh that sounded like a squeak and then he pushed me around the floor. He kicked the chair and I moved a few centimetres and then he pushed my legs and the chair came with me. He drew his foot back and landed a blow on my right thigh. I cringed in pain. I wanted to scream. I thought I'd puke but I'd be a dead man if I did.

He was smiling more broadly now. I felt like a helpless animal in a cage. I thought of Dagmara and then about Trish. I didn't want it to end this way. He cleared his throat, a serious look in his eyes. He stepped up to the table and picked up the baseball bat. He came over towards me and poked me. On my knees, then my shoulder and then my arms. I pulled at the chair again and he laughed.

He tapped the baseball bat in the palm of one hand as I heard a door open. I saw the perplexed expression on his face and then the face of Tomas as the light caught him. I didn't know whether I should be pleased.

When he raised a pistol and shot baseball-bat man I had my answer. The relief hit me and I pissed my trousers. The big man stood for a moment, looking at the blood on his chest. Tomas aimed another shot and this time it was right in the middle of his forehead. He dropped the baseball bat and it span along the dirt of the floor. He swayed for a moment and then fell. There was a dull thud as his bulk hit the ground.

I gasped for breath when Tomas undid the tape on my mouth and then the pain shot through my legs. He rummaged through the dead man's jacket and tapped out a message on the mobile.

'Lech think you dead now,' Tomas said. 'We go.'

A thousand questions swirled through my mind.

My legs felt like sponge and I tripped and lost my balance as we left the room. Tomas opened the door and led me out into a long corridor that eventually finished at a metal door, which he pushed with his shoulder. My legs were burning and my shoulder ached and I needed a shower and some clean clothes, but when the fresh air burst onto my face I fell to the floor and took deep lungfuls of breath. It was dark, but I had no idea of the time.

'We go,' Tomas repeated, tugging at my shirt.

I got up onto my knees.

'Where are we?'

'Lech's place,' he said, pulling at my shirt again. 'It not safe.'

I got to my feet and looked around. We were standing on waste ground near some factories and industrial buildings. It was dark: no street lights, just the barest outline of a road.

'This way,' Tomas said as he walked towards a tall building with streaks of light leaking around doors and windows.

I stumbled again until I fell into a slow pace, trying to catch up with Tomas. He strode on ahead of me until he ducked down under a broken fence. I followed him, my shoulder aching more when I bent down. Behind an old hut there was a Skoda that was unlocked, and he got in. I followed, pleased to be sitting down. He started the engine.

'What time is it?' I asked.

'Twelve.'

'Where is Dagmara?'

'England.'

'Cardiff?' I said.

'We need to leave now.'

'Where do we go?' I asked, struggling to think straight.

'England,' he said simply. 'Change clothes from bag in back.' He jerked his head to the back seat.

I leant over and pulled the overnight bag that I'd left at Dagmara's apartment onto my lap and found my clothes, a wash bag and passport with my wallet. I struggled to take off my dirty clothes before eventually pulling on a pair of trousers and a clean shirt.

The old Skoda had a good heater and soon the car was warm. I tried sleeping but no matter how I shaped my body in the seat I was uncomfortable. Once we'd reached the countryside the rain started and the wipers struggled to clear the windscreen.

'How long will it take?' I said.

'Many hours.'

After a couple of hours we stopped at services. I found the toilet but there was no soap in the dispenser and no hot water in the tap. I splashed cold water on my face and pulled wet hands through my hair. The coffee was strong and coated my mouth like syrup. We chewed on stale bread and pastries. From a chiller we paid for bottles of water and continued the journey.

By the early hours we were near the border with Germany and Tomas slowed.

'Sometimes police on border. Polish guards are pigs and German same.'

Once he was happy that the border was clear we drove on.

'German police on autobahn stop us always,' he said, and my fragile optimism waned.

Through his broken English I understood that the German motorway police liked to stop Polish cars and check their documents. Tomas had been stopped five times in as many hours on one journey. The autobahn was smooth, well lit and Porsches screamed past in the outside lane.

'Why are you involved?' I said eventually, my mind thinking about Dagmara.

'Special Forces with Michal and Leon,' he said. 'I was their friend; they saved my life. I could not save Michal or Leon.'

He spoke slowly and I pieced together the history of the unit that they'd all been in. They'd seen action in the

Central African Republic where their unit had been ambushed. It took an hour for Tomas to sketch out all the details. They'd been young soldiers together in the Military Police and their commanding officer had sent them on a routine mission, but things had gone wrong and soldiers from Ireland had been killed and others from Latvia badly injured. Occasionally, he stopped to take a breath or find the right word and sometimes he used the wrong word but I didn't correct him. It had been a bloody attack in difficult circumstances and for hours he had known his life was at risk. It was Michal and Leon who had saved him after risking their lives driving through hostile territory to reach them.

Tomas scanned the forecourt when we stopped for fuel, finding the pump furthest from the store. He seemed unaffected by the long hours of driving. I slept for a couple of hours, but I could still hear the traffic and the low hum from the radio. When I woke we were near the Belgian border and dawn was breaking behind us. Tomas stopped at the next services and when I left the car, pain shot through my back. I hobbled to the toilet and returned to the smell of greasy pizzas that Tomas had bought. After the service station the traffic built up, trucks and vans filling the autobahns.

He said we'd made good time once we were halfway through Belgium and he talked about catching the ferry to England. Coaches with Polish plates passed us on their way back to Poland, crumpled sleeping faces pressed against the windows.

'Coach much cheap,' Tomas said.

Another couple of hours passed; the burning in my eyes began to feel normal. Empty water bottles and plastic coffee mugs littered the rear. It had been ten hours since we'd left Poland and I wondered if baseball-bat man had been missed. If he had then we were in trouble. And

Dagmara was in more trouble. I didn't think Lech would make the same mistake twice.

On the dockside in Calais, trucks and articulated units had parked in tight formation. We paid for the ticket and pulled up alongside a French lorry. The ferry was half-empty and while Tomas went in search of more coffee I stretched out on the floor. I was asleep within seconds. The next thing I was aware of was Tomas prodding me in the thigh. He had chosen the spot with an enormous bruise and I cried in pain.

'Time to leave,' he said.

Once we were clear of the port I told Tomas to pull up by a telephone kiosk. I dialled Boyd's number.

'Where are you?' he said a troubled pitch to his voice.

'Dover.'

'How did you get out of Poland?'

'Just listen, Boyd.' I said, dictating detailed instructions for him and the others. He cut across me before I'd finished. 'You're in deep trouble,' his tone serious now.

'What's happened?'

'The Polish police are after you.'

'What?'

'They found a journalist dead. Tongue cut out and fingers amputated.'

'Yes, I know.'

'They have an eyewitness who puts you at the scene. They want to interview you.'

Chapter 37

'You smell awful.'

Boyd creased his face and inched the chair a little further away from me. I couldn't smell anything of course. I'd been sitting in the same clothes for hours.

'I need a shower.'

'And some clean clothes,' Boyd added.

It was early evening and the services on the outskirts of Cardiff were full of salesmen in sharp suits and girls on high heels in narrow skirts. Then I noticed some of the glances and whispered comments that must have been about me and Tomas, whose eyes seemed more sunken and his cheeks more hollowed out than before.

'Forensics have confirmed that Gerek was in the factory,' Boyd said.

I should have been pleased. 'Good,' I said. It meant we had enough on Lech to satisfy Cornock. 'Have you found out who the other men in the photograph might be?'

Boyd shook his head. 'We've had the images scanned into the computer and then the faces were picked out by this geek from forensics. At least we've got a rogues gallery. If we find the girls and they give evidence we might have a chance of getting the CPS to agree to prosecute them. The chances of them admitting to having sex with underage girls is remote.'

We had to find the girls first and even if we did, the gangs would reorganise and the trafficking would start again. The WPS would investigate, Amnesty would write another report. Things might get better. I had to hope so.

'I need a full alert on Frankie Prince. Everything. Somebody must have seen him.'

'So what happened in Poland?' Boyd said.

'Fucking mayhem. Dagmara and Markus acting like

a pair of vigilantes.'

'Markus is the journalist?'

I nodded. Boyd continued. 'The Polish police want to talk to you about his death. There's an eyewitness who puts you in the flat just before the body is discovered. What happened, boss?'

Tomas had been quiet until then. It was difficult to see if he was tired or not. 'I need food,' he said. Boyd went with him to buy some fast food and I used Boyd's mobile to call Cornock.

'I need to see you urgently.' Cornock's voice was wintry, a tone he kept for special occasions. But I wasn't feeling particularly special.

'I need to clean up and then I have to find Dagmara—'

'I want you in here before you go running all over Cardiff.'

'Her life could be in danger.'

'And the Polish police want to talk to you about a murder.'

'There's a computer somewhere that was hidden by Michal. It's important enough for Lech and Frankie to go about killing people, trying to find it or trying to prevent someone else from finding it.'

'Do you know where this computer could be?'

'Not at the moment, sir.'

I could hear the exasperation in Cornock's voice. 'Then you don't know where to look. So into Queen Street. Now.'

He rang off before I could respond.

I hadn't realised how hungry I was until Boyd returned with burgers and fries. I finished the meal without stopping, mumbling occasionally through a mouthful of food as Boyd interrogated me about Poland.

I didn't notice the traffic as we drove to my flat in the Bay. Tomas parked next to a man who was leaving his Audi. He pulled up his nose as we met him again near the lift. I muttered something about having a bad day at the office, but all he did was give Tomas a stare. I showered, had a change of clothes and brushed my teeth so hard the gums bled. But I felt more human and ready for Frankie Prince and Lech Balinski. On my way to the station I dropped Tomas outside the Catholic church, having spoken with Father Podolak on my mobile, grateful that he didn't ask for an explanation.

Sitting at the lights near Queen Street police station, I thought about going straight to find Dagmara and Anna and arresting them for obstruction or perverting the course of justice or anything that would mean I could take them off the streets. Boyd would understand but Cornock wouldn't, so I drove the car towards Queen Street.

Cornock fixed me with a cold stare and muscles in his jaw twitched. I gave him a summary of what had happened in Poland, ignoring the night in Dagmara's apartment.

He leant back in his chair once I'd finished.

'The Polish police want to interview you about the death of the journalist.'

'He was dead when I got there.'

'I appreciate that, John. But you were there and they've got eyewitnesses.'

'I need to find Dagmara.'

'This computer better be worth it. I should send you home and get Hobbs to take over the investigation.'

I stood up before he had time to make a final decision.

'I need to find Dagmara. She trusts me,' I said, hoping that would help.

'I'm sticking my neck out here, John.'

I was out of the door before he'd finished.

A woman with dreadlocks and a long flowing skirt opened the flat in Whitchurch. The air inside was so thick with cannabis smoke I could have sliced it and sold it to help reduce the national debt.

'It's for personal consumption only,' the girl said. The drug squad would have disagreed when we saw the five other people sitting on the floor in the small living area.

Boyd and I looked in every room and opened every cupboard. We found lots of scarves, but nothing to suggest Anna or Dagmara had been staying there.

'Sorry,' the woman said, her eyes barely functioning. 'I haven't seen her for days, maybe weeks.'

Time was obviously a difficult concept for this woman and, while arresting her and her friends might contribute to the statistics, it wasn't going to help me find Dagmara.

An hour later I stood by the back door of Anna's house. The pane had been replaced and there was fresh silicone around the new glass. I rattled the handle a couple of times.

'Looks empty,' Boyd said, taking a step back and looking up at the windows of the bedrooms.

I tried the mobile number I had for Anna again. And then I tried Dagmara's. With every ring I knew I should have arrested them when I'd had the chance and none of this might have happened.

We sat in the car outside the house and I lit a cigarette.

We watched a group of teenagers staggering home, and then a couple of taxis passed. The small hours were approaching and I knew I had to sleep. I could remember the sensation of the lumpy old bed in Dagmara's flat and the heavy sheet and the duvet. My eyes were burning now, but I was clean and my clothes didn't smell.

'Let's go and visit Frankie,' I said.

The gates were open and the lights on the drive were blazing. There was a BMW I recognised parked alongside Lucy Prince's Range Rover – LP 5: hard to miss. I didn't recognise the other two cars and I hoped that Frankie had arrived home.

I pressed the doorbell; a light under the CCTV camera lens flashed into life, and then I heard Lucy Prince's voice.

'What do you want?'

'I need to speak to you,' I said, as though calling in the middle of the night was routine.

The hallway was the size of a double garage and expensive paintings hung from the walls. Music drifted in from somewhere and then I noticed the small speakers positioned in the walls. The staircase behind Lucy Prince had intricate finials and balustrades that would not have been out of place on a haunted house film-set. But I could tell Lucy wasn't comfortable. She was wearing a tracksuit and a T-shirt that she must have kept from her time as a physiotherapist for a rugby club. She drew her hand casually through her hair.

'So, what do you want?'

'Is Frankie around?' I said, looking over her shoulder.

'No. And I don't know where he is.'

'Are you always up so late?'

'Do you always work this late?'

I decided that conversation with Lucy Prince wasn't going to be productive, so I marched towards a set of double doors.

'You can't do that. You have to have a warrant, or something,' she protested.

I pushed them open. Behind the doors were suitcases arranged in neat order and standing behind them, dead still, was Jim White.

'Jim,' I said, as though he were a long lost friend. 'I thought I saw your car. So when is Frankie going to join us?'

'We don't know—' White began.

'It's none of your business where Frankie might be,' Lucy said, standing in the doorway behind me.

'It is my business when he's a suspect in a murder case.'

'You can't prove anything,' she said, hands on hips.

I sat down on one of the two long sofas, each the colour of vanilla ice cream. They smelt clean and the glass on the coffee table in front of me sparkled.

I decided to consider the options. It was late. I was knackered and I wanted to sleep, in a bed. I had to find Dagmara and keep her safe. And Lucy and Jim White were being awkward. Lech was on his way to Cardiff, maybe even here already and I wanted to arrest Frankie so badly it hurt.

'You're both under arrest for obstruction,' I said.

Chapter 38

'Piss off, Marco.'

Working in the custody suite of a police station has a numbing effect on most police officers and the duty custody sergeant made no attempt at respecting my rank.

I was so tired I could barely speak.

'Help me out here, Boyd,' I said.

The custody sergeant stared blankly, first at Boyd and then at me.

'Inspector Marco and I have arrested Lucy Prince and Jim White for obstruction. We need to get them locked up for the night so we can formally interview them in the morning.'

When the sergeant realised we were serious he started the process. Did they want anyone notified they were there? Did they want a solicitor notified – I heard the name Glanville Tront mentioned. Did they want anything to drink or eat?

My mind was blank when I left the custody suite and I drove home, thankful that the roads were deserted. When I pushed open the door of the flat I smelt Trish's perfume. Then I heard her call out, demanding to know who was there.

'It's only me,' I said lamely.

There was a sound of hasty movement from the bedroom and she appeared in the sitting room, threw her arms around me, and then kissed me on the lips.

'John, I've been so worried. Why didn't you text me or call? I had no idea where you were. Boyd didn't tell me anything and Cornock refused to speak to me. I was so worried I tried calling the support team and one of the secretaries I know. What's happened? When did you get back? And your mother has called me every hour today.'

'I haven't slept for the last two days and I've just arrested Lucy Prince so I need to sleep.'

I sat on the edge of the bed and felt my body relaxing. I almost fell asleep where I was sitting. When I woke, Trish was prodding me and telling me to wake up and take an urgent call. I was dreaming of sleeping with Dagmara and having her body next to mine under the duvet in the cold flat in Warsaw.

'DI Marco.'

I recognised the custody sergeant's voice from earlier. 'Jason Brown wants to talk to you.'

'Who?' My mind was trying to focus.

'The Scotsman banged up for the Cyncoed burglaries.'

'What time is it?'

'Early,' he said. 'I'm going off shift in a couple of hours. Your two other guests have been well behaved, but I've had their brief on the telephone. Glanville Tront, no less.'

I glanced over at the clock, scarcely believing that I'd been sleeping for three hours. It felt like ten minutes.

Jason Brown smiled at me as I walked into the cell. He hadn't shaved since I'd seen him last and he kept swinging his right leg that was crossed over the other knee.

I'd rushed an instant coffee before leaving the flat, but I still wanted a double espresso and my patience with Jason Brown wasn't going to last very long.

'Inspector Hobbs is dealing with your case now,' I said.

'He's a fucking knob-head.' A Glaswegian accent made the insult sound worse. I was tempted to agree.

'Get to the point Jason. Why do you want to see

me?'

'I see really bad things.'

'You've said that before.'

'I mean really bad things. I was down by the river a wee while ago. I've got a favourite bench there. There's an old lady that brings me some tea in the morning.'

'All right. Get on with it.'

'If I give you any information, then will it help me? I want to know that I'll get a reduced sentence. I've got some really fucking useful info.'

They all say that. I didn't have time to go through the paperwork for a deal with Jason Brown; if he wanted to cough, he'd have to take a chance.

'I can't sanction anything. All I can tell you is that if you have any information that might be of assistance with an ongoing inquiry, I'd make sure you were given the recognition you deserve.'

He gave me sullen stare for a moment and then hesitated before resuming.

'It was before them Polish people started to get killed. And have their fucking tongues cut out. That was fucking grim I'll tell you and I've seen some bad bastards in my time. I was banged up in Long Lartin with them terrorists and they scared the fucking shite out of me.'

I doubted that the prison authorities would ever have classed Jason Brown a high-security-risk prisoner.

'It was one of them clear fucking nights and I was down the Taff but I couldn't sleep. It must have been in the middle of the fucking night.'

Jason had my attention and I waited for him to finish.

'I saw a big fucker and Frankie. You know, you nicked his fucking wife last night – there was shouting about her around the cells last night. Anyway, they were there by the Taff and I saw them push the body into the water.'

Suddenly I didn't feel tired.

'Describe the big fucker.'

Jason waved his arms and hands as he talked.

'He had fucking big, fuck off legs and he must have been seven foot tall. He had fucking shoulders as big as …. I don't know what.'

'How can you describe him so well?'

'The lights from the streets. I could see them. I was under the bench. I was so frightened I could have shat myself and then they passed me. Just walked away as if nothing was wrong. Laughing and fucking joking. Them Russians need to be locked up. Have you got a ciggy?'

I threw him my half-empty packet of cigarettes. I'd get some more later. It was going to be a long day, and five would be ten, probably, by the time I reached my bed.

'And you're prepared to make a statement about what you saw?'

Jason Brown nodded energetically. I wondered if he would be quite as enthusiastic if he knew about Lech Balinski.

Jason enjoyed the attention of being a witness and having a statement recorded; he even enjoyed the rancid-looking coffee the young uniform brought into the interview room in a plastic cup. Cornock had said evidence: not circumstantial, but direct, and now I had enough to charge Frankie and Lech. The prospect of making the arrest and charging both men contributed to the sense of elation in my mind.

I'd cleared my desk and I had the plastic pockets with the keys laid out neatly alongside Michal's belongings and the remains of Leon's life. A yawn gripped my jaw and I shuddered violently as I failed to stop it. Boyd sat staring at me, as though I were a specimen in a scientific experiment.

'You look a bit rough, boss.'

I nodded.

'Any luck in finding Dagmara or Anna?' I said.

'Joe and Phil were out last night and couldn't find either of them. They tried most of the factories where the Poles work and the Polish shops in town and the pubs where they drink. Nothing.'

'I just don't believe they can disappear like this. Somebody will know where they are and let's hope it's not Frankie Prince.'

'And Glanville Tront has been after you this morning. He wanted to know when you're going to interview Lucy Prince and Jim White.'

'When I'm good and ready.'

'He mentioned talking to Cornock. Thought it was an abuse of your powers of arrest.'

I laughed out loud and then it occurred to me to pick up the telephone and explain to Glanville Tront what exactly Lech Balinski and Frankie Prince did for a living.

Now I had an eyewitness to Michal's murder, but I doubted that the CPS would ever agree for him to be used as a witness. I could hear a defence barrister tearing him to shreds as a drunk and a fantasist. But challenging the evidence of Aaron French wouldn't be so easy.

I was reassuring myself that I really did have enough to charge Lech and Frankie when a uniform officer appeared in the door of my room.

'DI Marco?'

'Yes.'

'This message came in last night,' he said, handing me a piece of paper.

I read it quickly and the adrenaline pumped through

my body.

'And why the fucking hell wasn't this emailed to me or a text sent to me – or someone call me last night?'

The constable blushed and stammered that he'd just been asked to deliver it.

I shouted at Woods and Lawson as I marched into the Incident Room.

'Lech Balinski arrived in Bristol last night,' I said.

There was a brief silence.

'What next, sir?' Lawson said.

'We find him. And Frankie Prince.'

The telephone rang twice and I wondered where my mother could be. Eventually she answered, relieved to hear my voice. I'd said very little before she interrupted.

'You sound tired, John.' It's funny how parents know about their children from the slightest inflection – or lack of – in their voice.

'I haven't slept much in the last couple of days.'

'But you must rest. Trish told me about the case you're on.'

I thought about telling her what I was doing, when Dave Hobbs knocked on the door of my office, and I rang off, but not before my mother got me to promise to call her back.

'What were you doing with my case?' Hobbs said, narrowing his eyes. 'You know the protocol. You should have spoken to me before talking to Jason Brown.'

He was right of course, but I wasn't going to admit that to his face.

'Jason asked to see me. Said he had important information about the murders.'

'The protocols are there for a reason.'

The grip I had on my temper loosened.

'I've got four murders and you're preaching to me about protocols.'

'If we don't follow the right procedures then policing will go down the drain. We'll be getting a bad reputation and cases will be lost.'

I wanted to tell him to go back to North Wales and the mountains and leave us city folk in peace. I wanted to tell him to go and fuck himself, but it was against protocol. I wanted to solve the murders and bang up Lech, but he was getting in my way.

'I've just spent the last few hours being almost killed in Poland; then I spent sixteen hours travelling in a car over Europe and you're telling me I can't take a witness statement that might help. Fuck off, Hobbs.'

His eyes narrowed again and he picked up one of the plastic pockets.

'Are these the exhibits?'

I nodded.

'Looks like a key my father had for his yacht.'

Chapter 39

I switched on all the warning lights and kept one hand pressed on the horn as I darted the Mondeo between cars stuck in traffic.

Boyd was on his way and I'd spoken to Cornock as I left the car park.

Where no one would think of looking.

It made sense, hiding something in the gallery and then in the yacht. Nobody would think of looking there.

It should have taken me fifteen minutes to reach the marina, but I hadn't counted on the roadworks. When I slowed to a crawl I shouted, cursed and then I looked for Lech, and Frankie in the cars caught in the jam and, wondering whether they'd already left the marina, in the cars passing me in the opposite direction.

I was praying that Dagmara and Anna were somewhere safe.

The traffic hold-ups cleared and I found my way to the marina and pulled up alongside a gleaming Range Rover. I was out of the car in a second and looked around for Boyd, just as he pulled into the car park.

'What happened?' he said.

'Dave Hobbs saw the keys. Said they looked like something his father had on his yacht.'

I ran over to the office building, Boyd following me.

The marina manager was the sort of idiot they put in charge of looking at CCTV images all day, issuing tickets for marina berthing fees and having a mind that worked on simple straight lines.

'I can't give you access to the CCTV images.'

I flashed my warrant card.

'It's Freedom of Information and all that confidentiality business,' he said, crossing his arms, staring me out.

'A girl was taken on a yacht from here and drowned in the sea by a Polish guy with hands that would crack your spine in two. He's probably just been here and I need to know when and with who.'

He just carried on staring.

'Who's your supervisor?' I said.

He gave me the number and I made the call. I was calm and reasonable, which was a trial as the idiot was still sitting with a defiant look on his face. Then I handed the telephone to the idiot and I watched him nod. Eventually, he sat back.

'More than my job was worth you know,' he said, by way of explanation. 'How far back do you want to go?'

We sat and watched the screen, hoping that we didn't have to go back too far. We didn't have to wait long. My heart beat faster when I saw Dagmara entering the security code into the key pad by the gate. Then I noticed Anna standing by her side. It was early that morning; the shadows were long and workmen passed them taking kit down to the yachts.

I made a note of the time and then I got the idiot to advance the coverage and within half an hour I saw the familiar figure of Lech Balinski lumbering towards the gate. Frankie appeared and they punched in the right code and the gate slowly swung open.

'Fuck,' Boyd said quietly. 'They beat us to it.'

The time on the screen told me that another half an hour had elapsed before the image of Lech and Frankie appeared again. This time they were pushing Anna, then dragging her and she seemed to be protesting, waving her hands in the air.

Fear gripped my chest.

No sign of Dagmara. I glanced at my watch. It had

been a couple of hours.

We sprinted over the pontoons and my lungs were tearing at my chest when we finally reached Frankie's yacht.

A wheel-cover with the name *Esmeralda* lay piled in a corner. I knelt down and peered into the yacht, but it looked empty. I swung a leg over the rail and lifted myself over onto the deck. The doors of cupboards hung open, their contents strewn all over the cabin. There was a smell of bleach in the air.

I took out the keys from my jacket and sat down by the round, polished table, wondering how people could enjoy sailing when things were so cramped. Boyd was tidying the piles of sails and life jackets and high-visibility vests and odd pieces of rope into a corner when I saw the cover of a small bench, lying at a crooked angle. I leant over and beneath it was a compartment with a fancy lock.

I fingered the keys and gently tried pushing the first and then the second into the lock, without success. I sat at the table, my mind trying to focus. I must have missed something. I thought about the marina manager and the CCTV tape and how helpless I felt watching Dagmara and Anna walking down onto the pontoon. Then the image of Anna came to mind being pushed and dragged by Lech and I knew then what was missing.

'There must be another boat,' I said, reaching for my mobile as I scrambled out of the yacht onto the deck. I dialled the marina office number.

'Does Frankie Prince have another boat?' I said.

The marina manager hesitated.

'Don't you even fucking think of not cooperating.'

'Ah … yes. He's got one of those Sunseekers.'

'Where is it?'

I was beginning to clamber off the yacht, waving at Boyd to follow me. I ran as fast as I could until I saw *Esmeralda 2* gleaming in the autumn sunshine. I was praying, hoping that Dagmara had been able to escape.

I stopped, dead in my tracks, when I saw a scarf draped over a hand rail. I hauled myself into the boat, almost falling before regaining my footfall. I heard Boyd landing heavily behind as I fumbled with the keys. The larger key fitted perfectly and I pushed open the door and found myself in the galley with a smart sitting area. I quickly scanned for any sign of Dagmara, relieved that she wasn't there. Every cupboard door and compartment had been wrenched open. A small cupboard by my feet underneath the table had its contents strewn on the floor and I fingered the second key in my pocket before sliding it smoothly into the lock. My heart sank.

At the far end of the galley was a small doorway. I pushed it open before descending down the small flight of stairs. In front of me were two doors and I pushed the first open to find myself in a spotless bathroom that was larger than the one in my flat. I could feel my pulse beating on both sides of my neck; my head was pounding. I pushed the second door.

I gasped. Dagmara was lying on the bed, perfectly still, her dark hair falling over her face. I almost fell as I stepped over towards her and sat on the side of the bed, taking her arm, and feeling for a pulse as I pulled her close. I wrapped my arms around her, wanting to hold her close as I'd done during the nights I'd spent in her bed. I felt helpless, as though a part of my body had died. My chest pulled and heaved and I felt the tears pouring down my cheeks. I tried convincing myself that it wasn't really happening. That we'd have other nights where I'd feel her body next to me and taste the warmth of her lips.

I drew her hair to one side and ran a finger over her face; it was cold and it startled me. I wanted to scream at someone, at anyone.

I heard a noise behind me – then I turned and saw Boyd looking at me from the doorway.

'I'll call CSI,' Boyd said.

I was still holding Dagmara in my arms when he returned. It felt like seconds but I knew it was longer. He said something but I didn't pay attention. I tightened my hold on Dagmara as if the intensity of my grasp would change things, alter time itself.

'CSIs on their way, boss.'

I heard Boyd but said nothing.

'It's a crime scene, sir. We should leave. We need to find Frankie and Lech.'

It must have been the names that prompted my mind into some sort of clear thinking. I laid Dagmara back on the bed, stood for a moment choking back the tears, and left.

'Is this a good idea?' Boyd said.

I stood by the bar in The Captain Scott looking at the vodka in the clear glass that the barman had left alongside the half-pint glass of Brains. All I could think of was the fact that Dagmara was dead because I hadn't been careful enough. I hadn't taken the time to think things through. I should have told her not to get involved. I should have insisted ...

I ran my finger over the condescension on the beer glass. The mere sensation of doing that brought back memories I'd long forgotten. How the first drink tasted so good ... And promising myself it would be only one ...Then laying on the floor with puke all over my clothes.

I'd never see Dagmara again. Never feel her skin against mine or her breath on my lips. I pushed the change over the bar and lifted the glass a couple of centimetres.

Jackie would often arrive at this point and force the glass out of my hand. It never worked and I'd go back to the bar and order another and another.

'What now, boss?'

I heard Boyd, but I wasn't listening. He raised his voice.

'Don't fuck about, sir. We've got to find Lech and Frankie.'

It must have been hearing Boyd swear that made me look at him. The vodka glass was still in my hand.

'They're probably in some bolt-hole that Frankie keeps a secret.'

I put the glass down onto the bar, but my fingers couldn't quite release their grasp as I thought about the address Terry had given me. My pulse quickened; I scribbled the address onto a beer mat and thrust it at Boyd who looked bewildered.

'You go back to Queen Street,' I said, walking out of the bar. 'Get a countrywide alert into the system. We'll need the Armed Response Unit for this address, as soon as.'

'You'll need to talk to the Super,' he said, as I closed the car door.

A dark, empty feeling hung in my mind as I crossed over Cardiff for the comfortable suburbs in the north. The knowledge that I'd never see Dagmara again had left a raw ache that was turning to anger, and then a fierce rage that I had to find Lech and Frankie before they could kill someone else, particularly Anna. It felt as though I had so many things unsaid, with everyone; but with Dagmara there was no second chance. Stopping by traffic lights I fumbled for a handkerchief to wipe away the remains of the tears that had scoured my face.

Most cities have a clear divide between rich and poor, ethnic and indigenous, and Cardiff was no different. The docks and south of the city had the council flats and terraces and then from Roath Park the houses got bigger and the gardens longer. But larger houses didn't mean less criminality, just cleverer people willing to take risks. The sort of risks that got them photographed in parties with young girls. And wealthy people able to pay for the sort of protection and support from the likes of Frankie Prince who supported their charities and then collected when it mattered.

And then the likes of Anna came along and seduced Dagmara and Maria into believing that she could really conquer evil. I thumped the steering wheel so hard it shook.

I braked hard to avoid a car turning out in front of me while winding my way through Albany Road. I blasted the horn at every lorry that delayed my journey. Then I dialled Cornock's number and after a couple of rings he answered.

'I need the Armed Response Unit authorised immediately. Boyd's got the details but I'm certain I know where Frankie Prince and Lech are going to be.'

'You'd better be right about this, John,'

After the bustle near the centre of town, the traffic thinned and the roads widened. I slowed the car, hoping I wouldn't be noticed. Eventually I parked at the edge of the road. I could see the house; lights shone from the upstairs windows and the front gates were open. The street was quiet and I opened the window a couple of inches, enough for the smoke of a cigarette to escape. I was reaching for my lighter when the passenger door opened and I saw the toothy grin of Janek smiling at me. Then he pointed a pistol at my head.

Chapter 40

I had learnt never to argue with a man pointing a gun. Now, I was in a room with four men, all with guns. And I was tied to a chair, a habit I definitely wanted to kick.

A long table was pushed against the far wall; concealed spotlights cast a clean white light over the large room. It was vaguely familiar.

Anna sat on the floor, duct tape stretched tightly over her mouth, sweat beaded on her face and her eyes darted around the room. I could see she wasn't going to hold it together for very long. I hoped that we wouldn't have very long to wait.

Boyd would have finished with Cornock by now and the ARU would have had their instructions. Like most forces, the Wales Police Service had a team of specially trained officers ready to respond. There would be five, maybe more, in the team, all using Heckler and Koch semi-automatic carbines, issued and signed for with a specific number of rounds. There would be clear instructions as to when lethal force could be used. But I knew they had a problem. They had no idea who was inside the house, or its layout, and if it turned into a siege then things might get messy.

Frankie sat by the table, focusing on the laptop open in front of him and which was connected to an external hard drive. Lech stood over him, holding a gun and Janek stared at me with a fixed smile. Kamil leant against the far wall, cradling a gun.

Lech turned towards me. 'I thought we leave you dead for sure,' he said evenly.

'Take him with you,' Frankie said. 'Nobody will miss him.'

Lech stepped towards me. 'And who helped you

escape from Barzak?'

My mind was racing. My heart thumping in my chest. I had to get them to stay until the ARU arrived. I had to make sure I could arrest Lech and Frankie. I had to be able to tell Michal's family that we'd caught the men who'd killed their son.

Lech prodded me with his gun.

'The man who helped you is a dead man.'

'Did you find what you were looking for?' I said, frantically wondering how I could delay them.

'Mr Policeman.' Lech prodded me again. 'How did you find this place?'

'We need to go,' Frankie said, looking at his watch.

'I know. Maybe we take you back to Poland. We have place in one of the forests where we take our friends.' Lech said.

Janek snorted. Kamil just stared.

'And we take this girl back to Poland too. Maybe we have fun,' Lech said.

Anna blinked frantically.

'Why kill Markus?' I said.

'He very good and tell us code before he died. Michal very clever. He had taken much information from Frankie's computer onto the hard drive.'

I was counting the time in my head – had it been half an hour or more since I'd left Boyd? How long would the ARU take to get here?

'And why kill Maria and Leon?' I was making conversation, hoping that Lech would talk.

'The whores are all the same. Families want money but when they have to work they want to get freedom.'

Lech walked around the room and he stood over Anna. She tilted her head and looked at him.

'And this one.' He kicked Anna's shin. 'Useless piece

of shit.'

She grimaced in pain. And then he turned his back on her. 'And did you find your Polish whore?' he said, staring at me.

My wrists strained at the rope and the chair moved forward a couple of inches. 'You fucking bastard.'

Lech snorted.

I heard some noise on the first floor and then the sound of young girls talking, laughing and joking. Then it struck me why the room seemed familiar. It was in this room that Wing Commander Bates had been photographed, champagne in hand, lusting after a fourteen year old.

'I need to protect investment,' Lech continued.

'That's why you had Kamil poking around all the time?' I asked.

Lech shrugged his shoulders and smiled the sort of smile a man might make when he was contented with life.

'My friends back in Poland are very pissed with you. Barzak was good man. Good killer. He killed ten men with bare hands.'

Then I said the first thing that came to mind. 'There's another copy of the hard drive.'

'He's wrong,' Frankie said.

Lech came to stand in front of me. The jacket had a herringbone check running through it and the cloth looked expensive. It was the first time I'd noticed his face up close and he had two large lumps on the right cheek.

'How do you know?' he said.

'Maria told me.'

Lech leant back, scratched his jaw and the lumps wobbled. He was thinking about Maria. I was counting again in my head, waiting.

'I speak to Maria too. And she say lots before we take her tongue out. After that she speechless.' He smiled;

Kamil and Janek laughed right on cue. 'But she tell me truth and when I ask her about the hard drive, she say only one. So, Mr Policeman, you wrong.'

'It's in the same place as the photographs in the camera that Leon and Maria had.'

Frankie raised his head and looked over at me. I had his attention now.

'Don't listen to him,' Frankie said.

Lech narrowed his eyes and said something in Polish to Janek.

'You can't take that chance,' I said, getting into my stride. 'I found the photographs from what Maria told me and now—'

'Shut the fuck up, Marco.' Frankie was rattled.

There was a noise behind me in the passageway. Lech turned to look at the door, his eyes troubled.

The next few seconds happened in a blur, like a slow-motion scene from a Western movie. The door opened and the colonel burst into the room. He was dressed in combat fatigues, as was Tomas behind him. They had pistols already at chest height. I saw Janek getting up off the table and reach for his gun, but the colonel fired two shots and Janek's head exploded, blood and flesh flying everywhere.

Lech had stepped back towards the table and picked up the gun near the computer. Kamil had his feet wide apart and as he pumped two, then three shots, into Lech's head, there was a loud thud as the giant body crashed to the floor.

Frankie didn't have time to hide the sheer terror on his face.

He stood for a fraction of a second with the gun in his hand, Lech on the floor by the table and Janek's blood splattered all over his white shirt.

Two shots rang out and then Frankie's body heaved

upwards in a twisting motion, as the force of the bullets dragged his body towards the wall, already covered in Janek's blood.

My heart was beating so fast it was likely to tear out of my body.

Kamil came over and untied me. I fell off the chair as two more men in combat dress filed into the room, carrying body bags. I got up and fell down again. My legs were like jelly but I got over to Anna, untied her, and carefully took off the duct tape.

She started crying and shouting and after a couple of seconds she took off her fleece and tossed it aside. I sat down on the floor next to her and pulled her close.

The air was thick with cordite and the hot smell of blood and flesh.

I watched as the colonel and his men dragged the lifeless bodies of Lech Balinski and Janek into the bags. Kamil stood by his side and they started talking and looking at their watches.

'Have you always been working for the colonel?' I asked, as I thought about Kamil's attempts to get information from us.

Kamil narrowed his eyes and nodded slowly.

'How long do we have?' the colonel said to me. 'Backup is on its way, yes?'

I wanted to say – yes, it fucking is and then I'll arrest the whole fucking lot of you. But I settled for a nod and a mumbled confirmation. It took four of them to move Lech's body. Once they'd got the body of Janek out of the house, the colonel stood in the middle of the room with the hard drive in his hand.

'This is what we came for,' he said, tapping the metal box in his hand.

He pulled the door closed behind him. I bent down

and cradled Anna's face in my hands, staring at her intensely. She was still sobbing as I gave her clear, precise instructions.

Chapter 41

When the Armed Response Unit crashed into the room, Anna started to scream again. Then she seemed to notice Frankie lying near her feet, his head shot to pieces and she put her hands to her eyes and drew herself into a ball.

Boyd followed the ARU officers, his body armour tight against his chest. He stopped for a moment and looked at the carnage in the room.

'What the fuck happened?' he said, and then immediately, 'Are you all right, boss?'

I nodded, but said nothing.

Boyd continued. 'This is a crime scene, sir. We need the CSIs here.'

It was going to take some time explaining this to Boyd, but he was right and he made the call. Alvine would love this, I knew. Three different DNAs and only one body.

Other officers streamed into the room. I could hear footsteps running up the stairs, voices on the first floor and shouts for assistance. A woman police officer appeared and knelt down, covering Anna with a blanket before getting her to her feet and taking her outside.

I was on my feet by the time the ARU team leader, a thin, wiry sergeant with a heavy jaw and deep-set eyes strode towards me. 'Are you responsible for all this blood?' His tone was almost complimentary.

'Call an ambulance,' I said. 'And the pathologist.'

'I've got protocols to maintain and reports to write. If you've discharged a firearm, Inspector Marco, I need to know.'

'I was unarmed.'

'So this is a crime scene.'

'Yes.'

He looked at the blood on the wall and on the floor.

'Looks like more than one victim.'

'It's a crime scene.'

He hesitated. 'So who's the SIO?'

'I am.'

He narrowed his eyes. 'What can my team do to help, Inspector Marco?'

'There are young girls upstairs that need to be taken to safe houses, then interviewed through interpreters and their families contacted. And they need to be treated as human beings. I need family liaison officers on duty to help – and get social services involved and any other fucking agency you can think of that might be able to help these girls.'

He barked instructions into his radio as he left the room. Boyd was at my side as I walked outside. Anna was huddled under a blanket when a car arrived and they left for headquarters. The cool October weather was fresh on my skin. I thought about a world without Frankie Prince or Lech Balinski. Boyd was coordinating the work needed on the crime scene. Paddy MacVeigh arrived and gave me a long, hard look and emerged minutes later.

'What the hell happened in there?'

'It's a long story.'

'Going to the Bluebirds game next Saturday?'

I hadn't thought about football for days. I hadn't thought about anything except work for days. I didn't even know who they were playing.

'I'll buy you on orange juice and you can tell me all about it,' he said.

I nodded.

My last cigarette had been cut short when Janek pointed a gun in my face. Now I took my time to enjoy a smoke. Maybe I had even got down to less than five a day. My mother would be pleased.

Alvine Dix was the next to arrive and from the look on her face she'd heard what had happened. She squeezed out what sympathy and concern she was capable of, but I could see she was finding it a trial.

'Are you all right?' she said.

I nodded again and pulled on the cigarette. 'It's a crime scene.'

'Frankie Prince in there?'

'Shot in the head. Lots of blood and guts.'

'Any other bodies?'

'It's a long story.'

I walked through to one of the interview rooms at the custody suite and, passing Glanville Tront, told him I was going to talk to Lucy Prince on my own. His mouth dropped open and I heard him tell the custody sergeant he wanted his complaint noted.

A night in a cell had messed up her hair and her make-up was smudged. None of her false eyelashes flickered. Her eyes didn't well up. There was no handkerchief dabbed to her cheek. She didn't blink.

Lucy took the news of Frankie's death as though she'd been given the latest turnover figures for the Four Seasons.

'Who killed him?'

'We don't know.'

'I told him not to get involved.'

'Involved with who?'

She gave me a long look. Maybe there was the start of a tear in one eye.

'He wanted to make lots of money. He didn't tell me the details. I didn't want to get involved, but I didn't like those men from Poland. They always smelt and their clothes

...'

I left her sitting in the room by the plastic table with the tape recorder and the walls lined with cork and found Glanville still standing before the custody sergeant's desk.

'We can bail her for now,' I said to the sergeant. 'We'll interview her again.'

Glanville glared at me, 'What did you say to her? This is quite improper.'

I turned and left.

I smoked two cigarettes on the way home. By the time I pulled into the car park by the apartment, tiredness hit me like a train. I was yawning heavily and my eyes were burning. I'd tried Trish earlier, but there had been no reply so I'd sent a text but she hadn't replied. I turned the mobile through my fingers, thinking I'd text my mother but I doubted my ability to tap in the right words. She sounded worried at first but then relieved, and after telling her I was going straight to bed she made me promise to call her in the morning.

I scrubbed my hands in the bathroom sink and noticed the traces of blood in the soapy water. Frankie's blood or maybe Lech's or Janek's. I stepped over into the shower and set the temperature to high. The water poured over my face, I scrubbed my fingers hard, and then my face until the last traces of anything from today, the blood or flesh or body bits, was gone.

I didn't even watch any *Top Gear*.

I sat on the bed and then fell asleep.

Chapter 42

I stood at the back of the neighbourhood watch meeting wearing my new suit.

Superintendent Cornock sat by Hobbs's side and the Assistant Chief Constable, a woman with broad shoulders, a severe hair cut and comfortable shoes, chaired the meeting. I was on hand ready to fill any gaps and press the flesh after the meeting was over.

Dave Hobbs gave me the occasional nervous glance as he explained that the WPS was still no further forward with the complex investigation. Different threads had to be followed up. Murmurs of approval and nodding of heads followed Hobbs's reassurance that enquiries were still ongoing.

It helped that Jason Brown had pleaded guilty to a sneak-theft charge involving a handbag from a kitchen table. Now he was in Cardiff prison enjoying three meals a day, regular exercise, daily showers, a warm bed and television in his cell.

There were a couple of awkward questions about policing policy and whether regular patrols would be commenced in the streets of Cyncoed, which the ACC answered with the sort of diplomacy that justified her pay packet.

Once the evening had finished I sipped on an orange juice, ate some chicken wings and sandwiches that a woman, with a loud voice, told me were home-made. I recognised the faces of magistrates and solicitors and their wives with careful hairdos and immaculate manicures.

I made my way over to Wing Commander Bates and when I had the chance, I took him to one side. He went an odd colour when I showed him the photographs, before giving me a pathetic, pleading look, designed to appeal to my human decency. What he didn't know was that there was nothing I could do. But he'd never have that certainty and it was comforting to think that I could keep the images for an emergency.

I left him standing at the makeshift bar drinking two glasses of wine, one after the other. Later I saw him talking to Judge Patricks who gave me the briefest nod of acknowledgment. I found Dave Hobbs refilling his glass, his cheeks already flushed and a contented look on his face.

'How's it gone, Dave?'

'Very well indeed. I think they all appreciate how much effort I've put in to the investigation,'

'Of course.'

'Judge Patricks is *very* pleased.'

Before I could reply Cornock was standing by my side, his dress uniform recently pressed.

'John,' he paused. 'Thought you might like to know that Wing Commander Bates is withdrawing the complaint. He thinks it's inappropriate in the circumstances. He went out of his way to praise the work you've been doing.'

'Thank you, sir. Always good to be appreciated.'

I smiled at Hobbs.

Cornock continued, 'And the ACC wanted me to congratulate you as well.'

I gave a slow, regal nod.

I noticed that the aquarium looked newly cleaned as I walked into Cornock's office. I sat down without being asked. He looked me straight in the eye.

'Meeting went well last night, don't you think?' Cornock said.

'I thought Detective Inspector Hobbs spoke very well.'

Cornock narrowed his eyes for a second and turned to the papers on his desk.

'So you didn't arrive until after all the shooting?'

'That's right, sir.'

'Anna thinks she saw men in combat fatigues.'

'Poor kid. She took it really badly.'

'Her witness statement is *rather* confused.'

I frowned and shook my head. 'She's a wreck. Do you think she'll be all right, sir?'

'Well ...'

'I expect some rest and a good holiday will help.'

He narrowed his eyes again. 'But she's adamant that you weren't there. Said it several times.'

'She must have been relieved to see me after witnessing that carnage.'

'Yes, I expect she was.'

'Could she identify the men involved?'

'It happened so quickly and she covered her face. We're not going to make much progress. At least the IPCC won't be involved.'

'And Frankie Prince is dead.'

Cornock sat back in his chair and clenched his jaw. I'd said what was on his mind.

'He was killed with a Russian made machine pistol. Apparently, it's commonplace in Eastern Europe.'

I raised an eyebrow.

'And the blood and flesh traces found in the house aren't on the DNA database. We're waiting to hear from the Polish police about their records.'

Somehow, I knew what the Polish police would be telling us. The colonel would see to it.

'DCI Banks rang me this morning,' Cornock continued.

'Really?'

'Stanislaw, the Polish guy who runs the shop in Cardiff, has disappeared and the whole business has closed down. Apparently there were other operations in other towns throughout the UK and suddenly they've gone.'

'Sounds like a good result all round.'

'The Serious Fraud Office has been on the telephone. Something happened back in Poland. The Polish police just decided not to proceed with anything else.'

'Good news,' I said. 'And what's happening with the girls from the house?'

'The Home Office sent a liaison officer.'

'Really?'

'A couple want to cooperate and they've made statements. Five have gone to London to *stay with friends* – whatever that means – and the rest are going back home to Romania and Hungary.'

Cornock sat back and smiled. 'Janet Helm resigned from the Ember Vale Foundation.'

'I saw something in the newspaper.'

His smiled broadened as he continued. 'I'd heard that the leader of her party has given her a dressing down.'

'Couldn't happen to a nicer person.'

Cornock grinned. 'And the CPS have authorised the prosecution of Lucy Prince and Jim White on charges of human trafficking, living off immoral earnings ...' He waved a hand in the air. 'All the usual stuff.'

'I wonder what Glanville Tront will make of that?'

'Case is GTi-proof. Good work, John.'

I sat in my office reading the messages in my Inbox for the first time in days. A district inspector in Bridgend had emailed asking me to review a case of a man alleging that he'd been assaulted in police custody. A dozen files that needed case reviews had landed on my desk. I read a complaint about 'strange goings-on' in a multi-storey car park in the middle of town. It probably meant that the drug squad needed to be informed.

My telephone call to Jackie had been easier than I'd expected and we finalised the plans for my trip with Dean to see the next QPR game without argument. The tickets were propped against the Gaggia coffee machine at home.

Boyd stood by the door when I was halfway through deleting most of the emails. I noticed one from Dave Hobbs telling me he was on annual leave in the Scottish highlands.

'Are there midges in Scotland this time of year?' I said to Boyd.

'Don't think so.'

'Shame.'

'New suit, boss?'

I was wearing my second-best suit; it had recently been cleaned which accounted for Boyd getting confused.

'We've got a complaint about groups of youths milling around in that multi-storey car park near the railway station,' I said.

'Probably drugs.'

I looked at my watch. 'And I'm having lunch with my mother at that Italian place near the National Gallery.'

We agreed a time to meet and I left Queen Street early. It wasn't raining, nor too cold.

17487076R00194

Printed in Great Britain
by Amazon